IOMANTE

A Black Sun Novel

Shawn Brooks

Cover art by Boris Groh.

Published by Ninja Nomad Press.

Print ISBN 978-4-9913671-2-0

Acknowledgements

Iomante is the first book I launched a Kickstarter campaign for to help me fund the cover art. I want to give a special thanks to everyone who supported me and helped me see this vision through!

Thank you to Chris Swinger, William Weiss, Solocosmo, Jonas Sværke, Stephen Logan, Michelle White, Eileen, Joey Logan, Clifford Clark, Jeremy Hayes, Caroline Coriell, Joy Gredvig, Kimberly Byrd, Scott Lang, Vince Losacco, and Marc Waters.

Hope you find this book as dreadful as you hoped it would be.

About the Black Sun Series

Iomante is the third Black Sun book. These stories take place in the same universe, in Japan specifically. All of them are based on Japanese folklore and mythology, and occasionally real-life events. They can be read in any order. Each book is a standalone story, though you can find hints for the other books in each one if you're looking closely enough. The only Black Sun book that has to be read in a certain order will be the last one, book five, titled "Black Sun." Coming out late 2025. This will be the only book that ties everything together, with past characters making appearances throughout.

The Black Sun Series:

Endless is the Night (out now)

Under the Amber Wave (out now)

Iomante (out now)

Dead Roots of the Earth (coming Fall 2025)

Black Sun (coming early winter 2025)

Other books by the author:

What Dances in the Dark: a short horror story collection (out now)

Pine Haven: an anthology (coming May 2025)

Stay up to date at: shawnbrookswrites.com

IOMANTE

LONG NIGHTS

DECEMBER 1915, HOKKAIDO, JAPAN

Yayo Inoue sliced the radish with a butcher's knife in her shaking hand. If she wasn't careful, she could cut her knuckles. Snow raged outside the small home. The winds battered against the walls and even shook the log rafters overhead.

But it wasn't the cold that made her shiver. It was the sound of gunshots and screaming from somewhere just outside her front door. A door that was locked with a sliding iron bar and built with heavy oak. Her home was one of the better-off ones in the village of Kamuy-Kotan. Not too hard when there were only ten families who had tamed this forested wilderness together.

What did that soldier say right before he left her here?

They were devil's eyes.

That's what the young man said, with bloodshot eyes of his own and a tremor on his lips. Right before he ran off into the night to chase down that bear.

That accursed bear.

The one who injured the Otani family, all seven of them, killing three of the children. The one who slaughtered poor Miyako-san as she was drying her linen on the line in broad daylight! To add salt to that wound, she was pregnant.

Was.

Yayo shivered even more and had to put down the knife.

The bear assaulted the tiny community for an entire week. If it didn't stop, there would be no one left. That's why her husband was out there now. Out in the dark storm. Hunting it along with the rest of the men. There was even a nearby detachment of imperial soldiers that Mayor Tetsuya—*ha! what a title for this hamlet*—had convinced to come and assist.

So now, there were over forty men in those woods. With guns. Even dynamite. Hunting the bear. She should have felt safe in her home—*my home*—kneeling by the hearth. The light of the fire mixed with an overhead whale lantern's orange radiance. But instead of filling her home—*my damn home, not that animal's*—with that special kind of comfort you get sitting by a fire when the outside world is nothing but dark and cold, instead of that, the lights cast shadows in the corners of the room. Long and erratic things danced on the walls. She could have sworn she saw something, something large and hairy, moving just out of sight, crouching in the kitchen. But when she looked, nothing but shadows and light.

Her baby boy, strapped to her back in a straw harness, gurgled and wriggled, bringing her mind back to reality.

Yes, reality. Keep your mind away from these delusions.

Her daughter sat in the room's corner, under a writhing shadow, playing with a doll made from corn husk. The three of them were safe. They were sound. Sealed away from the snowstorm. Warm and dry and about to eat dinner.

But those shouts? The gunfire? So many of them rang out. How many did it take to bring down one bear?

Yayo shook her head free of those thoughts. Picked up the knife. And began cutting the radish into thin slices. Grabbed them. Tossed them into a pot of boiling water hung over the hearth.

Her baby fussed and let out a brief cry. Yayo took a leftover slice of raw radish from the cutting board, crushed it in her palm, and reached back to give it to him. She heard him munch away as he settled.

A shiver of frost dance on her spine. She fidgeted on her knees and rubbed her lower back. She was safe, safe, damn it. The men were taking care of things. Armed as they were, how could they fail?

She looked at her daughter, a girl of six, as she fiddled with her makeshift doll. An overwhelming wave of feelings welled up in Yayo's chest. It was the need to protect. The need to hold. The need to keep those she loved safe. The need to run and hide. She gripped the knife tightly in her left hand. She didn't know why she did this. They were safe. It was perhaps that shadow off to her left, near the front door. A flicker of flame caused the darkness at the top of the door to dance. Looking, just for a moment, like the head of a bear.

Gunfire. Several shots. Far away. Further away than last time.

She exhaled the stored up the breath she hadn't been aware she was holding. She relaxed her shoulders. Of course she feared for her husband, and the further out that they went, the more dangerous it could be, out there in the forest. But it also meant that danger was moving away from her home.

"My home," she said under her breath.

Her daughter perked her head up and looked at her mother. Yayo saw her open her mouth to say something, maybe to make fun of her for talking to herself, when the girl's face went white as bone.

She was looking at the kitchen window.

Yayo turned quickly. So fast that her baby laughed, enjoying the ride. The kitchen itself was empty of anything aside from onions hanging from the rafters, crates full of potatoes and rice, and a steel washbasin. Snow beat against the window, almost like rain. Splattering itself against the glass and leaving behind streaks of ice. Beyond that was the void of night.

Yayo put her hands on the floor and pushed herself to her feet, balancing the baby on her back.

She was still holding the knife. Now held out in front of her.

She walked over to the kitchen window.

Looked out.

At first, she could see nothing but the white whirlwind of the snow and the vague dark shapes of trees beyond. If it didn't move, she would have never noticed it. The large black mass, just outside the reach of the light from the window. Yayo peered closer, fogging up the window with her breath.

And recoiled when she saw them.

Animal eyes reflecting the minimal kitchen light. A brief glint, a momentary shine, before night swallowed them.

The mass rushed forward.

Breaking glass.

Window frame splitting.

Screaming.

Running.

Water pot upturned.

Hearth flames doused.

Steam rising.

Lantern knocked to the floor and shattering.

Darkness.

Yayo slashing the knife out into the darkness. Yelling for her daughter to follow her voice.

And more screaming.

CHAPTER 1

December 16th, 2024, Hokkaido, Japan

Across the blank canvas of the snow, every action left its mark. Every thought and every intention was laid bare before this naked world. The footprints of a hiker. The dirt and oil from a car's tire. The blood of a fresh kill.

A cobalt blue sky shone above as the sunlight glistened off the freshly fallen snow like thousands of diamonds. The snow was semi-hard and crystalline, the kind that breaks with a satisfying crunch of a foot punching through it. The air in northern Hokkaido tasted pure and untouched by humanity.

Anastasia Timurovna Kadyrova crouched behind a frost covered bush. Her hands gripped her rifle. Even through the wool lining of the gloves, the cold bit at her fingers; and her face, and even her lungs. It stung her flesh and made her feel alive. Her breath came out in clean puffs and floated away. She poked her head above the bush and looked into the forest.

Everything was silent. The snow absorbed any and all sounds. She heard a ringing of tinnitus in her ears.

And then there was movement. Ahead and to the right. She saw it leap behind a thick grove of elm trees. A pair of antlers, a flash of red and gold fur.

She hurried after the deer, keeping low to the ground. The trees here grew far apart from one another. Her feet only sunk down to her mid calves in the snow. She knew soon it could be up to her waist or even higher. The winter was a mild one so far, but the forecast for the week ahead spoke of off and on squalls and even a possible blizzard. Better not waste time. Not if she ever wanted to bag a deer before the season ended.

The cold air burned her lungs as she walked, nearly jogging. It brought tears to her eyes and evaporated them quickly. When she reached the spot she saw the deer disappear from, she slowed down and came to a stop. She listened to the forest. Drops of melting snow exposed to the direct sunshine. The groan of the branches. And the breaking of snow, not too far away.

She got on her stomach and crawled in between two trees with branches overloaded by snow, which gave her some cover. Her white Gore-Tex jacket shielded her from getting wet, and from being seen. Peering out through the brittle leaves of the branches, she saw the buck, far off but within firing range. He was meandering away without a care in his head and would soon be out of sight. But she knew from her failures this month that it was better to wait than to act too soon.

She arrived in Japan over a year ago to finish university. In no rush to go back to Russia, it was her dream to live in Japan for a few years. Get some space from that old life. She graduated and worked her ass off to get a hunting license, showing that all those years studying Japanese were worth something. Not that it helped her too much with the local dialect. It sounded more Korean than Japanese to her. She had to shadow a local hunter for a month before she was awarded the license. A man by the name of Ogoto. The town drunk and an idiot. But she liked him enough, anyway. Kind of reminded her of Dad. Blunt and dumb, but deep down a good guy.

She saw the buck walk off and behind another thicket of trees. But he was in no hurry. And neither was she. As long as she got to him before the heavy snows fell. Today, though, was a sunny day with no care for things like deadlines.

Anastasia pulled herself up to her feet and crouched low. She walked toward the deer. The snow melted off the branches overhead and the water tapped against the hood of her jacket. *Rap-atap-tap-tap.*

She held a hunting license back in Russia—and had held one for ten years now—but had never shot an animal before. Somehow, she thought it would be easier here, far from home, far from the reasons behind her failures.

Ogoto teased her about constantly about this.

"You know how to shoot, girl, I'll give ya' that. But you've shot nothing living before? Why even bother hunting?" he said, a dribble of *sake* still on his chin's stubble. "I thought Americans grew up shooting things all the time."

She told him she was Russian, not American, but he would always forget, or, to him, all foreigners were American by default.

"And you look Japanese but can't speak Japanese," he said and laughed his howler-monkey laugh back at her cabin. "I don't understand you."

This was something that was slowly grating on her. Her family was from eastern Siberia, with roots going back to China, Korea, and even Japan itself, so she did, in fact, look Japanese. Something that most people took as guaranteeing her intimate knowledge of the language and the culture. Until she opened her mouth, that was.

"At least I can hold my drink better than you," she fired back as she downed her fourth shot of sake. That was a lie. She couldn't hold it, but Ogoto didn't need to know that. What she could hold better was her poker face. A lifetime of not smiling in front of strangers was good practice.

"Anoosootsjyah," he would call her. So she told him to call herby her nickname Asya instead. He couldn't pronounce that either, so her new name, Ashiya, was born on the lips of a drunk in the middle of a frozen wood at a desolate cabin's dinner table.

"I don't need to hold my drink if it holds me," he said and winked at her.

She laughed at him. "That doesn't make sense, old man."

"Don't need to make sense if sense is something that can't be made."

Tracking the deer now through the quiet woods, Ashiya almost laughed. Her best friend in this unfamiliar country was an old man—*sixties maybe?*—that could hardly say her name.

She passed by a thin birch tree and paused.

Something carved five claw marks into its flesh. She checked the snow for tracks. None but her own and the deer's. No droppings either. The cuts looked fresh, but bears should have been hibernating by now. She shrugged it off as her mistake. The marks must be older than she thought. There were no bark pieces on the snow either to show that it had just happened, though it did snow just yesterday.

She came out of the thickest part of the woods, and a clearing opened up before her. She saw the deer tracks in the snow. They led across the open meadow and into the next tree line. She stared into the forest on the other side and saw him. Right in front of a pair of elms, his back to her, grazing for what little green he could find.

Ashiya took a knee and shouldered her rifle. She peered down the scope and lined up the shot. The buck lifted its head and sniffed at the air. She didn't make a sound. The buck went back to foraging for grass under the snow.

All it would take now was a single pull of the trigger. A single second and the deer would go down, she was sure of it. Then she would have gotten the only thing she really cared to get out here in Hokkaido. She took a deep breath and held it. She could feel her heartbeat in her ears.

Time slowed down. She could see the individual snowflakes as they danced their way down from somewhere out of the blue sky and alighted on the buck's antlers, getting absorbed into the bone.

Her right hand started shaking.

Come on, Anastasia, get it together. Just pull the damn trigger and it will be done with.

The buck turned around and locked eyes with her.

It's just an animal. Come on. For Alexei.

The deep brown eyes of the deer bored into her own. Those eyes did not speak of intent, they did not speak of fear or hate or love; they were cold and silent, like the forest itself.

She had a perfect shot. But the wind was blowing. And the deer was looking at her. And how was she going to get its body back to her cabin? How was she going to dress it? How was she going to feel about it when it was done?

And why didn't I pull the trigger back when it really mattered? Then maybe Alexei would still be alive. Did you ever think about that?

Her index finger curled around and softly tugged at the trigger. Then relaxed. She put the rifle down and let out a sigh.

The deer bounded off into the trees.

She sat down in the snow and laid the rifle on her knees.

She watched as the buck disappeared.

Lost another one. Five so far. How many more you want to lose, huh?

She laid down on her back and looked up at the sky. The sky was blue, but snow blew in from nearby treetops, falling gracefully on her. A single crow cawed, but there were not others to respond to it.

The forest was desolate. Mostly bereft of life.

Ashiya got to her feet and made her way back to the cabin.

Lost in thoughts that were submerged under the crunch of the snow, she walked back the way she had come, stepping on her previous footprints. She passed the tree with the claw marks, giving it a second glance.

Those marks do look fresh.

Ashiya passed the frozen ravine, skating across it, careful not to crack the ice. She walked along a ridge top overseeing the old lumber mill, down in the valley to her left. She didn't know for how long it had been abandoned, but rust covered the metal siding of the mill, with holes of various sizes—some big enough for a person to squeeze through, most not—pockmarking its walls. The roof had caved in from years of heavy snow and neglect. Two derelict tree harvesters sat buried under the snow, ghosts of their former selves.

Her brother's face came to her mind. He had done some work cutting down trees back home in Yakutsk. His company didn't have machines as big as the harvesters though, they had to do it the old-fashioned way with axes and chainsaws. His naturally crooked smile and his bright hazel eyes—both compliments of their mother's side of the family—filled her mind. The last time she saw that face—alive—was in a winter field just like this, seen through the scope of a rifle.

But it wasn't the last time she saw him, was it?

In the frozen halls of her memory: a patch of red grass swaying in the wind. A herd of caribou, racing away. A pile of teeth—

A branch snapped.

The sound rang out loud and clear in the hermetic silence of the snowy woods. It broke her out of her melancholic daydream. She was only a few minutes away from her cabin, but picked up her pace. It could have been a bear, one who had awoken too early from hibernation. That made them dangerous. There were no other animals out here to fear aside from a wild pig every once in a while. Monkeys and foxes were a joke.

Even so, let's get home quick.

She rounded a cluster of spruce trees and stopped. The scent of iron filled her nose. Sour. Painted across the clean snow in front of her was a lake of glistening red, with a lump at its center. It took her a moment to process what she was seeing. It was a doe. Surrounded by her own blood. Something had ripped the body in half at the waist. It looked like an animal had taken a massive bite out of its midsection. The spinal column barely connected the two halves together. She gripped her rifle, pulled off her hood, and lifted her beanie off her ears. No sound in the air and no movements in the trees. She circled the grisly scene for tracks.

And found none. None from the bear she believed had to have done this. None from a person, though, that would have been more disturbing to find.

And what really chilled her blood then: no tracks from the deer itself. All the snow around the mess of blood was otherwise untouched.

It was as if the doe had fallen from the sky.

CHAPTER 2

Ashiya drove her beat-up '98 Jimny into the nearby town of Kamuy-Kotan. The roads were clear of snow, but she took the dark corners slow. Never know when a spot of black ice could spring up from the shadows and spin your car out into a tree. She knew a guy, Anatoly, back in high school. Straight laced, never broke a rule type of guy. Even asked her out on a date once and she said yes. She spent the most boring ninety minutes of her life in that cafe listening to him talk about sci-fi movies. Well, he ended up smashing his face into a cement divider one day because he took a corner too fast. One simple mistake undid a life of promise. No more talk about sci-fi or anything else ever again. Can't do that from the grave.

This would not be her. Her life would not spiral out of control.

She thought of the deer.

The doe disturbed her. At best, a bear had woken from hibernation and killed it. If that was the case, then she'd have to be more on guard when she went out to the woods. At worst; she didn't even know how to follow that train of thought. She imagined a psychopath butchering the deer and leaving it out in the woods for her to see. Most of the people in Kamuy-Kotan knew she was out there in that cabin all by herself—she was one of only two foreigners in town as far as she knew—and the deer's body was only a minute's walk from her front door.

But it was ripped completely in half.

And why didn't you notice it when you went out there that morning? You would have seen it on the way.

And where were the tracks?

Many questions. Little in ways of answers.

Elm trees and Sakhalin firs dotted the roadside, their branches hanging over the road. Ashiya's cabin was a ten-minute drive into town and she made the trip in every few days. She had planned on living off of the deer she would shoot but was forced to, in utter humiliation, do her shopping at Saito's Market instead. At least once a week.

The road turned hard to the right, and she slowed down to take the corner, letting the car glide into it without force. The trees thinned out, and she drove past a wooden signboard on the right written in both Japanese and English saying, "Welcome to Kamuy-Kotan, town of the gods." To the side of the sign was a cutout of a brown bear with big blue cartoon eyes that made it look like an anime character. Something meant as a serious warning but was too cute to have the desired effect.

She passed a frozen lake to her left, the name unknown to her. Saw a man out in the middle, sitting down on a lawn chair, holding a fishing pole.

It was Ogoto. She rolled down her window, honked her horn, and waved her hand at him. He lifted a fish and waved it back at her.

Such an idiot.

She smiled and kept driving.

Ashiya drove past the lake and took the next right onto the main street of the town. No idea what the name of that was, either. She had noticed that none of the streets had names and wondered how people could navigate without resorting to Google Maps. Most of the buildings in town were residential. A few shops and restaurants and even a few convenience stores here and there. The homes were old on the outskirts, becoming more modern yet smaller towards the center of town.

Smoke trails snaked their way out of chimneys, hinting at the life hidden away behind those walls. Nobody was out walking the streets.

Kamuy-Kotan was a town that you'd drive through completely in five minutes and barely even register that you had done it.

Ashiya came to Saito's Market, a detached one story building with a signboard looking like an old American wild west saloon. Christmas lights strewn over the front glass of the store with a plastic life-sized Santa Claus by the front door.

Her car hit an ankle high ice berm and bounced over it. She parked the car in the five-spot lot out back and went inside the store, high-fiving the Santa on her way in. He rocked in place as if nodding at her.

The market was a tiny thing. Three aisles of goods with a meat section in the back. A plastic Christmas tree stood by the only register. Two elderly women were the only shoppers she saw strolling through the store. One was staring at a carrot like it would tell her the secrets of eternal youth. The other one was shuffling down an aisle, talking to herself.

Ashiya wanted to be in and out. Avoid all small talk. Get back to the cabin and plan her next outing. That would be difficult because Hikari Saito, the owner's daughter, was on the register today. She had tied her hair—a pink streak running through it—back in a ponytail. Hikari had three piercings in each ear, and Ashiya suspected she had tattoos—something Ashiya knew was taboo in many parts of Japan. Hikari looked out of place in this small, conservative town. Ashiya wondered why she lived here, but never took it upon herself to ask her. She was here for deer, not friends.

Hikari spotted Ashiya and waved at her. Ashiya meekly waved back and forced herself to smile. Her smile probably looked deranged; she rarely smiled at strangers. Nobody back home ever did that. With friends and family, sure, but with people she barely knew? But she was trying to not be rude.

Ashiya grabbed a basket and got her supplies; a head of lettuce, two bottles of plum wine, a bottle of sake, a thick cut of beef, a loaf of bread. She made her way to the register, preparing herself for the onslaught of pleasantries.

"Ashiya! So good to see you today. How are things?" Hikari said through her ever-beaming smile.

"Good," Ashiya replied and placed her groceries on the conveyor belt and Hikari began ringing them up.

"Wow, alcohol again? You buy way too much of this for being such a small girl. I could never drink this much, not even in a month."

"Yeah."

"*Yeah*, she says. You've been coming here for months, and that's about all you can ever say. I know your Japanese has gotten better by now."

"Maybe."

Hikari smiled wider. She was a beautiful woman, maybe thirty years old, and Ashiya even kind of liked her. Just that she had an overactive Golden retriever type of energy that Ashiya was ill-equipped to deal with.

"You know, I've been meaning to ask you for weeks now, but I didn't want you to feel awkward about it. But, you should come over to my place for dinner tonight. My husband is coming back from a Tokyo trip and I thought it could be a good way for you to make some friends. I've been meaning to invite you for a while, but just had a loaded schedule of taking Ren to Sapporo for his exams."

Ashiya looked at the old woman with the carrot and never so badly wanted to trade places with somebody else than she did at that moment.

"Well, I'm kinda' busy tonight."

"*Busy* she says! I know that's a lie. Come on, just this one time, and I promise I'll stop bothering you about it. Who knows, you might actually enjoy yourself. Let me get your number and I'll send you the details after my shift."

"But I need to plan for tomorrow. I do that every night."

"Come on, it's just one night. I promise that whatever it is you do out in those woods will still be there for you, whether or not you plan for it."

Ashiya didn't know why, but she felt compelled to tell Hikari her number. This woman had some kind of magnetism about her. Ashiya liked her but would never admit that to anyone. She paid for her groceries and told Hikari her number. Then hurried to grab her bag and leave. Hikari made a move to say more until an old woman came scuttling in, jabbing the carrot in front of her face.

"Why is this carrot so orange? The ones last week were more yellow," the woman accused more than asked.

Hikari put her hand up to the woman in apology. Ashiya laughed.

"Hey, you can smile. Looks good on you."

Ashiya's face went hot, and the smile turned to a grimace.

"Bye," she said as she rushed out of the store and back to her car, shoulders hunched up, trying to hide her face. The carrot woman's ranting growing louder by the second.

Ashiya unloaded the bags in the back and got into the driver's seat. She reversed—hit the ice berm, the lettuce head fell out of the bag and landed on the floor—and came back out onto the street.

Dinner with the Saito family. Ashiya racked her brain for an excuse to make up later and have to cancel on them. She didn't dislike them at all.

In fact, she had harbored a certain fondness for that family. She'd run into Hikari and her son Ren, maybe ten years old, dozens of times at the store. Met her husband, Itsuki, there twice. They were kind to her, and Hikari always went out of her way to try to make her feel welcome.

But I didn't come here to make friends.

I came here to get his face out of my head.

As she drove back home, she thought about the last time she saw Alexei before they buried him. An Orthodox priest was blathering away, his heavy gold cross necklace swinging like a mace as he swiveled around in his gold and white robes.

Ashiya was fifteen back then. Sitting silently in the back of the church. Didn't hear a single thing that was said. Not even when her mother told her it was time to go up to the front and say goodbye to him. Mom had to grab her arm hard and fast to snap her out of her funk.

"What?" Ashiya said. Hardly able to see her Mother through tear-blurred eyes.

"Anastasia, come up now and pray for you brother!" Mom's voice rose, and some guests looked over at them and started whispering.

It wasn't a closed casket service. Though it really should have been. Ashiya heard from Dad later that the mortician did the best that he could, but it wasn't good enough. Mom objected, said she didn't care what he looked like. Everyone needed to kiss his forehead before burial. Dad was against that, but they eventually compromised and left just his forehead visible, the rest of his face covered with a red satin cloth. Dozens of flowers blanketed his chest.

Ashiya walked up the aisle with her Mother still gripping her left arm. Her nails dug into Ashiya's skin, but she accepted it. She deserved any pain she felt.

Mom leaned in and said, "If you don't look at him now and say goodbye, he will haunt your dreams forever."

When they reached the coffin, the priest standing to the side, staring at them with intensity, Mom let go of her arm, bent down, and kissed Alexei's pale and waxy forehead. She looked up at her daughter and in her hard stare said, *Get your ass down here now.*

Ashiya stepped up to the platform and looked down into the coffin. Her knees became water and her breath came in fast. She saw the red cloth, the flowers, and the forehead that looked like a porcelain doll. Mom tugged at her dress and tried to pull her down. She could hear the whispers of disapproval from her relatives in the aisles. The stare of the priest burned a hole in her own forehead.

Then she turned and ran out of the church. Mom screaming after her to come back.

That was her last memory of her brother before they buried him.

But it wasn't the last she saw of him.

CHAPTER 3

Toi Ogoto was staring into the hole he had cut out of the ice two hours earlier. The water was wavy and blurry to him. Like he was looking at it through a plastic sheet that somebody was waving around like crazy. He lifted his eyes to the rest of the frozen lake around him. That was blurry, too. He put his hand out in front of him.

Holy shit. The world's gone all fucked up and sideways.

No, it couldn't be the world that was losing its shit. He looked back at his hand and took another gulp of his beer, crushed the now empty can in his hand, and tossed it into his bag.

Maybe I've had too much. Blurry water and hands and, oh shit, I can't stand up.

He tried, though. And immediately fell on his face onto the grating ice. Ogoto never could tell what that line was, the one between excess and enjoyment. The two worlds were one and the same for him. Maybe that's why he was still single and late into his sixties now. Though that didn't stop him from flirting with Kaede down at the town's only bar every Saturday. One day, he might just get lucky.

Of course, he never confronted the real reason behind his bachelorhood; doing the same shit he was trying to do with Kaede now, only back then he was a married man.

He pushed himself off the ice. His face stung a little, but was mostly numb.

From the beers or from the cold? Fuck if I know.

He sat himself back in his lawn chair. His fishing pole was hooked up to the chair. He suddenly remembered why he was out here.

Fish!

He looked back into the water. The line didn't move.

The sound of a car engine purred to life from the road. He looked up and saw that Jimny that American hunter girl was driving. All dented up and muddy and an ugly lime green color. She honked the horn at him and put out her hand to wave.

Ogoto grabbed a stuffed fish from his pack—a child's toy, one he always brought with him for good luck, though today he had caught nothing, not even a single bite—and shook it above his head, laughing. He didn't even know why he laughed. He didn't find it particularly funny; it was just something he felt like doing. Like most of his decisions in life.

Anoosootsjyah really ought to get that car washed up proper.

He reached for another beer from his backpack. All gone.

"Damn it."

He tried to stand to his feet again, but his head felt like a bowl full of water sloshing around, the contents shifting over the side, ready to spill over. In a rare moment, common sense won the day, and he kept his ass in that chair. Though if he didn't move it sometime soon it'd be night and he'd end up getting frostbite. He'd seen the signs before in some kids who got lost on a school outing some five years back. Ogoto was called in to help find them because he was the best damn tracker this small town had, sober or otherwise.

Found those kids in just under an hour. One of the boy's hands was already a reddish purple. When Ogoto felt the skin, it was waxy and smooth. That's how he knew it'd have to get chopped off.

Damn shame.

He looked up into the sky. No clouds out. But that winter night was coming in fast. So too several days of erratic snowstorms if he could believe the weather report. The forest itself was dark while the tops of the trees caught that last golden shine of day.

Best be packing up.

Ogoto rocked himself forward in his chair and swung himself out of it. His feet slipped, but he caught himself from falling this time.

He saw the tail-end of the Jimny pass the lake as it turned away into town.

He worried about that girl. Gave her shit every chance he got, but that was just his way of fooling around. He was sure she knew that. But it didn't sit right with him. A young girl at what, twenty-five she said? And a foreigner who spoke shit Japanese. Sure, she proved herself capable out here. Didn't scare easy. Could take care of herself.

Lot more than any other woman I've seen in my life.

But still. A man worries about these things.

Ogoto zipped up his rucksack and reeled in his line. He broke his pole down and strapped it to the side of his bag. Just then, a fish jumped out of the water and disappeared just as quickly into the icy blue.

"You little fuckers."

"Ren! Get your toys off the table, now!" Hikari shouted into the bowels of her cold home. Can't be wasting money on heating until absolutely necessary.

"Just a minute Mom, I'm at a really important part!"

Her son's voice was almost drowned out by the sound of whatever video game he was playing.

I swear, that kid has so much potential and he's wasting hours away on that thing.

"No way, buddy. I said now."

No response save for some *digital* gunfire. Hikari stomped her way up the stairs and barged into his room.

Ren was lying on the floor in front of the TV that displayed some nonsense. His hands flew over the controller, his eyes fixed on the screen as if he were trying to land a space shuttle on a dime. His friend Ben was lying next to him. The son of an American man and Japanese woman in town, but the boy had grown up in Kamuy-Kotan his whole life.

Hikari walked across the room, stepping over the boys, and turned off the TV.

"Mom! Do you know what you've done!?"

Ben's jaw looked like it was about to the touch the floor it had dropped so low.

"Do *you* know what you've done? Or haven't done is more like it. We're having a guest over in an hour and you still haven't cleaned up. And you," she looked at Ben with narrowed eyes. "You staying or what?"

Ben meekly said, "Ren said I could, if that's okay with you, Mrs. Saito."

"Of course it's okay. Ren, you'll walk him home afterwards, yes? It is a school night."

Ren's face matched the red blankets on his bed at that moment. Hikari wanted to laugh at the unintentional camouflage but kept her strict I-mean-business Mom-face.

"You heard me, yeah?"

"Yeeeeaah," Ren let out like a deflating balloon. He rose, head bobbing down, shrugging his shoulders, trying to look upset. Hikari smiled and held out an open hand to him. "Come on, my guy, give me a hug."

His face went from red to Thermo-nuclear. He hissed out, "Mom, not now."

She ignored him and pulled Ren in for the hug, anyway. He didn't fight back. Hikari knew he liked the displays of affection, of course not in front of his friends, but she was never one to shy away from how she felt. She was the one to propose to her husband. She was the one to confront the parents of that bully that tormented her son back in preschool. People always said her personality fit Osaka with their in-your-face-attitude. Not the chill and quiet countryside of Hokkaido.

But everyone needs a little fire in their life from time to time.

She released Ren from his indentured affection and shooed the two boys downstairs. Ren grabbed his toys—a figurine of Ultraman, a baseball mitt, a bunch of playing cards—from the dining table and handed them over to Ben.

Hikari checked on the stew she had going on over the stove. She had no idea what people ate in Russia, but she assumed it had to be meaty and salty. She hoped so, at least, because she was not a master of producing anything other than a salty dish. Her husband didn't seem to mind, never said as much if he did. Ren could suck it up and eat what he was given. But with Ashiya and Ben over for dinner tonight, she was more careful about what she was making.

Or tried to be anyway.

She stirred the lamb stew and took in a whiff. It smelled more sweet than salty.

Success?

Ryoji Tetsuya sat in his leather armchair, smoking his mahogany pipe. He swirled a glass of whiskey in his left hand and stared at his wall. Aside from a pair of satin boxers, he was otherwise naked. He had a slight pudge hanging over his underwear, but was mostly fit for his age. How many men in their mid-forties had veins that bulged while they worked out? How many had tans? How many could sleep around with whoever they wanted to?

His wall displayed deer heads, bear heads, fox heads—even a rhinoceros head from those trips he wasn't supposed to talk about. Their glassy eyes didn't blink. Had they done so, he wouldn't have been scared. He'd see it as a sign he was on the right track.

Ryoji put the glass down on the table by his chair and stood up. He walked over to a polar bear's head mounted over his roaring fireplace. He pat the fur and ruffled it like he would do to a beloved dog.

"You were a bitch to put down, weren't you?"

A knock at his door.

"Yes?"

The door opened and his assistant Rina came in. He wasn't too fond of how she kept on fucking up his appointments, but she did always wear that tight skirt, even when it was subzero out. Bless women like that. Today, she had wrapped herself in a towel—even better—and had done her hair up to avoid getting it wet in the shower. Her husband wouldn't appreciate her lies about why her hair was damp after a day at the office—or Ryoji's residence, to be more precise.

"Sir, the festival committee wants to know what time you will make your speech tomorrow."

He took a slow and deliberate inhale on his pipe, not breaking eye contact with Rina. She blushed and looked away.

"Tell them five o'clock. Unless I get word that it's been spotted."

"If that happens, what should I—"

"Don't tell them anything. If I show up, I show up."

"But it's your—"

He put his finger over his lips and shushed her. "Honey, don't worry about it. It'll work out."

She gave a nervous bow and left the room.

Dumb bitch. If it wasn't for that skirt, I would have tossed her out years ago.

Ryoji turned back to the polar bear's head. Even as the Mayor of Kamuy-Kotan, he had bigger things to worry about. That brown bear he shot last week and didn't kill. It had to still be out there, and he had to be the one to do it in.

Ryoji's father and his father before him were famous for killing bears. Ever since that attack back in 1915, his family took it upon themselves to kill as many bears as possible as a tribute to the fallen. Grandad shot and killed that original bear, but not until it had slaughtered seven people, most of them women and children. He remembered the old man's stories about how it took several shots to the head to do it. How it wasn't like normal bears.

Ryoji's father bagged fifty of those fuckers during his tenure as mayor.

They said it was to avenge the dead. Ryoji cared little for that. He was in it for the thrill.

Last week, he tracked a bear that had woken up from hibernation. A local farmer called it in to his office, as Ryoji preferred that any such calls would be. Said he was worried it might kill his sheep. Ryoji went out by himself and found the bear in under two hours. It was emaciated and confused. Not much of a challenge. Shot it right in the neck and it ran off. Never found the body. The bear had a unique mark over its left eye. A white stripe that looked like a lightning bolt.

Ryoji looked at an empty wall space next to the polar bear. He imagined putting that pretty lightning-eyed face there.

"Don't worry," he said to the polar bear. Its eyes beheld him impassively. "You'll get some more company real soon."

Ashiya lit the furnace, and it grumbled to life with a rattle. Soon her one-room cabin would fill with heat. She preferred the wood-burning stove and the seeping warmth of the flames. The crackle of the wood helped her fall asleep. As did five or six shots of sake.

Ogoto helped her get a deal on several hundred pounds of firewood from some hermit that lived off the grid. The two of them spent several days splitting it all and stacking it on the side of the cabin. She'd rather grab several logs and start her nightly drinking session by the fire and pass out on the floor.

But tonight she had plans.

Fuck.

There was no way she'd leave her cabin unheated while out all night. Hokkaido wasn't nearly as cold as Yakutsk, there really was a difference between -10 and -40 degrees Celsius. At first she felt like a champ in Japan. While everyone else complained of the cold weather, she purposefully walked around the town in a T-shirt. It was petty, but the looks of the locals at her bare arms in winter, tatted up to the shoulders with skulls and wolf heads, were worth it.

But people adapt to their surroundings. In just a few short weeks, she shivered at a mere zero degrees! What would Dad say about that?

The furnace was in full swing now, and she went to the bathroom to wash her face. She would not be putting on any makeup. It was enough that she was leaving the house—at night!—what more could people ask of her?

She grabbed her parka with the fur lining and her car keys. Turned off the lights. At the moment the lights went out, she saw the outline of a man over by the stove. She quickly turned the lights back on. Nothing out of the ordinary.

She turned the lights back off and shut the door. Locked it—even though Japan was safer than back home, old habits and all.

Got into her car and turned it on.

Drove down the road trying not to think about what she saw by the stove.

But she knew that smile. It was crooked. And above it, wrapped around the rest of the face, was a red sash.

Just my imagination.

CHAPTER 4

Dinner was extremely salty. No amount of water or beer could bring her taste buds back from the desert grave that the stew had sentenced them. Ashiya made an excuse halfway through to use the bathroom and washed her mouth out in the sink. But nobody else seemed to notice the taste. They ate it like it was nothing!

Are they all psychopaths?

She braced herself for another potential round of salt stew and returned to the dining room of the Saito home. To her surprise, Hikari was already cleaning up the plates. Itsuki was looking at his phone and absentmindedly sipping at his coffee. Ren was taking out a bag of trash, his friend Ben in tow.

"Hey, sorry about dinner, you didn't like it," Hikari said as a statement more than a question.

"No, not at all. It was great." Ashiya forced a smile onto her face. She was getting good at that. Even if she had to brave another bowl of lamb and salt stew, she'd gladly suffer that rather than be seen as a rude guest. Someone inviting you into their home was never to be taken lightly.

"I could tell by the way you ran out of here looking like your face was going to explode." Hikari gave a half smile that dipped into a frown.

"Well, it may have had a bit too much salt."

"You know, everyone always says that, but I've never believed them before."

She is a psychopath.

"Tasted fine to me," Itsuki muttered from behind his phone and mug, the steam of which fogged up his glasses.

"It was fine. Don't worry about it. Let me help you with those," Ashiya made a gesture towards the sink and the pile of dishes resting precariously on the counter's edge.

"Now that would be rude if I let you do that," Hikari smiled and lightly slapped Ashiya's hand away.

"Hey Ashi," Itsuki said. He had taken it upon himself to give her yet another nickname. *Is my name really that hard to pronounce?* "You smoke?"

"Of course she doesn't," Hikari insisted.

"Umm, yeah, I do."

Hikari's eyes widened in surprise.

"Sounds right," Itsuki grunted as he took out a pack of Winstons. He pulled out a chair for Ashiya. She sat down and took the cigarette from his hand. She looked around to see if it was okay to light up in their house and in front of Hikari's judgmental eyes. Hikari slid the door shut to the kids who had gone into the living room. She walked over and took one from her husband and lit it up as well. Now it was Ashiya's turn to look surprised.

"What?" Hikari asked. "A girl's gotta de-stress somehow."

Ashiya laughed and took a puff of the cig. For the entire meal, she sat straight up, chewed with her mouth closed, refrained from making any minor mistake. Now she could finally relax.

The Saitos owned a two story home. One of the modern ones in town. No lack of central heating. They built the walls from proper timber, not flimsy wood and paper. The electric heated flooring and the heated driveway was the picture of pure opulence to her. Her own home back in Russia was a simple apartment. Like her cabin here in Japan, it relied on more rustic forms of heating.

She found it funny how her view of wealth all came down to how well a home could be heated.

"So, how long you staying here?' Itsuki asked, finally putting his phone down. His dark eyes and bony face gave him an intimidating look.

"Until I shoot a buck. Can share some of the meat with you guys too. Then I'll probably travel around the country, get a job somewhere."

"I could never shoot anything. I mean, stare the thing in the eyes and it knows it's coming, right?" Hikari asked.

"Ogoto says you haven't killed anything yet," Itsuki said. Then to his wife with a grin, "So you don't need to worry about her actually shooting anything."

Don't be rude, Anastasia.

"I can shoot better than anyone in this town, Ogoto included."

Damn it.

Itsuki took a long drag. Like it didn't matter how long she had to wait for his rebuttal. "I don't doubt that. But the will to kill something, that's what's lacking. Can I ask why it's so hard?"

Ashiya squeezed her cigarette too hard, and it broke in her hand.

"Hey, who wants dessert?" Hikari got up to grab something from the fridge.

"I had a brother. Alexei. He died because I couldn't fire my rifle in time. So I guess that's why I *lack the will*." Ashiya emphasized that last phrase stronger than she had intended to.

Hikari stood at the fridge, her mouth mimicking the wide-open door.

Itsuki's face softened, and he handed her another smoke. "Shit. I'm sorry. You don't need to talk about it."

"No, it's okay. It happened ten years ago, so it's not worth bringing up anymore."

Her lips quivered, and she felt the rush of seawater in the back of her throat.

It was as silent in that room as the woods had been this afternoon. She could almost hear the thoughts racing through their heads. Hear the words that would come, *Hey it was nice to meet and all, but we won't be meeting again.* She didn't mean to snap like that or bring up Alexei. Ashiya wanted to blame it on the beer she had for dinner, but she wasn't even tipsy. She wanted to blame it on Itsuki's insistent questioning, but that wasn't it either.

It was a lie that Alexei's death was old news. Kind of hard when you dream about him every night. Ashiya's mind raced for a way to change the topic, to break the awkwardness, to escape.

Hikari came back to the table with three slices of cheesecake and put them down. "I'm sorry that happened. If you want to talk about it, we're here." She took Ashiya's hand in her own. Ashiya became instantly aware of how cold her own hands were once Hikari's warm palms enfolded them. She blushed again, just as she had done back at the grocery store.

Itsuki put out his cigarette in the ashtray. "Hey, I was out of line with pushing you like that."

"Let's just... forget it, okay?" Ashiya said.

"Done," Itsuki replied.

"So, I'm not good at awkward situations like this. Let's talk about what really matters now, shall we?" Hikari said as she took her hands away from Ashiya's. "I heard you're single. I have this cousin I think you'd get along great with."

Out of one fresh hell and into another. But at least this one was more tolerable.

Itsuki laughed out and told his wife to cut it out. That she was the last person to give romantic advice. She had married him after all, right?

Ashiya felt the stiffness leave her muscles, and she relaxed. Even smiled a little. One that wasn't forced. She might end up liking this sort of thing—a social life—after all.

Ashiya stayed for another hour. They didn't talk about her brother anymore. The little that she let out was enough. They smoked and drank—she kept it minimal because she'd be driving home in the dark and the roads would be slick by now. They talked about how the couple had met: Itsuki was in university down in Osaka, though he grew up in Hokkaido. Found Hikari sitting on a curb, smoking and drinking with her friends. Worked up the nerve to talk to her, and that was that.

They talked about the tsunami that hit Aomori just a few months prior. Ashiya had just finished university in Sapporo city and moved up to Kamuy-Kotan. Half of Aomori prefecture swallowed by the sea. A national disaster of apocalyptic proportions. Most of the water had receded, but the northernmost tip, the one nearest Hokkaido itself, remained submerged. Nobody knew what to make of it. A freak accident of nature not seen for millennia. The Saitos donated money to the Red Cross and even Ashiya felt like she should do the same thing as soon as she could.

Hikari tried to steer things back to Ashiya's love life. She got out of it by pointing at the clock.

It was now eleven at night and Hikari suddenly realized they forgot to send Ben home.

"Oh shit," she said. "His mom is going to kill me. Ren!"

She went up the stairs to get the boys. Ashiya put her parka on and stood by the door. She shook Itsuki's hand. Hikari and the boys came flying down the stairs.

"You gotta go home now, Ben," she said and threw the boy's jacket at him from the coat rack. He caught it and put it on.

"Hey, I can drive him home," Ashiya offered.

"Oh no, we couldn't ask that," Hikari said. She made to put on her own jacket but stumbled. Clearly had too much to drink. By the watery red look in Itsuki's eyes, he too. Ashiya was as fine as if she'd been drinking water.

"No, you are drunk. I'm not. Where do you live, Ben?"

"Down the street like two blocks, I think."

Ashiya smiled, and the boy blushed. "You think? You don't know where you live?"

"He's down the street if you take a right out of our drive, two blocks. His house is the big blue one on the right with all the Christmas decorations out," Hikari said.

"Got it. Alright, come on, kid."

Ashiya and Ben left the house. The Saito family waved them off at the door. She opened the car door for Ben and almost had to help push him up into the passenger seat. It was a few inches too tall for him. But he made it on his own with a jump. Something fell out of his pocket and landed in the snow. She bent down to grab it.

"Hey, you dropped this."

Ben almost fell out of the car, reaching for the blue CD case.

"Thanks," he muttered, not meeting her eyes.

She closed the door for him. For a moment, she thought about digging deeper into what he was holding.

Not my business. Not my place.

She drove him home.

CHAPTER 5

Ren Saito lay awake in his bed fighting sleep. He thought about Ms. Kobayashi's language arts class and how she always picked on him for the answer.

"Mr. Saito, do you know which is the correct Kanji for subway system?"

He wanted to say, "We don't have subways here, so why do I need to know that?"

Instead, he kept his mouth shut as the other kids laughed at him. Fire burned in his cheeks and tears welled up in his eyes.

That class was first on the docket for tomorrow. Well, technically, later today.

He thought about Nana, the prettiest girl in class who sat next to him in science. She had thick-rimmed glasses and braces and was a bit of a dork. But she smiled at him once and he felt like he could float off into the clouds and never be found after that.

He even thought about the mean dog that lived down the street. He would never admit it to Ben, but the big white Akita scared him. So much so that he wouldn't walk home straight from school, though that was the faster route, he would loop around the block to avoid the animal.

Mostly what he thought about was how it was Tuesday night and school was fast approaching. Dread filled his stomach. How could he waste all these precious free hours on sleep? Wasn't his whole life dictated by school, by Mom, by her weighty expectations over his future?

And sleep? He could do that when he was dead. Mom forced him to go to Sapporo for his special tutor on Saturdays. School forced him to join the soccer club. Soccer in winter! He'd rather stay inside and play video games.

Which reminds me.

He rolled out of bed and pressed his ear against the door. The house was dead silent. He looked at his bedside clock: two in the morning. He crept up to his TV and turned it on. The electric whine of the static screen was quiet, and it filled his room with a ghostly white light and stung his eyes. He turned on his PlayStation 5 and lowered the volume all the way down. Just enough to hear something, but not loud enough for his parents to catch on. He may not have been good with Kanji or science, but he did have practice in the matter of skirting Mom's watchful eyes and ears.

He and Ben had been playing that new Biohazard game for hours on end that day but didn't get to beat the last stage. He knew he should wait for his friend to come back tomorrow and then the two of them could claim victory together. But the game was calling to him. No way he could just go back to sleep when all these zombies needed their heads blown off. It was his civic duty if you thought about it hard enough.

The console loaded and showed the menu screen, but no game. Ren's heart picked up its pace. The game wasn't in the machine. He hit the eject button. There was an electric whirring sound, but nothing came out. Ren pushed over the pile of game discs set up in a haphazard tower. He picked each one up. None of them was the game he wanted. He knew he left the disc in the machine. Never bothered to download it onto the console itself. He could swear on his mother's life—well, maybe that was too harsh—he could swear on Ms. Kobayashi's life that he did not touch the disc.

Could it have been Ben?

He felt ashamed for thinking his friend could steal from him. But then he remembered how Ben wanted to come over just to play it. How Ben had been texting him all week about it. How hungry his eyes were while they played. How sad he looked when he had to go home.

Ben's mom didn't let him keep his phone on him at night. Something dumb about it rotting his brain. It was somewhere on his parent's bedside table and he would not risk texting. Ben only lived a five-minute walk down the street. Sure, it was late out and freezing, but he could be there and back in ten, fifteen minutes, tops. Ben slept on the first floor. All Ren had to do was sneak up to his window and tap on the glass. He'd done it dozens of times before, hadn't he? The last time was a month ago when he and Ben snuck out to throw snowballs at passing cars. They never actually hit anything, but it was fun to try. And if Ben didn't wake up, he could just open the window anyway and climb in. Not the best option, but he was a desperate man.

Or I could just go back to sleep now?

A part of him wanted to jump back in under his covers. Shut off the lights and sleep warm and safe into the night. But that other part, that part that couldn't wait until the game was finished, no, even deeper than that, that other part that needed to confront his friend and see if that friendship actually meant something; that part won out.

Ren put on a red ski jacket over his Spider-Man pajama tops, his ski pants, his gloves, his scarf. He opened the door as if any undue pressure would trip off an explosive. The door creaked some, but he didn't hear his parents get out of bed. He walked down the hallway one methodical step at a time. Came to the landing of the stairs. He didn't dare turn on a light and wake his mom. Dad would probably just send him back to bed, but Mom would berate him, and not just in the moment, but for the rest of his life.

Darkness enveloped the staircase. Like a black maw ready to swallow him whole. He never liked his house at night. Once he swore—again on Ms. Kobayashi's life, sorry not sorry—to Ben that he saw a ghost looking back at him from the top of the stairs one night when he got up to get some water. Its face was ashy and pale. Its smile was black, like the rest of the house. Sure, it was probably just his imagination. But on nights like this imagination beats fact. Anything was possible when everyone else was asleep.

He descended into the dark, feeling the stair railing and then the downstairs walls for where to go. He came to the front door. Opened the shoe locker. Put on his boots. Unlocked the door. Carefully opened it, walked outside, and closed it.

It was much colder than he thought it would be. To be fair, he'd never been outside this late at night in the winter. But this was something else. It felt like his face was being pulled off by the cold. Like tiny icy hooks were tugging at his skin. The air stung his eyes, and he imagined his tears freezing into little icicles that would hang over his cheeks. Like a mutated walrus.

The stars shone beautifully in the clear sky. He realized he never really appreciated them before. But his eye-level surroundings were in near total darkness.

He walked down his driveway and triggered the sensor light above the garage. He slipped once on the ice but caught his balance. There was one streetlight to the right of the driveway that offered some hope. But from his house to that light was an ocean of night; he couldn't see anything in that gap. He held his breath and hurried through the dark, unable to see anything near him, careful to not slip, eyes fixed on the streetlight ahead and its angelic white glow.

He made it. Let out his breath into vapor that rose like a dying ghost. He started shivering despite all the layers he wore. His teeth actually chattered. He thought that was just a dumb thing cartoons did.

Ben's house was another two streetlights away. Each interval of darkness between them expanded the length of an entire block. Homes to his right. Some had a light or two on, shining through tiny windows. Most were shut up and quiet as a tomb. To his left was the forest. He couldn't look that way. He imagined all sorts of horrible monsters in the woods. All eyeing him with their hungry red eyes. He thought of the zombies from his game. Now all that didn't seem so fun anymore. He questioned whether he would even play it once he got it back.

He looked back at his home. The sensor light had died, and it too was lost to the night.

I can go back.

No. Don't be a wuss. You can do this.

He held his breath again, not quite knowing why he did that, and shuffled his feet—careful to not lose his balance on the ice—into the next wave of night. His heart suddenly beat quicker. He kept his eyes on the light ahead; not the thick, almost living, dark around him. He felt suffocated by the lack of light. It could have been his holding in of his breath. He let it out and gasped.

That was it. Dummy.

He heard a cracking sound. Like breaking glass or somebody stepping on thin ice. He looked into the forest. Nothing but darkness. He picked up his pace and made it to the next light. The mayor's house was to his right. A four-story mansion with lights on in at least five of the rooms. He was filled with a sudden urge to run up to those giant white doors and start pounding away. Get to safety and to warmth.

He kept walking forward.

Halfway through the next batch of darkness, he could see Ben's house just past the next island of light. But there was something else, off and to his left.

The only color of that world was black. Yet somehow, two distinct obsidian orbs glistened back at him. Like they were shining. Not that they were reflecting light, because they weren't. No, this was a bright darkness.

Another crack of ice.

A low rumbling. Like the growl the mean dog did at him. But it was *heavier* than the dog's. So was the air. It felt like all those stars above him were now pressing him into the snow. Like an invisible hand was squashing him. His head started to hurt.

The wind picked up and shook his bones with its frost. He let out a whimper and started shuffling his feet back to the last house he passed, the big one with all those lights on.

Please mister, please open up, please help me! He wanted to scream that out, but his voice lost its way coming up to his throat.

He thought about his warm bed and his stupid school work and Nana's smile. He even thought about how angry his mom was going to be. And he wanted that. All of that. Anything but what was out there in the dark, looking at him now with those black-yet-bright eyes, breaking the ice now, quicker than before. And was it picking up speed? Was it running now?

Ren screamed. He broke into a run.

As something lifted him off his feet.

CHAPTER 6

Ryoji pulled his red tie tighter across his throat. He was looking in the mirror, not blinking. He liked the sharp tug of the tie and the way it bit into his neck. If he pulled it tight enough, he could feel the sensation of suffocation. He braced himself to do just that. This wasn't just a sexual urge of his, this was about something else he couldn't quite put his finger on.

Power?

A knock at the door.

Can't get any fucking privacy.

"What!?"

Rina opened the door. Her heavy eye shadow covered up the purple skin around her right eye. "Officer Kawamoto is here for you. He's waiting in the lounge."

"Did he say what about!?" he growled.

She flinched at the grating sound. "He said it's urgent. A child went missing last night near your house."

"Tell him I'll be out in a minute."

She bowed and closed the door. As he watched her go, he smirked at the sight of her new short skirt. She was annoying, but yeah, still had her uses.

He loosened the tie to a socially acceptable degree. The skin around his neck was bright red, but it would calm down in a moment.

The day's plans annoyed him. His speech at the town festival was to be given in just a few hours. The town's winter solstice festival; a time when all the old bums and hags of Kamuy-Kotan said their prayers at the shrine, cleaned their homes, remembered the bear attack of 1915, and made offerings to the spirits for good health. His father told him that this time of year was when the sun was at its weakest, therefore all the dark things of the spirit world had easier access to ours. Many believed that's what that bear attack was; a demon that had slipped through because of the lack of sun and the lack of piety. Some old fools even prayed to the bear god for forgiveness. Ryoji didn't believe in any of this shit, of course, but he was still mayor, and he still had to give a speech and offer a prayer at the shrine for the good health of the town.

But he had other, more important, things to attend to. Things he wished with all his heart to do instead. Ryoji kept a line open with the forest management agency in case the bear with the white-lightning face showed up again. Nothing so far. Which meant he had to put on a fucking suit and talk to a bunch of geriatrics about why their town was so damn special. What irritated him more was the job left undone. Hunting, aside from banging his secretary, was about the only joy he found in life.

Missing kid?

Last night came back to him. He had spent the entire night in his trophy room. Drinking. Fucking. His wife was out of town all week in Okinawa, coming back in a few days, so no need to worry on that front. He was looking out a window just past two in the morning. He thought he heard something that sounded like a scream. When he went to look, nothing.

He put on his suit jacket and walked out of the room and into the adjoining lounge.

Officer Kawamoto was sitting on the edge of the leather sofa, like his ass wasn't allowed to touch it. He held his navy police cap in both hands. He looked bewildered, out of place, nervous.

"Kawamoto, I'm sorry to hear about the missing person. What can I do to help?" Ryoji stamped across the hardwood floor to the officer and gave him a brisk bow.

Kawamoto stood up. "Ren Saito, a ten-year-old boy, went missing last night."

Ryoji shook his head. "Terrible. Terrible news. Sorry to be rude though, but what has that got to do with me?"

"It's just, uh, there was—"

"Out with it, man."

"The boy is a neighbor of yours. A few homes down the street. We found his footprints in the snow. They stop in front of your house here and—"

"Un-fucking believable. You're accusing me?" His plastic smile melted away quickly under the heat of perceived accusation.

"No sir, not at all. But there was some blood found on the road. I have another officer out there right now checking things out. You didn't notice it this morning?"

"I haven't left the house since waking up."

"What about your assistant?"

Shit. Come on, Ryoji boy. Truth or lies.

Fuck it, lesser of two evils.

"She slept here last night."

Kawamoto raised an eyebrow. "Ah, I see. Well, if you wouldn't mind, sir, could you accompany me outside?"

"I do fucking mind. I have a speech to give across town soon."

Kawamoto looked around the room and gripped his cap tighter. He was a small town cop way out of his league. He said, in a wavering voice, "I'm sorry, sir, but you really don't have a choice."

The balls on this guy.

Ryoji laughed. He couldn't decide if he hated this man or loved him. "Alright, but it's gotta be quick."

Ryoji bent down and examined the area in front of his home. The town's only two police officers and an ambulance were there. Yellow tape cordoned off the road on both sides.

Can't believe I didn't notice this earlier.

The Saito family was behind the tape talking to the other officer, Rei, he thought the name was. The woman was hysterical. Sobbing and falling on her knees. Her husband held onto her arms and was trying to lift her up. His face was shell-shocked and white, not looking like he was even hearing what Rei was saying. Next to them was a young woman standing stiffly, close to the woman and looking uncomfortable. She looked Japanese, but Ryoji knew she was that Russian girl. He had a vague memory of seeing her at the city hall to get her hunting license. Caused quite the scene as everyone scrambled to figure out exactly how to process a foreigner's ID into the system.

The foreigner went to put her hand on the mother's shoulder. Mrs. Saito accepted it, but her body stiffened.

Ryoji looked back down at the snow. The boy's footprints were obvious. They came from down the street on the left, passed his house by a meter, and then arched like he was heading back the other way. They snaked their way into Ryoji's yard and became chaotic. Large impressions on the snow like a body had fallen down. But they were too big to be from the boy. Or an adult at that.

There were four bright red spots in the tussled snow. Blood. Not much, but enough to not bode well for what happened here.

Ryoji already pointed out to Kawamoto that there were no tracks leading from his house to the street. He hadn't left in a few days and there had been one dusting of snow last night to cover all his, and Rina's, steps. The only tracks were from Kawamoto leading up to the front door. That seemed good enough for the cop. For now, at least.

What concerned Ryoji at that moment wasn't what Kawamoto thought. It wasn't the distress of the Saitos. The woman's sobs were annoying him. Deep down, he knew this had to be a bear. Not too unusual for one to be out of hibernation by chance. The one he shot last week was proof of that. They could be driven mad by hunger and being thrown off their natural rhythm by waking up too early.

He secretly hoped it was the same bear. Good old lightning face. It would give him a chance to finish what he started.

There was a doubt gnawing at his mind, though. Aside from the boy's tracks, the impressions, the blood, there were no other tracks—bear's or otherwise.

It was like the boy vanished from the spot.

Like he was plucked up into the sky.

Ryoji smiled, hiding it from the grieving family, showing it only to himself. He turned to Kawamoto. "We'll need to get a search party together for the boy right away."

Kawamoto fumbled for a response. Ryoji picked it up for him. "We'll start here."

He nodded towards the woods.

Ryoji put on a grave face, but inside he was beaming. He'd get out of his speech after all.

CHAPTER 7

Whoosh.

The arrow left the bow and sailed through the air. It raced past the cabin and struck the bag of straw. Its head buried deep in the neck of the crudely drawn man that was scribbled onto the bag with a black marker that was running out of ink.

Ashiya walked over to the target and pulled the arrow out. She walked back to the front of the cabin and turned around. Breathed in through her nose—five seconds—held it, five seconds, let it out, five seconds. She did this for two more rounds. Strung the arrow. Lifted it up and aimed it at the bag-man. Another round of breath work.

Her eyes were still wet and blurry from earlier and if she didn't focus and shoot that bag, the tears would come again.

Ashiya hoped Ren was okay. Even though Hikari didn't say it, Ashiya could sense a thin cloud of apprehension around her.

Did she suspect me?

Ashiya understood. The one night they invited the loner, the stranger, the foreigner, into their home, was the same night their son went missing. It didn't look good.

More than her ego or her hurt feelings, she worried for the boy. She knew the chances of somebody surviving a night out in this cold, with no special gear or training, unscathed, wasn't good. He could live through it for sure. Maybe. But she feared he'd be frostbitten or have gotten hypothermia.

She pulled the arrow back. Imagined that the bag-man was all her rage and hurt and pain. That's why she drew the goofy grin and the bucked teeth. Before she let loose a loud car horn made her jolt. She aimed the bow up, let go of the arrow, and it flew over her cabin; hopefully landing somewhere in the snow and not in her car's tire.

She spun around and saw Ogoto's banged up truck in her driveway. She saw his stupid grin through the dirty windshield. Very much like the bag-man indeed. Too bad she couldn't use another arrow on him.

She stomped her way through the snow and up to the truck. Kicked the driver's door.

"You idiot! I could have hurt myself or shot you!"

He went to open the door, but she kicked it again, shutting it.

"Hey it was a joke," he shouted from inside the truck. "You gonna let me out?"

"No."

He crawled over some food wrappers and old clothes in the passenger seat and opened the passenger door and got out. He fell out of the truck and landed on his side. Muttering to himself, he stood and brushed the snow off his clothes and took a bag out of the seat.

He walked around the front end of the truck. "I'm sorry. I thought it'd be funny."

"Not forgiven."

"I heard what, I mean, I brought beer."

He patted the bag.

"Sure."

Ashiya was pissed at him, but that was nothing new. Still, this was literally her only friend. She didn't expect the Saitos to be up for her coming around anytime soon.

She opened the door to her cabin and let him in. Her place was a one-room cabin built back in the sixties by some land developer from Tokyo who wanted to play at winter wonder land living. It was probably very nice back then. She saw evidence of a large yard, now overgrown with dead trees. Of a treehouse, now a pile of stone and rotted wood. The interior was dusty when she moved in. Spider webs clogged up every corner and every doorframe. She even found a centipede under the bed.

That was back in Autumn so at least now the winter freeze put an end to most of those nasty things. She spent weeks cleaning the place out, replacing rotted floorboards, installing lamps—there was no electricity—and buying cheap rugs, pillows, curtains; anything to liven the place up a bit. She only planned on being here for the winter, but that was no reason to live like a pig. Ogoto helped her do all these things, besides letting her shadow him for the hunting license.

Fairly quickly, he must have realized that she was a better shot than he was and better prepared to live out in the woods. But she said none of that to him. Never made him feel less.

The fire was going. The lamps cast an orange glow. There was even a string of cheap Christmas lights strung around the room. She was never a big celebrator of the holiday. Even so, it reminded her of home.

She pulled out a chair by her tiny table in the kitchen corner, and Ogoto joined her. He flopped the bag on the table and took out two beers. He handed one to her. They cracked them opened and Ashiya took a sip while Ogoto took a gulp.

"Thanks," she said.

"No problem. So, I heard people are blaming you for what happened. I mean, that's what everyone is saying."

She raised an eyebrow. "Everyone?"

Ogoto drank the rest of his beer in one go, crushed the can, and grabbed another one out of his bag. He offered one to Ashiya, but she raised her hand to block it.

"Yep."

"It's not even been a day," she said.

"Word travels like wildfire here. People don't mean ill by it. Just the way it is. Went down to the Saito market to pick up some food, but they was closed as I figured they'd be. Two women were out front, looking real sad like because they couldn't get in, talking about that Mongolian girl living out in the woods by herself. People real suspicious about you."

He laughed and slurred some of his words. This was definitely not only his second drink of the day.

"Mongolian?"

"Hey, I stepped on in and defended you. Said she's American first off, and second, that she's a good woman."

"I. Am. Russian," she said through nearly clenched teeth.

"Same thing. Anyway, point is, I know you and I know you had nothing to do with that kid going missing." He drank half the beer in his hand, keeping his eyes on Ashiya as he drank. He placed it down on the table. "Did you? I mean, if you did, I wouldn't tell nobody."

"Of course I didn't."

He seemed satisfied with her resolve and stared into the fire. "So, what you going to do?"

"What do you mean?"

"The mayor is putting together a community search party to look for the kid today. They didn't bother asking me to join, even though I know these woods better than any of them, but I get it. I'm useless, today at least." he pointed to the now empty beer can in front of him. "No harm, no foul, right? But the people goin' ain't worth their shit. The mayor knows how to shoot 'cuz he's always going on these overseas safari type hunts. So he knows how to use a rifle. But tracking? How to navigate around trap doors or tree wells in the snow and not fall in? None them know about that."

His slurring and his thick dialect were getting to where Ashiya had to focus with all her attention to understand his words. But his meaning was beyond her, even had he been speaking Russian.

"Your point is?"

"You should help them."

She almost spit out the beer she just took a swig of.

"You're joking? I... the Saitos wouldn't want me there."

In her mind, despite the Saitos saying nothing of the kind, Ashiya felt the suspicion in how Hikari nearly flinched when Ashiya touched her shoulders earlier.

Ogoto's perpetual grin straightened into a grimace. "No, I'm dead serious. If this was a run-of-the-mill search and rescue, sure, maybe. There's enough men in town who could pull that off. But—" His eyes and his words got lost in the flames now. Ashiya could see them dancing in his dark eyes. "I have this feeling. Deep down like. That they'll be needing someone who knows how to survive out there. How to really survive."

"Well then, that's not me. Aren't there more people coming in from the city to help? How many people are joining the search?"

"Maybe forty people out there right now. But a blizzard is coming tomorrow morning. Will be touch and go for a few days after that. The city can't spare anyone until at least tomorrow and no one is driving in then. All the roads will be snowed in for sure. Maybe they can send a helicopter tomorrow, but that will not do much with all the tree cover and the boy will be dead for sure, if he ain't already."

"Even if I went, what could I do? Yeah, I could follow tracks, but that's about it. If we ran into anything, I can't even shoot. I'll be about as good as any of them out there. And if there's this rumor about me, won't that just make things worse? I don't think people want me anywhere near this."

"Like hell they wouldn't. Don't be a pussy about it. Your feelings are hurt because the whole fucking town blames you? Too bad. You are the one to do this job. I know it. And if you can do it, do it. Not for your pride or for their feelings. But for the kid."

Ashiya went silent. Took the words to heart. Looked on the man, the town drunk, the clown in tattered clothes, and marveled at the wisdom that somehow found its way crawling out of his mouth.

"But they've already left, right?"

"Yep. Ryoji—that's the mayor—took the group into the woods across from his house. He lives—"

"I saw the spot."

"Alright, good. They left about an hour ago, which gives 'em about six hours before sunset. Be coming back before then. They're not stupid enough to be out all night. But still, I think you should go and do your thing, whether or not you join with the group."

Ashiya set her beer down and turned her body towards the fire. It was safe and warm here. Things were under her control.

And look where opening up got you? You wouldn't be involved in any of this if you just stayed home last night.

She saw Alexei's face in the fire. His crooked smile. She even heard his sarcastic laugh as the wood popped in the flames. The way the wood turned into red coals almost looked like the red sash on his dead face.

"Okay. I'll see if I can do anything. But I'm not expecting I can."

Ogoto nodded his head.

"Alright, I'll get going. Just wanted to see how you were and let you know my thoughts. You stay safe, Anoosootsjyah."

CHAPTER 8

Ashiya's feet broke through the hard snow with a satisfying crunch, though getting them out again wasn't easy. In some places, they didn't even break through and she could walk on top of the snow itself. That was better. She held her backpack straps with both hands and kept her eyes looking ahead. In the bag was an emergency space blanket, materials for getting a fire going, first aid kit, water bottles, and even a small lean-to tent setup. The rifle attached to the outside of the bag by a bungee cord. Bright orange hunter's vest over her white ski jacket.

Always be prepared.

She had on her best thermal underwear and her Gore-Tex snow gear. A white wool face mask that left only her lips and eyes exposed. She felt fairly warm, for now. She remembered her father's story about how he went on a two-hour hunt near their home when he was a teenager. The day was sunny, with no clouds in sight. Got trapped in a sudden snowstorm anyway and had to spend the night out in the fields with no light, no tent, no fire. He made it. But his left pinky and ring finger didn't.

This was all before she was born, so she grew up used to her father's stunted hand. But the image of the nub just above the knuckle still burned its way into her subconscious.

That would not be her.

The sun was high in the pale blue sky. But dark clouds loomed over the horizon. The snow reflected the sun's glare, slightly dimmed by her sunglasses. The birch trees stood out of the snow like bones ringed with black circles. There was no sound in the air. No birds. No wind. It was tranquil yet foreboding. Like the air itself took in a breath and was preparing to speak. Whatever it would say couldn't be good.

She was following the set of tracks before her, left by the search party maybe an hour or so before. Dozens of people, some with big boots on, some with basic tennis shoes. They walked in pairs, carving multiple different paths, all going in the same direction. All leading into the deep forest. She knew this area well, but had never strayed too far into the woods before. The deer were abundant even close to the residential areas and there was no need to go further in.

The search party started at the tree line next to where the police found Ren's footprints and the blood. Ashiya parked her car further down the street. She was afraid people would see it and the rumors would catch fire even more. So she went into the woods from several hundred meters away until she caught up with the path.

She wondered at what tracks the search party could be following. She saw the double indentations of deer hooves here and there. The tiny, almost human-like paws of tanuki. But nothing else.

She thought about what could have happened to Ren. Him running away was doubtful. Ashiya had done that once back in high school. Ren didn't seem the type and even if he was, there was nowhere for a ten-year-old boy, without money, to go to in the middle of the night out in the middle of nowhere. That left one other option: someone took him.

If it was a bear, there would have been paw prints. More signs of a struggle in the snow and more blood. So it couldn't have been that. She imagined a man in a dark van pulling up to him on the street and taking him inside. There were tire tracks on the road, but those could have belonged to anyone living on that street. It was hard to imagine that sort of thing happening here. The town only had two cops and a handful of stoplights. Sure, evil could be hidden behind any door in any home, but why would it come out now? As far as she knew, this sort of thing had never happened in the town before.

She thought about Ben dropping that CD and the way he refused to look her in the eye afterwards. She figured he took something from Ren, but it wasn't her place to prod somebody else's kid about being a thief.

But if I did, would Ren be missing?

She guessed he must have been out that night to get his game back from Ben. She could have stopped it. But she didn't. Now another person was paying the price for her inaction.

She tried to tell herself that it wasn't her responsibility, that she was being too harsh on herself. And maybe she was. Didn't help to unload the guilt. Didn't help to bring him back.

But *she* could. If he was out here in these woods, she could find him. So long as he wasn't taken in that van in her imagination and carted off to a different town. As long as he was out here in this forest, she had confidence. But if it wasn't done quickly, she shuddered at the thought of his state when she did find him.

She walked in between two large Sakhalin firs. Their green needles gave a splash of warmth to the otherwise dormant forest. Most of the trees were elms, devoid of leaves, stretching out of the earth like shriveled claws and tendrils, reaching for the blue sky. Like the buried dead longing for life above the surface of their graves. Seeking to take hold of it and thrust it down to the depths.

She saw droppings near the base of the fir on her left. Too small to be from a bear; maybe a monkey's or even a boar's. Neither of which could have taken the boy.

Ashiya wasn't nervous about running into a bear. The brown bears in Siberia could grow as big as a Kodiak, but usually didn't. The Ussuri brown here in Hokkaido were bigger. Not as big as a Kamchatka, but still pretty damn close. Boars though, those bastards could come running out of a bush anytime of the year and gore her.

She walked in silence for several minutes. The only sound was the breaking of the snow under her boots and the wind rattling the dead branches of the trees.

She came to a small clearing. The path of the search party ran straight through it. She walked halfway across the meadow and stopped. Some movement in the trees ahead caught her eye.

At first, she thought it was the search party and almost called out to them. But the shadow in the forest was moving erratically. First on two feet and then falling to four. She judged the size was too big for a man. She dropped to a knee and shouldered her rifle.

Looking down the scope, she caught sight of dark brown fur. It darted behind a tree and she lost it.

Something about that movement seemed too fast, too deliberate, too mechanical, to be an animal. It was almost as if a person had spotted her and was trying to hide; albeit a person who also moved unnaturally. But the size of the creature and the fur coat convinced her she had been wrong.

There was a bear out here.

And it was heading towards the search party.

Ogoto had given her the mayor's cell number before she left. She took her phone out of her jacket breast pocket and called him. It was too awkward to do so before, and she was confident she'd catch up to them, anyway. But now there was an obvious threat. No time for social ineptitude.

He didn't answer the phone.

She put her phone away and stood up. Picked up her pace with her rifle held out in front.

She entered the next tree line and came to the spot where she thought she saw the bear.

Aside from the human ones, no other tracks.

Ashiya half questioned her sanity. Did she really see what she thought she did?

The path made by the group continued forward, and she followed it. The trees grew closer together in this part of the forest. A few times, she had to turn sideways to get past them. Both the evergreens and the dead branches crowded the sky, dimming the light underneath their arms. It felt like the temperature had dropped significantly. She shivered.

As she walked forward a few more meters, she came upon a fat oak tree. It had a bear claw mark scratched onto it. The marks went deep. Splintered wood lay atop the fresh snow.

Rifle up.

Walking forward.

The air felt heavier now. Almost as if she were quickly rising in elevation. The pressure filled her head, and she yawned to pop her ears. No relief. The air seemed to shimmer and wave like it does on a hot day.

But her blood ran cold.

It was as if something was here. Watching her, even standing right next to her. Unseen and unheard, but very much real and present.

Something huffed in the dark spaces of the forest ahead. The snort of a large animal.

The hair on her neck stood up. The cold air felt like needles being pushed into the skin that was exposed around her face. Her heartbeat drowned out the sound of her footsteps in the snow. She saw the animal. Far off ahead, but no mistaking it for anything but a bear. Facing her. On its hind legs. It didn't move. It stood still. Too far away to tell for sure, but it looked massive.

She raised the scope to her eye.

The bear was gone.

She pulled the scope away and scanned the horizon with her naked eyes.

Not a trace.

CHAPTER 9

Hikari Saito lit the incense and placed it in the fixture by the altar. She closed her eyes and clasped her hands together in front of her face. She prayed—no idea to who—God? Buddha? Her ancestors?—whoever would listen, really.

Never had she prayed from her heart. Never had she dared to believe in its power. She wasn't sure if she even did now. But what else was there to do?

Itsuki was out with the rest of the community volunteers looking for their son. She stayed home just in case Ren came back. She had fought with Itsuki on that, wanted to be out there right now and look for him. But reason won out. If Ren was out there, lost, and came stumbling home, she wanted to be there waiting for him. Besides, there were dozens of people out there right now. They had to find him.

Please.

She opened her eyes and looked back at the smiling Buddha statue on the shelf in her home. The smoke of the incense wrapped around his golden, chubby, indifferent face. Did prayers reach him? Did he care? She turned and went to sit down at the kitchen counter.

There was nothing more to do.

Everyone she could think of had been called. She knew Ren must have been going to Ben's house, given the direction of his steps. After just minutes of getting Ben's father to interrogate him, she found out that he stole a game from Ren.

That's it? A stupid fucking game is why he's missing?

She stared at the blank white wall of the adjoining living room. There had not been tears since she broke down on the street. There was nothing but a numbness left in her. Like she had been in the cold for hours without protection.

And what did he have on now? A simple ski jacket and gloves?

She got that jacket for him last month. He needed a new jacket every year. He grew so fast.

Would she ever get to buy him another one?

You don't grow while frozen in the ground.

Where did that come from? She shook her head and clasped her hands in prayer again.

She fell to her knees on the linoleum.

"Please, please bring him back to me."

No answer but the ticking of the clock on the wall and the hum of the AC unit.

This is stupid. I have to do something.

But what can you do?

She got off the floor for starters. Wandered around the living room like a wraith of her former self. She couldn't bear to look at the framed pictures of him on the fireplace mantle. In a way, that would be admitting that he was gone.

Because I'll see his face soon is why.

Hikari walked over to her front window and looked out at the forest. She never enjoyed living so close to the wilderness. She was a city girl through and through. But Itsuki wanted a quiet life out in the country, near his parents. A safe place to raise a family. To see their children be happy and grow old.

She couldn't continue the thought.

I'm going for a walk.

She put on her jacket and boots and went outside.

The cold didn't even bother her. It could consume her for all she cared. Swallow her whole and spit out the bones on the street. She walked down her driveway and turned left onto the street. Shuffled her feet down the road, away from the spot where her son disappeared from. Earlier that day, when she woke at six to a mild hangover, she got out of bed to make some breakfast for the family. It wasn't unusual for Ren to want to sleep in on school days—any day, really—and she would let him. As much as she pushed him and got mad at him for being lazy, she didn't actually believe in any of that. She knew her son was as diligent as could be expected from a ten-year-old.

When she went up to his room at half-past six and knocked on his door, no response. She opened it and did not find him inside. For a moment she thought he might be up already, but then she would have seen him. It didn't take long for the panic to set in when she couldn't find him anywhere in the house.

And now he was out there somewhere. She looked at the gray trees and cried. Her tears felt like burning ice as they rolled down her cheeks.

Hikari knew she'd be useless out in the woods. As much as she wanted to be there, she left that to the volunteers—mostly men who knew how to move in the woods and a few women, the sporty types who could handle a hike, and that was not her. She'd just get in the way. But she couldn't stay here anymore. Sure, the police told her that Ren might show up, so she should stay home to meet him. But she didn't believe that. Not in this moment. Whatever, whoever, had taken her son was out there. Never had she felt so inept and useless than at that moment. Her chief skill in life was her ability to keep on talking about anything to anyone. And what could words do in this situation?

She suddenly snapped her head up. Hikari had walked three blocks and not even realized it.

To her left was the Okawa family's tiny cottage. Smoke billowed up from the chimney. Their two cars in the drive. Everyone home and safe and warm.

To her right was the forest and, just ahead, parked onto the berm, an ugly lime green Jimny covered in mud splotches.

Ashiya's car.

Rage. Fear. Shame. Panic. All these emotions flooded her mind and made her dizzy. The world swayed and shifted like it wasn't actually there, like she was looking at a picture of life and somebody was shaking it back and forth.

She regretted what she felt towards Ashiya despite saying nothing of the kind to anyone, not even to Itsuki.

It's your fault.

What did you do!?

She knew deep down that it couldn't have been her. She knew people, and she knew Ashiya was one of the good ones.

But still. Her son goes missing on the one night this stranger comes into her home? Who could blame her for what she felt?

And what was her car doing here? Parked so far away from where she had any business being.

Hikari climbed up the berm and stood on top of the churned up ice and dirty snow. She saw footsteps leading from the car and into the woods.

"What are you doing out here?"

She imagined all kinds of horrible things. Was she out there to throw the search party off the trail of her son? Was she there to hide something? To hurt somebody? To help?

Hikari had no answers. She wanted to believe that it was a mistake. That she and Ashiya could go back to last night, smoking and laughing at her kitchen table. When eating too much fucking cheesecake was an actual worry in her life. But more than anything, she wanted her son back. And if it was this woman's fault, and if she was doing anything to prevent the party from finding Ren, she would not allow that.

She took out her phone and called her husband. It kept on ringing, but he didn't pick up. She texted him: WHERE ARE YOU?

She stared at the screen, but he didn't read the text. She thought about just calling Ashiya and having her explain herself. Her thumb hovered over her contact icon.

No. No more being useless. Hikari jogged home, grabbed a heavy duty ski jacket, scarf, and gloves from the hall closet, and went back outside. She returned to Ashiya's car, climbed up the berm, and entered the forest.

After taking a few steps past the first trees, she felt a sudden rise of pressure in her head.

CHAPTER 10

Ashiya heard a group of people talking. She climbed up a small hill and looked out to her right. Far off, down in a flat part of the forest, she could see someone in a red jacket walking with someone else in a bright blue one. And beyond them, a dozen more people walking. They were yelling, their voices echoing off the trees. The search party.

She reasoned she should check the part of the forest the volunteers were not in. They could keep to that side, and if they found Ren, great. Meanwhile, she would search her side of the woods separately from the group.

Her side was hilly. The trees grew close together. The snow wasn't hard here, but soft. She sank to her knees with every step. By the time she climbed another hill and could hardly hear the yells of the search party, she was exhausted. At the crest of the hill, she leaned up against a tree to catch her breath.

No tracks anymore. She had followed those of the volunteers to this point, but there were no animal tracks; not even from deer. No child's tracks either. She felt useless. What was she supposed to be looking for? What if Ren had been abducted and wasn't even out here?

She pushed herself off the tree and walked down the hill. Ashiya looked at her watch: three in the afternoon. Sundown two hours away, but in an hour it would get dark. She could always come back tomorrow, first thing in the morning, but by then it would be too late for Ren, wouldn't it? She had the gear to survive out here for a night.

Then that's what I'll do. Unless he's found *earlier, I won't leave the forest until at least tomorrow night.*

The pressure in her head never really left her. It made her stomach heave, and she felt dizzy. Still, she pressed through it and moved forward.

A flash of movement up ahead.

Rifle out.

She saw the bear. For just a moment. It was running away from her direction and vanished behind a thick wall of trees. She stepped forward.

BAM!

Bark rained down on her, and she laid herself out on the snow. The sudden explosion of sound ricocheted all around. She heard men shouting. Footsteps quickly advancing.

"I think I got it!"

"I see nothing."

Ashiya looked up and saw two men approaching her, not looking directly at her. Maybe they couldn't see her? She was wearing her white jacket, but she had an orange vest attached to it. One man was portly, had a thick gray beard, and a faded green jacket. The other one was a police officer. Not the one who questioned her and the Saitos, but the other guy who went into the mayor's house. Tall and skinny, his eyes wild with fear.

"Don't shoot!" she shouted.

"Shit, it's a person!" said Gray Beard. He had a rifle. The cop had a pistol in his shaking hands.

Ashiya got to her feet. "What are you doing!? You could have killed me!"

Gray Beard's eyes opened wide, and he stuttered, "We thought...I thought...you were a bear."

Ashiya grabbed her orange vest and shook it at him. "You couldn't see this!?"

Another man came running up to the group from behind. It was the mayor, Ryoji. Ashiya recognized him from posters hung up around town on store fronts and some people's homes. He had a beaming smile, bleached white. But no smile lines by his eyes. Her grandmother always taught her to look for those lines. *A smooth face is a false face,* she said.

"What's happening?" Ryoji asked.

Gray Beard stuttered some more and even sputtered like a broken sprinkler.

"This guy almost shot me," she explained.

Ryoji looked her up and down. "And what are you doing out here? I know you're that foreign pet of Ogoto's. You're in the way."

"I just... wanted to help find Ren."

"By getting yourself shot? Wandering over here by yourself will do that. And why are you carrying that gun? Kawamoto!" He looked over at the cop. "Is that legal?"

"Umm, yes, I think so. She has a license and me and Rei are aware of her. So, as far as I know, I think—"

Ryoji held up his hand and cut Kawamoto off. "Fine. But I don't trust you, girl. If a person took the kid, who do you think prime suspect number one is?"

"Well, that's not official and I can't really say..." Kawamoto began and cut himself off this time.

"I saw the bear," she said.

At this, Ryoji's eyes lit up. "Where?" No hint of doubt in his voice as she had expected. He was more than eager to know.

Ashiya pointed in the direction she saw it running.

"You're not lying?" Ryoji asked. Ashiya shook her head. "Fine, let's go," he said.

"I'm coming with you," Ashiya put in.

Ryoji looked at her and scoffed. "Whatever. But you stay in the back. Don't need a foreigner, a woman who can barely hold up her rifle, fucking this up. Kawamoto is going to check your license and your visa after this. Make sure you're supposed to even be here."

Kawamoto said nothing, just looked at the ground as if expecting the snow to save him from the situation. He followed Ryoji and Gray Beard as they took the lead in the direction Ashiya had pointed out.

Ryoji got on his phone and told whoever was on the line to not bring everyone over. No, the gunshot was just a mistake. Don't worry about it. He hung up.

Rage simmered in Ashiya's chest. Ryoji lit every fuse in her in a matter of seconds. And now he was taking the lead on the information she had provided.

It's not about credit. It's about Ren. Calm down.

She told herself this and tried to let the cold air soothe away her temper. Did her breath work—five seconds in—hold it, five seconds, *fuck this.*

It didn't work. Her mind raced too fast to concentrate on her breathing.

They walked on in silence for several minutes. Her head still felt stuffy. Something she ignored until she saw Kawamoto yawn and shake his head a little.

So they feel it too?

The branches overhead grew thick and blocked out the sunlight. Everything in front of her turned an ashen gray. She checked behind them and to their sides for movement. Kawamoto and Gray Beard kept their eyes forward. She knew they were scared. Ryoji held his head up and scanned the forest. He was an asshole, but at least he looked more competent than the other two.

The pressure in her head grew more intense. Shadows of the trees bled out over the path.

Gray Beard put his hand to his head. "Fuck, my head hurts."

So did hers.

The air shimmered and flexed. It somehow seemed darker and colder than it was just a second ago.

Ryoji said nothing and led them to a near-black tree. It looked charred as if by numerous lightning strikes. Rotten even.

Ashiya's pulse quickened. Each rush of blood felt like the beat of a drum.

Or did she actually hear that just now? A drum beat. Rhythmic pulsing. Was that an actual sound or just in her head?

"Do you hear that?" Kawamoto asked. No one responded.

Real it is.

Ryoji walked around the black tree and stopped.

Gray Beard came next and dropped his rifle in the snow. Then fell on his ass and screamed. Kawamoto froze in front of Ashiya, not even rounding the bend to see what the other two had seen. Ashiya pushed him out of the way and waded through the deep snow to see what was happening.

And then she saw it.

"Oh my God," were the only words that could escape her throat.

But God had no part in this.

CHAPTER II

Splayed between two trees was the skinned corpse of a deer. The deer's limbs were spread in almost a mock crucifixion style. Its feet were impaled on short branches. The meat glistened in the falling light.

The snow beneath it was a deep red, thoroughly soaked through.

Its spinal column and ribs were exposed by what looked like a single bite wound, akin more to a shark's than a bear's. The head—still furred and antlered—impaled on a stick that had been driven into the ground in front of the body. Eyes wide open and black. The rest of its hide was nowhere in sight.

On the trunks of the two trees that held up the body, deep slash marks from a bear. The bear's bloody claws made red rivets in the marks as it scratched the tree. That, or the tree itself, was bleeding.

Aside from their own, no other tracks in the snow.

Gray Beard scooted back on his ass over a bush. Whimpering.

Kawamoto stayed where he was, around the bend of the tree. He hadn't even seen it yet.

Sweat appeared on Ryoji's forehead.

"I've seen something like this before," Ashiya said. Swallowing her spit with great difficulty first. "By my cabin, over by that lake, the one just outside of town. I saw a deer with a bite mark just like this one, but smaller. But no tracks in the snow to show what did it. Just like this." She walked closer to the deer and gestured at the jagged rips in the meat. "But it wasn't skinned or decapitated like this. Just bitten."

Nobody replied to her observation. That drum beat—what could have been her own heart—pulsed louder in her head.

"What does this mean?" Gray Beard asked, still scrambling away on his backside, slipping as he tried—and failed—to stand.

"Oda, get your shit together!" Ryoji barked at him, face still drained of color. He went over to the man and grabbed him by his jacket and forced him to stand. Ryoji yelled at Kawamoto to come over, and when he did, his skin turned whiter than the snow, his lips bluer than the sky.

"I think it's obvious we are not dealing with a bear," Ryoji said. He stared hard at Ashiya. "We are dealing with a sicko. Whoever did this might be the same person who took the boy."

"I sh-sh-should call this in," Kawamoto said and reached for his walkie-talkie. He flipped the switch on, but all that came out was a screeching, static cry. He tried to hail the Officer Rei, but no one replied.

The sky grew dark in an instant. Through the gaps in the branches above, Ashiya could see thick, almost black storm clouds cover the sky. A rumble of thunder that sounded too much like a cacophony of drum beats to her. Snow suddenly fell heavy and fast. The wind picked up and slammed into their faces. Ashiya even felt the slight sting of graupel.

Oda screamed something about bad omens and took off running back the way they came. Ryoji yelled after him, but the man disappeared into the blanket of snow; so thick it was getting hard to even see the trees that were right in front of them. Kawamoto turned on his flashlight, but the reflection of the falling snow made it even harder to see. He switched it off with shaking hands and almost dropped it. Ryoji took a few steps after Oda, himself almost vanishing into the storm.

"Hey!" Ashiya yelled above the howling wind. "Calm down. It's just a storm." *Yeah right.* "We need to keep our heads or we'll get lost." *Or run into whoever strung up this deer.*

She didn't believe that whoever had skinned and strung up the deer had also killed it. An animal had to have taken a bite out of its midsection. But the bite was too big to be a bear. None of this was making sense to her. All the while, her head pounded to the rhythm of the drums.

Darkness seemed to seep down from the branches overhead, bleeding into the near-whiteout snowfall.

"What do we do?" Kawamoto asked, moving closer to Ashiya as if seeking her counsel over Ryoji's.

"If we stay, we might freeze to death," Ryoji said.

"We wait until the snow clears up a bit!" Ashiya snapped. "We won't find our way back in this. One of us could fall down a tree well. There's lots of them out here under the snow. I have supplies that could be enough for all of us in case we need to wait it longer than an hour."

"I'm h-h-hearing voices," Kawamoto sputtered out. "There's something speaking in the wind. Can't you hear it?!"

Ashiya could not. But the drum beats, which had faded to a low pulse, were still present.

Kawamoto went on, "It's not natural. That deer is not natural. There's something evil out here!" He screamed those last words and nearly turned to flee in the way Oda had gone.

Ashiya grabbed his arm and held onto him. "Sir, do not go. Not yet. It's not safe."

"Bullshit," Ryoji said and walked up to the deer. He grabbed it by its legs and tore it down from the branches that held it up. "All that's out here is some sick fuck messing with us."

"No," Ashiya said. "I mean, yes, somebody put this body here. But, I saw a bear. It was huge. Look at this bite mark. Do you know any bear capable of that?"

Ryoji looked down at the corpse at his feet. "No. No, I don't."

Ashiya took Kawamoto by the hand and pulled him close. She reached out for Ryoji's, but he held it back, furrowing his brow at her.

"We need to stay close and keep warm for now. Come on."

Reluctantly, Ryoji moved forward and the three of them huddled in the middle of the squall. The snow lashed at them like it was personal. Ashiya could see ice wrapping around Kawamoto's thin beard and the eyelashes of both men.

Just then, a sound that filled her with dread. Above the howl of the wind. The low moan of a bear. It puffed out air and growled. Mixed with the wind, it was too hard to tell where it was coming from. And she couldn't see shit. It sounded like it was circling them.

Kawamoto shook even more, and not just from the cold. She hoped he wouldn't wet his pants. It could freeze to his leg. She and Ryoji turned outward from their huddle and faced the heavy snowfall with their rifles out.

Another growl to her right. Nothing to see but the white static screen of the storm.

A sudden rush of footsteps. Directly at them. Kawamoto cried out and fell to his knees. Ryoji fired his rifle into the snow. Ashiya waited. Wanted to see what she was going to hit. No sense in killing somebody by mistake. She imagined Oda running back to them and getting shot.

A puff of air. A snort. Just beyond the veil of snow, she could see the dim and faded shadow of something large. Moving from right to left in front of her. Good enough. Ashiya took aim to fire just as the shadow receded back into the storm. Her hands shook. Her breath came in fast and heavy. She was lightheaded.

She wanted to believe that she would have pulled that trigger if it got any closer.

Ryoji fired another shot.

In the lightning crackle of the rifle, Ashiya saw Alexei's face in her mind. Not the wry, crooked smile he always flashed at her to get his way. Not the red sash that covered him at the funeral. She saw him as she did that final time. The last time she truly saw his face.

Or what was left of it.

She saw the broken teeth lying in the frozen grass—painted red and shining wet. She remembered creeping up to that grass. Seeing more teeth. All of them shattered save for one molar, the whole tooth, standing upright in the dirt. She could still remember the grooves of that tooth, even now. It had six. The shading of white and slight yellow of plaque. Alexei was never good about brushing his teeth. To the side of the teeth, the red mass. He was still twitching.

She turned to face him and screamed.

And then she was back in the storm. Kawamoto kneeling in the snow. Ryoji, yelling obscenities at the wind.

Until it all died down. The snow fell more softly. They could see the trees now. The sky was gray, but not as black as it had been. The wind still blew, but it whispered now more than howled.

"Ren!" They all heard it from the depths of the forest. The voice of a woman.

"Ren!"

It was Hikari's voice.

CHAPTER 12

"Ren!" Hikari shouted.

She trudged through the snow, following Ashiya's footprints. But things had gotten all weird and confused. She never deviated from the trail, but now the footprints were nowhere to be seen.

Snow was falling hard, and the sky had grown darker.

Just then, ahead of her, a figure stepped out from behind a tree. Even amid the snow—like a thick white fog—she could see it clearly.

Red jacket.

Ren.

It may have been her imagination, a hallucination or delirium, but she thought she saw him smile. With teeth too big for his head.

He turned and ran away from her.

"Wait! Stop!"

She picked up her pace and tried to run after him. But running through the snow was like wading through thick mud. She fell face first and felt a stinging pain in her face. She pulled herself up.

Wet. Cold. Can't see anything.

"Where are you!?"

She started crying. Her heart beat ramped up. Her adrenaline ran her body momentarily hot.

She didn't know where she was. Where the path was. In what direction home was. And why was Ren running away from her?

And what is that sound? Like a heavy breathing, right next to her ear. Like a build-up of pressure crushing her brain.

She screamed and thrashed her arms out. Nothing was there, as far as she could tell in the muted light. But it sounded so close. She felt the heat of breath on her face.

She knew if she panicked; she was dead. But that thought just made her panic all the more.

She walked forward with her gloved hands outstretched. The blinding heaviness of the snow grew heavier still. The snow bit at her face. She couldn't feel her cheeks or forehead anymore. Save for the slight sensation of warmth behind the numbness. The body flooding blood to her extremities to keep them warm. The onset of hypothermia.

The red jacket appeared again. A flash of color in the storm's maelstrom. She pushed forward, no longer able to yell out Ren's name. The wind stole her voice and replaced it with the scream of the storm. The trees came in closer now. They appeared right before she would have walked into them. She reached out and grabbed them to have some anchor point in the white void.

The wind blew the snow harder into her face. She had to squint and could no longer see the jacket.

A new sound carried on the wind. Not the roar of the wind itself or the cracking and crashing of the branches. It was a child's laughter. Her child's. But it was filled with mockery and devoid of the warmth Ren's laugh always carried.

"Hikari."

Her name was called from a voice that could not have been further away than right by her side. It pierced through the hurricane of sounds. It was a whisper in her ear.

She ran.

With whatever strength she had, she barreled through the snow that was piling higher now.

And then she was falling. Rolling down a hill. Not seeing anything but spinning white.

Her body slammed into the side of a tree.

The moment of impact brought a sharp awareness of every sensation in her body. Like she was some detached spirit, observing it all from an ethereal plane. The needle-like pin feeling of numbness on her face and in her fingers and toes. The cold air rushing into her dry eyes. The tree trunk, white with brown horizontal stripes across it. And then the cracking of something in her leg. The lightning pain that surged through her whole body.

And did she see the dark brown thing standing on two legs? With what could have been fur covering its entire body? With what could have been two black eyes that shone in the snowfall.

She screamed and held onto her leg.

Another sound cut her cries short.

"Mom! Help me!"

Every nerve was firing in pain. Her body's only desire was to shut down, curl into a ball, and die. But something else rose inside of her. Set on fire by the cry of her son.

It was love.

She called back to him. His screams answered her back.

The tall thing with black eyes wasn't there anymore. A delusion. A phantom brought on by extreme stress, surely.

She tried to stand, but the pain was too much. She dragged her body across the snow, using trees and bushes and stones to help pull herself across.

Something cut short Ren's screams.

Crying, chest heaving, yelling out his name, she pulled herself faster. The fire shooting through her bones was worse than what she felt giving birth to Ren. She never knew that could be possible. She did not look at her leg, afraid of what she might see.

She pulled herself into a creek without seeing it first. Her body broke through the ice and the water soaked her clothes.

A jolt of adrenaline pushed her out of the creek. She grabbed onto a rock and raised herself up on her uninjured leg, trying to keep the hurt one lifted.

It stopped snowing. Moments after the fat snowflakes had finished falling to earth, she could now see a clearing in front of her.

And what she saw in that meadow made her scream.

CHAPTER 13

Hikari's screams lit a fire in the group. To her utter surprise, Kawamoto sprang into action and ran towards her. Ashiya and Ryoji followed him through the snowdrifts. Snow sprayed out like sea foam as they raced through it. Some of it was up to her waist and for that she was thankful that the other two were faster than she and somewhat cleared a path for her.

Terror seized Ashiya's heart. Those cries were not screams of fear. She had heard them before. She had made them before. The day she found Alexei lying in that field.

They were cries of sorrow and mourning.

Ashiya's mind raced. Why was she out here? What had she found?

Anguish and loss and pain were added to the indifferent whispers of the wind.

More than anything, Ashiya wished she could be anywhere else. In front of her fire, playing her guitar and drinking her sake. Alone and content to remain alone for all of time. Because what she feared to see on the other side of the trees Ryoji just ducked between was too much. Wind blew snow from the branches and it curtained the clearing she had just run to. The snow was a white veil between knowing and not knowing. Between keeping things the way they were and discovering a new and horrifying reality. She didn't ask for this. She didn't want to go through this again.

Soon, dark objects took shape in the white void. Trees and stones. The world's blank canvas gained a new color as she walked forward, fighting the urge to vanish into the blizzard. Red. A bright scarlet hue covered the ground in front of her. It made the scene look unreal. Like this was not supposed to exist out here. But much like the deer near her cabin and the one strung up earlier—a warning? A ritual?—the blood was unmistakable.

Two shadows took shape ahead. One of them hunched over and cradling a smaller shadow, a heap of something on the ground.

The two men got to Hikari first and stopped a meter from her. The wind cleared away the snow blown from the trees. As if to mock her wish to not see it. As if to give her the best conditions to see it, the clouds overhead broke enough for some golden light to shower down.

The light caused the snow crystals in the air to sparkle. The golden rays fell on Hikari Saito, holding her broken son. It seemed almost sacred, almost holy, like they should not be witness to this.

Ren was dead.

His blood splashed over the snow and the trees and the stones.

Hikari sobbed as she held his body.

Ashiya felt sick and lightheaded. Ren wore a red ski jacket and pajama pants. No tears in the fabric. But it was easy to see where all the blood had come from.

Ren was missing his head.

That night Ashiya was back in her cabin, just like she wanted. But she wasn't alone. Her thoughts and the memories of the day were with her. Like Alexei's, another face had joined her nightmare roster.

They found Ren's head on the other side of the meadow. His face was blue and his eyes were open.

Although the fire was hot, Ashiya shivered. Poured another glass of sake and downed in. Ren's face showed no pain, anguish, or terror. Any of those would have been enough to haunt her waking moments for the rest of her life.

No. He was smiling. As if he were having a restful dream. This unnerved her. Not that she wanted the boy she barely knew to have suffered, of course not.

She stood up and paced around the cabin.

It took them only an hour to get out of the woods after finding Ren. The weather, as if finished playing with them, released them without further obstacles.

Ryoji and Kawamoto had to pry Hikari's arms off her son. Ashiya could only look on with horror and sorrow.

Hikari had a broken leg. Some of the bone was showing, though at first it was hard to notice with all the snow. Ryoji may have been an asshole, but he took off his jacket and had her sit on it. He had some climbing rope in his bag, tied it around the jacket sleeves, and pulled Hikari out of there on the makeshift sled. When Ryoji became too exhausted, Kawamoto and Ashiya took turns pulling her.

As Ashiya helped pull Hikari across the snow, the sky no longer emptying snow on them, the sun setting fully and the stars coming out clear and cool across the sky, she couldn't make eye contact with her.

Hikari said nothing. Didn't cry, didn't whimper in pain. She was a husk of her former self.

They left Ren's body until Kawamoto and Officer Rei could go back to the scene and cordon off the area. It may have looked like an animal attack. Ren's body had obvious bite wounds on the neck. However, the nearby deer made it impossible to rule out human involvement. No tracks were found in the clearing, though that wasn't too unusual given the blizzard.

She couldn't help but feel the accusation in the eyes of those around her. Especially Ryoji. No one said anything. Maybe they believed she was innocent. After all, Ashiya had willingly gone out into the storm to assist them in finding the boy.

At least Oda had, if not the decency, at least the presence of mind to get an ambulance brought around after he fled. A few neighbors were even waiting with hot tea, hot chocolate, and heat packs for the returning party.

But she was still the outsider among them. The one no one actually knew. Officer Kawamoto asked to see her ID after they all made it back to the street and ushered Hikari into the waiting ambulance. Itsuki came soon after, dazed and like a walking corpse. He had been on the other side of the forest, that group having returned right before the squall got bad.

Ashiya hadn't brought her wallet, but Kawamoto showed no patience for her. Threatened to cite her for failure of not having her residence card and visa on her. She wanted to laugh in his face, but didn't have the heart to.

She stood by her cabin's window now, looking out into the dark.

A murderer? A bear?

That didn't explain things fully, did it?

Ren looked like a bear had mauled him. A bear large enough to not only rip the head off, but to have thrashed the body across the meadow.

That's what would explain Ren's blood covering not only the ground but the tree branches as well. And she had seen such an animal through her scope. But there were no paw prints in the snow. Nothing had eaten any part of the body.

And what about the ritualistic hanging of the deer?

She remembered what people back in Yakutia used to say, the ones who lived out in the tundra and the Steppe, the ones who still lived life in the way of the nomads. The ones who still believed in shamanism and evil spirits.

Decades of Communism couldn't beat the fear of the dark out of the people. No amount of atheist dogma could fully wash the minds of those who had claimed to see things out in the night and in the wild places.

They spoke of the *abaasy*, demons born of dead spirits. Eaters of the living. Bringers of destruction. Appeased only through blood sacrifice.

Her grandmother believed in such spirits and warned Ashiya, when she was a girl of five or six, to be careful of the lonely places of the world and the graveyards where the abaasy congregated, looking for souls to devour. If they ever caught her, they'd eat her whole.

Ashiya shook her head and forced a laugh. She didn't believe in any of this shit. The abaasy were also supposed to be one legged, one-armed, one-eyed things with metal skin that rode on two-headed, eight-legged dragons. The image of them hobbling around and their dragons scurrying like bugs was too ridiculous to take seriously.

Just superstitious faerie tales to explain the unexplainable.

After the tide of her forced laughter passed, a cold sinking feeling in her stomach.

Looking out into the dark forest that surrounded her cabin, it was easy to believe in such things.

The bear. The way it moved. The way it looked at her with shining black eyes.

Ashiya moved away from the window and laid down on the small couch in front of the fire. She bundled herself up with blankets and drank the rest of the bottle of sake, half full before she touched it. Tomorrow's headache be damned.

She hoped that being drunk and falling asleep to the soothing rhythm of the fire would help her to not see. Not see *them*. The popping and the crackling sounds could wash all thought away.

Could help her.

To not see Alexei's teeth in the grass.

To not see Ren's blue smile.

To not see what the red sash kept hidden.

As she fell into her dreams, those faces were all she could see.

CHAPTER 14

DECEMBER 18TH

The next day, the Saito family held a wake for their son.

The invitation surprised Ashiya, given the rumors about her. An elderly neighbor of the Saitos lent a black dress to Ashiya for the event. Ogoto got it from the neighbor and passed it to her. She showed up at the house at eight a.m., along with dozens of others.

All the men wore black suits and ties. The women in black dresses and few older women in black kimono. The atmosphere was an oppressive silence.

She almost wished they had been crying. But the people held a stoic muteness, pain only seen in their eyes and only if you looked hard enough.

Ashiya stood at the back of the living room, hands pressed awkwardly at her sides, talking to no one.

Hikari and Itsuki came over to her. Itsuki was in the black suit like the rest of the men, Hikari in a black kimono, sitting in a wheelchair, being pushed by Itsuki. She looked stunning and incredibly sad all at once, even with her leg sticking out awkwardly in the cast. She had dyed the pink stripe in her hair to a jet black and removed all of her piercings.

"Ashi, thank you for coming," Itsuki said and bowed. Hikari did the same.

"Thank you for coming," Hikari said. She tried to smile, but the action nearly broke her resolve. Tears welled up in the corners of her eyes and it stung Ashiya's seeing them. "I know there's a lot of... *things* being said about you. I want you to know I don't believe them."

"I'm so sorry for your loss. I'm here if you need anything from me," Ashiya said and bowed deeply.

Hikari lifted her hand, and Ashiya took it. They shared a moment of silence and pained smiles. The couple thanked her and returned to their son.

They laid Ren's body out in a coffin at the head of the room. Closed casket, of course. Unlike Alexei's. A picture of Ren in a bright blue soccer jersey, right foot on the ball, smile wide and beaming, standing on top of the coffin. A nearby table had three oranges stacked on top of each other and a stick of incense burning beside them.

A Buddhist monk was on his knees next to the coffin, fumbling his fingers around a set of beads, chanting a mantra. Some elderly guests sitting behind him were doing the same.

She saw Ben sitting in a chair in the front row, eyes wet and chest heaving. His mother had her arms around him and his father, a tall white man, stared ahead blankly. He was the only other foreigner in Kamuy-Kotan, but she doubted they had much in common.

Ashiya had heard that the body would stay a night or two with the family according to tradition before being cremated. The accepted narrative was that it was a bear attack. No need for an autopsy or further investigation, at least according to Kamuy-Kotan's finest. A man who literally shook in his boots. The same man Ashiya saw falling apart in the woods. But the people hadn't fully accepted that. Ogoto told her what he heard at the market. That bears don't rip the heads off of people—for one—and without eating the body—for two. Which left the rumor that it was murder.

She was glad to hear kind words from the Saitos. They lit a fire of relief in her heart. The rest of the town was not so kind. She felt the eyes on her as she stayed in the back of the room. Several people kept craning their necks backwards to look at her. Leaning to their sides to whisper in their neighbors' ears.

She heard the words "foreigner" and "did she?"

She felt like running out of there. The dress was too tight, and she felt too exposed in it. She hated how the skirt restricted her legs and made her feel trapped. It also smelled of stale perfume and mildew from the woman who lent it to her. Undoubtedly, she had it buried for years in the bowels of her closet. At least it looked clean.

"Why are you here?" She heard a man say next to her.

She turned and saw that it was Ryoji. His black hair slicked back like he was a Wolf of Wall Street wannabee. The overpowering fragrance of cologne that was more expensive than anything she had ever purchased in her life, plane ticket to Japan included.

"They invited me."

He clicked his tongue at her. Something she came to know from Ogoto meant disgust or irritation at someone. "I wouldn't show my face here if I were you. The whole town thinks you had something to do with the boy's death. I would be too ashamed to show up."

She fought back both the anger boiling in her lungs and the fresh sting of tears in her eyes. "Whatever you think is irrelevant. We are all here to honor him."

She turned her face away and tried to not show any hint of emotion to him.

Like a dog refusing to give up its toy, he continued, "A foreign girl thinks she can just play at hunter here. Gets a kid lost and killed. I know you have something to do with it—"

"Ryoji, shut up," Ogoto said as he stumbled over to them. He wore a black suit that wasn't wrinkled and stained as Ashiya thought all his clothes were. He still had a five o'clock shadow and slightly red eyes and his breath, if you were close enough, still reeked of stale alcohol. But aside from that, he cleaned up nicely.

Ryoji smirked and scoffed. "The town idiot and full-time drunk defending the weird foreigner. How special. Did he tell you, girl, why his wife left him?"

Ogoto didn't say another word. He gave a look that said, *Show some respect.* That and, *One more word and I'll shut your mouth up for you with my fist*. Ogoto fixed his tie that had somehow got twisted behind his back. He stretched out his arm and led Ashiya away from Ryoji.

Ryoji didn't chase after them. Instead, he just leaned back against the wall with his arms crossed and surveyed the crowd in front of him.

Once they moved to the other side of the room, away from Ryoji and nearer the coffin at the front, they stopped.

"Don't listen to trash like him," Ogoto whispered. "He's just bitter because he won't get re-elected next year. Everyone knows he's been screwing around behind his wife's back and the people here like things done the old way, conservative-like, you know? Anyway, you are welcome here."

Ashiya bit her lip and looked at the carpet. "No, I don't think I am."

"What are you talking about?"

"You said it yourself yesterday that everyone was talking about me, how they thought I had something to do with Ren going missing."

"Fuck 'em. Isn't it obvious it was a bear?"

Not as obvious as she had hoped.

"People will say I did something. I led him out of his room or some shit like that."

Ogoto reached into his front shirt pocket, presumably for a smoke, and finding nothing, a look of depression came over his face. "Well, then they're idiots. Why does that matter to you?"

"It doesn't," she said. It was a lie, of course. Despite her cold demeanor, she cared a great deal about what others thought about her. Always had. Even as a high schooler, she picked up smoking and drinking because that's what all the other kids did, not because she liked any of that. Not then, at least.

She went on, "I think I should go home."

"The wake is still for another hour. We can leave then, and I'll bring some drinks to the cabin."

"No, I mean back to Russia."

Ogoto looked like she just slapped him in the face. At least he didn't bring up her supposed American heritage.

"No," was all he could get out. They stood there in silence for a few minutes. Ashiya watched as the Saito family sat by their son, no longer crying, or talking to anyone, or receiving condolences. They were dead to the world and existed in a floating void of their own numb pain. Ashiya knew that world well.

"Well, if you go, I'll help you pack," Ogoto said. "But you should stay. We're bringing in a professional bear hunter tomorrow. We gotta put it down after what happened and, well, I'm useless, and Ryoji is nothing but a trophy hunter. And if you won't be here, we're shit out of talent. The roads are clear for the moment, so I'm leaving tonight for town to see if I can talk him—bear hunter guy—into coming. He grew up here, and we were buddies, so I'm sure I can convince him. Sure you don't want to come? Or..."

He trailed off. She was looking straight ahead at the wall above Ren's coffin. Counting the grooves in the wallpaper. She may have looked like she wasn't paying attention, but she was storing every word in her heart.

She turned to him. "Why are you so insistent on me staying? When I was out in those woods, I saw the bear and I couldn't even shoot it then. This hunter guy of yours, he can do it."

"Because," he looked down at his hands, appearing as if he wished he had a beer in them, "I'm afraid. I'm afraid that something is terribly wrong. And we need everyone we can get. Don't you feel it? Something is out in the woods and I don't think it's a bear. I can't explain. It's like this feeling I got. Haven't had it since I was a kid and Ma' left me alone in the woods behind our house. Never thought I'd get back home on my own, and it was gettin' dark, and I thought I heard my name being called from the trees. That was the last time I've felt like this. Scared."

She wanted to say "fuck off." She wanted to say he was already drunk and didn't know what he was talking about. She wanted to ask him what Ryoji meant about Ogoto's wife. Ashiya wanted to ask him many things.

But mostly, she just knew he was right.

No tracks in the snow.

Bodies skinned and hung from the trees.

The bear. Large and imposing. Here one moment and gone the next.

She didn't believe in faerie tales or monsters. It could be a man out there doing all this. Regardless, whatever it was, it was evil.

She looked Ogoto in his eyes. Didn't say a word. But the message was clear.

I'm scared too.

She saw Alexei's face in her mind. She saw Ren's face. Now lying under the cedar coffin lid.

Her brother's body was long ago reduced to mummification. Ren's would be cremated in a few days' time. But she knew they would visit her dreams. As she saw Alexei standing in a corner of a dark room from time to time—*my imagination*—she knew the boy would join him.

Even now, in the room's corner to the left of the coffin, she saw a man in her periphery. Crooked smile. Something red tied across his face. She knew it had to be her mind playing tricks on her. Yet, the thought of looking at him and him actually being there terrified her more than any bear ever could.

She blinked hard and looked at the opposite side of the room.

She had one way to escape their accusatory stares. It was the same need that drove her out to Japan.

Pull the fucking trigger.

Take revenge.

Against the animals of the world that took these lives.

Against her own inaction.

CHAPTER 15

Ogoto wandered the alleyways of Sapporo City. The streets were slick with ice and he had already fallen twice on his ass. At his age, that could put him in the hospital with no way out again.

That would be the death of him. No more freedom.

He was drunk, but far from wasted. He held off from his flask full of gin until he had made the mountain road drive into the city. Ogoto was stupid, but not stupid enough to navigate those roads drunk. But once he arrived in the city and parked his truck, out came the flask, and away went the memories of his wife. It was almost as if she were riding shotgun with him the whole way. He didn't believe in ghosts; but at night, on those roads, sober, he couldn't bring himself to look over at what must have been an empty seat.

He knew what Kamuy-Kotan really needed. Sure, the girl was a good tracker and would probably help them find the bear, or whatever it was out there, he hoped. But if the animal was what he feared it could be, they'd be needing somebody with more experience and skill in these matters.

He stumbled down another alley and bent down to look under the *noren* cloth over the doors of the bars and the *yakitori* restaurants.

The smell of grilled meat made his mouth water.

He emptied the flask hours ago. Wished he could just duck into one of these bars and drink himself into oblivion.

But first, find him.

Taro Ishida texted Ogoto while he was at Ren's wake, telling him the name of the bar to meet him at. Something to do with Marlin or Tuna, or some fucking fish, that's all he could remember. And he was too blitzed to remember to take out his phone from his pocket and check just now.

He stopped in front of a bar called the Robin.

Was it a bird?

Logically, he should say no, given his earlier conviction. But his gut told him yes.

He lifted the cloth over the front door and walked in.

A rectangular counter took up the center of the room, with customers sitting around it on all sides. The lighting was low and orange, giving the illusion of warmth to the place, but inside it was drafty. Fish nets and dried puffer fish hung from the low ceiling. The walls exuded grease, and that's how he knew the food must be good. The lone man behind the counter wore dingy blue coveralls and a dirty white rag around his forehead.

He looked at Ogoto and waved his hand for him to come in.

"You Ogoto, right?"

"How you know me?"

"Taro told me to look out for you. He's in the back around the counter."

Ogoto hadn't seen Taro in over twelve years and had forgotten how on top of shit he could be.

He walked around the compact bar and looped around the counter.

He saw Taro sitting in a dark corner, head down and staring into a half-drunk bottle of something brown. The corner wasn't actually darker than any other point in the joint, but it seemed like it was. As if Taro was a sponge sucking in all the darkness of the place and keeping it held there. And it looked like he was okay with that. He was sitting down and, even though he was short, his broad shoulders made him look too big for the table. He wore straw boots and a fur jacket—bear most likely—like he was living in the Edo period still, like he was some fucking frontiersman.

The wall behind him had a pair of deer antlers nailed into it above a grimy mirror. A bear's pelt next to it, stretched across the wall, nailed down, the head still attached, mouth open in a dead roar.

Taro raised his head and nodded at Ogoto. He had that jagged scar across his right eye that bled down into his cheek and even the tip of his chin. Though faded, his blue-gray eyes focused intently. Blue because Taro was Ainu, not Japanese. Didn't speak the language as far as Ogoto knew—did anyone anymore?—but he looked the stereotypical part. Broad shoulders. Thick beard. Light eyes.

As Ogoto sat down, he could smell the sweat coming off the man. Which must have been something powerful if he, of all people, could smell it. Come to think of it, it looked like the other customers were leaning away from him.

"Taro! You're looking good. You smell like shit though," Ogoto said and laughed his good-natured idiot laugh.

Taro grunted back at him and held his eye contact until Ogoto had to look away.

"How you been all these years?"

Taro took a long sip from the bottle. It felt like an entire minute passed before he spoke. "You got a job for me?"

"Yeah, shit sorry. We got a bear in Kamuy—"

"So what? Can't handle it yourself?"

"It's different than most."

"How?"

"Killed a young boy yesterday."

Taro looked back down at his drink. Ogoto couldn't tell if the man was bored or just more interested in his drink. "And it didn't leave any tracks in the snow. As in, not a single fucking one."

"Because you couldn't find 'em."

"Fuck off. Because there weren't any. Not even from the boy. The snow around his body was smooth and not touched by nothin'."

At this, Taro lifted his head. It didn't seem like the man blinked at all. "That's not all, is it?"

"They boy's head was taken off. Same with a deer earlier, all strung up and shit on a tree. Maybe nothing to do with the bear. Fuck, how can it be? But it is strange, right? And we gotta' take care of it. Before somebody else gets hurt."

One could easily mistake Taro's face for a stone you found in the woods, or even a tree trunk. Motionless. Wrinkled and scarred. Weathered almost as if the man slept outside in the winter. Fuck, he probably did.

But at the mention of the tracks and the bodies, a glimmer of animation returned to that ancient and passive face. A slight raising of his eyebrows and a slight lifting of his upper left lip. It could have been the evolutionary beginnings of a smile.

"I'll take it."

Ogoto clapped his hands and laughed. "I knew you would! The pay—"

"Damn the pay."

"You... you don't want to—"

"I'll get paid when it's done. I'll say what the job is worth after I done it. And if I can't do it, you don't pay me." He lifted the rest of the mystery liquid in the bottle and drank it as easily as Ogoto could beer. But the smell was more akin to gasoline, something even he wouldn't touch.

"Well, I'm not paying you. The city will. I'm sure they'll agree after you bag the bear." He thought of Ryoji's face when confronted by Taro over not paying the man. It brought an odd joy to his heart to imagine that man on his knees before Taro, begging him not to beat his face in.

Silence returned to the table. The chatter of the surrounding people seemed like a dream. People laughing about that co-worker they thought was weird, that couple fighting over who paid for the last date, those drunk businessmen singing K-pop songs over their beers.

But these two men sat in the bubble of darkness and sweat that shielded Taro from the outside world. After all these years of being able to talk with Taro again, he knew he was dealing with a different breed of human. The kind that used to take down mammoths with spears and wrestled saber-toothed cats with their bare hands. And these weren't the men for casual conversation.

"Kesagake," Taro said.

"What is that?"

"Dangerous bear."

"No shit."

Taro leaned back into the shadows of the corner until darkness shrouded his light-colored eyes. "Demon bear."

Ogoto rolled his hand to encourage Taro to continue speaking.

In what must have been a rare moment of talkativeness, he continued, "Remember that incident back about a hundred years ago? That bear that killed all those people?"

Ogoto nodded his head. Who didn't know that story? The town had erected bear statues all over the place to drive in tourism. They even built a giant bear statue looming over a hut out near where the event actually happened. For just 500 yen you could come in, take pictures, and say cheese in front of the spot where children were literally eaten.

"Seven people killed in one week. Mostly women and children. They eventually killed the thing," Taro said.

"Everyone knows that."

"But they don't like to talk about what those people saw. What they told their kids and passed on, do they? Not just the bear ripping into their children. They don't like to hear about how the bear moved. It would just vanish, they said. They even spoke about finding a skinned sheep hung on a tree, but none of the big papers made a connection there. People say the bear was a demon. It laughed in the wind. It left no tracks. Was created when the bear was out, minding its own business, and got shot by a local farmer. The bear didn't die. It suffered. Harbored hatred in its heart. Attracted... things to it."

The lights seemed to dim even more. Ogoto chuckled. "A story told by pioneers who couldn't even fucking read. The same people who believe that foxes can possess you."

"Maybe. Kesagake, they called that bear. Even if it was a demon, they still eventually killed it. Took just one shot to the heart and then three to the head. Maybe I'll get that lucky too."

Ogoto felt a chill blow through the already freezing bar. He shivered. Must have been just him since nobody else seemed to react to it.

"Not saying I believe that, but why would it become a demon?"

"No idea. But it sounds fun."

CHAPTER 16

That night, as Ogoto sat with Taro in that seedy bar, Saho Nakatani was listening to music in her room. Band-Maid was blasting through her bright pink ear-muff headphones. She was drawing a picture of a skull wrapped in blue roses. Mom didn't like her music, too loud and too vulgar she said. Mom also didn't like her art; all she ever drew were skulls, gravestones, cats walking with ghosts. Mom thought it was morbid, Saho thought it was beautiful.

Take the skull-rose: beauty that can rise out of something as horrible as death.

She wasn't a typical twelve-year-old girl. Especially out in the middle of nowhere, as the village of Ota was. The nearest town was Kamuy-Kotan, about an hour's drive through the mountains, and even that place was a tiny town. But at least they had stores and restaurants. Ota had... cows and rice fields and forests.

Dad wanted to move out here from Sapporo two years ago. Saho and Mom, in a rare moment of agreement, told him to stay in the city. Mom liked her nail appointments too much and Saho, her friends. Dad wanted to live a rustic life. They had saved up enough money to buy this cabin and try their hand at farming. Mom nearly had a nervous breakdown. Saho adapted fairly quickly, though she never would have admitted it.

Saho bobbed her head up and down to the hard rock beats. She was at her desk, which faced the open air living room, her room being a loft in the second story with no walls, a ladder leading down from it to the living room. Saho didn't mind the lack of privacy. There were no other rooms on the second floor, and the ladder made it difficult for Mom to come up here. Ever since the move, she never left the house. Her eyes were constantly red, never did her hair, and smelled more and more of what Saho assumed to be the stink of alcohol.

Dad seemed to not notice. He busied himself out in the yard and the fields all day. Didn't bring home much money from what he could sell, but their expenses were small.

Saho could stomach living out here. She even liked her view now: across the gap from her loft, over and above the living room, to the large pane of glass that made up the entire front wall of the A-frame cabin. It was pitch-black out, but the falling snow squished against the glass. They looked like flowers to her. She drew in some snowflakes falling over the rose-skull.

A hand slapped her shoulder and Saho jolted up.

It was Mom, towering over her, hair frizzed out, still in her bathrobe—as she always was.

Saho took off her headphones.

"I have been calling you for minutes!" Mom yelled, slightly out of breath. Climbing the ladder must have been the most she'd moved her body in weeks.

"Sorry," Saho said as she leaned her arm over her drawing. Mom saw it and smirked at her, but thankfully, said nothing.

"Dad wants you in the front yard."

"Why? It's snowing and dark out."

Mom said nothing but raised her hand. Saho flinched. A new habit she never had in the city.

Mom turned around and descended the ladder. Saho hoped she'd fall and break her neck. Then felt guilty about those thoughts. For as much hate as she had against that woman, she still loved her. Still wanted to be loved by her. After Mom reached the bottom floor, Saho grabbed her pink jacket and black beanie with the skull and cross bones on it and followed.

Saho walked across the living room, lit up by the roaring fire next to the window, and saw Mom asleep in her armchair. It was one of her many useless talents; Mom could fall asleep in seconds, even while you were talking to her, even while she was on her feet.

Saho put on her boots, went outside, and was blasted by the cold air. She shut the door behind her.

She saw flashing yellow lights off to the left side of the front yard and trudged through the snow to get there.

When she got to the side of the house, she saw Dad driving the tree harvester. He was swiveling it back and forth, the front end of it stuck in the snow. The tractor was supposed to be for cutting down trees and stripping off their bark. It looked like a snowplow with a long robot arm, complete with two chainsaws at the end. The blades could either cut into a tree from the side and fell it. Or, take a tree in between the two bladed rollers and rip off the bark.

Robot Chainsaw Arm. Great name for a band.

The problem before her was obvious. Dad thought he could outfit a moldboard to the harvester and turn it into a makeshift snowplow. He was trying to clear the snow from the side of the house and had gotten stuck.

"Dad!"

She yelled at him once more and he finally saw her and killed the engine.

"Hey Bean, come on up," he said.

Saho waded through the snow, put her right foot on the tank-like roller, and lifted herself into the cabin.

Dad was smoking but threw the cigarette away into the snow right before she came up. But the smell lingered.

"What's up?" Saho asked cheerfully. She may have had issues with Mom, but Dad was still cool. She thought he had no idea what he was doing with farming and home maintenance—and hybrid harvester plows—but she loved him all the same. Best of all, she never had to wince when he moved. She thought about telling him many times. Dad was never home when it happened and Mom never left marks on Saho's face. But she couldn't. Didn't want her family to fall apart because of her.

"I need you to retract the arm while I loosen a few bolts."

"Did you leave the chainsaw on?"

"No, of course not. They're out back. But something is stuck and I need you to move the arm while I check it out. Remember how?"

"Yep."

"Good Bean." He ruffled her hair, and she told him to quit it all while hoping that he never did. He jumped out of the cabin and walked over to the arm, half buried in the snow it was stuck in.

Not many twelve-year-old girls knew how to operate a harvester. Then again, not many also loved drawing skulls and hanging out around cemeteries. Dad had nothing to do with her love of the macabre, but he taught her all the ins and outs of the farm. Little as he knew, he passed it on. She felt she may have actually known more than he did at times.

"Okay, pull it back!'

Saho grabbed the drive shaft and eased it back, all the while keeping her hand on the emergency release switch. Had to hold on to it or nothing moved.

"Okay, stop!"

She did.

Dad bent over the arm and tinkered away with a tool she never saw him take out. Saho grew bored waiting for him to finish. She looked around at the dark forest that surrounded her home. The rest of the village sprawled out in front of the house down the hill, all dozen homes of it. But behind and to the sides of their cabin was nothing but woodlands. There's was the closest home to the wild. The snow fell lightly, looking like falling stars against the black expanse of the forest.

She hummed the Band-Maid song—Protect You—she had been listening to. Didn't know what the words meant, they were in English, but she knew the what the words were, *bring the thunder.*

She tapped her gloved hands against the drive shaft and the seat. Hummed a little louder.

Saho stopped.

Leaned forward in her seat, looking out at the forest.

"Almost done Bean, hang in there!"

"Dad, I see something—"

"There! Done!"

Dad stood up and cracked his back.

Saho rushed out of the cabin, nearly falling over herself.

"Whoa, hold on there," Dad said, looking concerned.

"There's something moving in the forest. Let's go inside."

Dad looked out across the meadow that was behind their home. A barren white moonscape. "It's just a deer Bean. But you go on ahead. I need to keep working."

He patted her on the back and ushered her towards the front yard.

She looked back at her dad as he bent down under the harvester's arm.

Maybe it was just a deer.

As she walked by the side of the house, out of view from her father, she heard something from the nearby trees.

A humming.

Someone humming a song.

A beat.

Bring the thunder.

CHAPTER 17

December 19th

The next morning Ashiya woke before the sun poked through the black sky. She awoke with a vague feeling of guilt like she was missing something. Like she had an exam or an appointment she had forgotten about but couldn't quite place it. There were faint memories of faces in the dark. Blue lips curling into a fanged smile. Red sash tightening across a face until it bled.

She didn't bother with starting a fire or turning on the furnace. She wouldn't be staying long and doubted that she'd be returning that night.

Ogoto texted her at around midnight the night before. It was a message so riddled with mistakes that even had it been in Russian or English, she would have struggled to understand what he was saying. She called him and he answered, in a heavily slurred voice, kitschy pop music playing in the background, dishes clanging and people shouting.

She could decipher the gist of what he wanted to say.

We're hunting the bear tomorrow. Taro is coming. Gone for days. Spending the night in Ota Village. You in?

She was.

She got dressed in her thermal underwear, woolen socks, sweater, snow jacket and snow pants, thick insulated gloves, wool face mask, and sunglasses. Attached her snowshoes and of course her rifle outside her bag, and her large fixed blade hunting knife in her jacket pocket.

Ashiya packed her bag; enough dried food for three days, Sterno stove for melting snow for drinking water, a sub-zero sleeping bag just in case. The bag was heavy but better than being caught off guard.

Remember Dad's fingers.

Ogoto said they were staying in Ota, which she had visited before. She assumed at someone's home since there were no hotels or inns there. The one time she went was back in November. There was a light layer of snow at the time while the trees were still going through their autumnal transformations.

A tiny hamlet deep in the woods. No stores. No police station. Nothing but a collection of fifteen homes. Mostly the elderly who refused to move into bigger towns after their children abandoned them and a few younger families, taking up government subsidies to go and re-populate the countryside.

Who else would join? She and Ogoto's bear hunter friend for sure. She imagined Ryoji wouldn't pass up the opportunity. Spending another minute with that man was a prospect that made her shiver more than the cold ever could. She hoped this Taro was at least not as bad.

But none of that really mattered. All that did was to take care of the animal so that no one else would get hurt or killed. She had no hate for the bear, anymore than she hated the caribou that trampled her brother. What she hated was her inaction. She knew others would say there was nothing she could have done in both cases; she didn't believe that. Ashiya saw Ben acting suspiciously with the CD. She could have said something, could have marched him back inside, and then Ren would still be alive.

She could have shot that caribou right before it stomped the life out of Alexei.

But she didn't.

She could see her breath the moment she opened her front door. The sun was peeking out over the trees and spreading a pale pink light across the deep-sea blue of the receding night. A few stars were still shining, but the oncoming wave of sunrise was eroding away their light.

She shouldered her backpack. Closed the door behind her. Got into and started her car. The engine failed to turn over twice, but on the third try came to life.

She drove down the forest road, the sunrise now full of warm orange light. As she let the warmth of its rays wash over her face, she made a promise to herself.

No matter what. You will pull that trigger.

CHAPTER 18

Nobody spoke for over an hour. The sun warmed the snow as they walked, making it slushy in some places. Thankfully, their snowshoes kept them from falling into the melting snow most of the time. A cawing crow occasionally broke the silence. Other than that—and the scrape of their snowshoes—it was silent.

They were following the only set of tracks near Ren's house. They found a single bear paw print right next to the road where Ren disappeared. Nobody saw it the day of the first search party. And there were no other tracks near it. It was odd, but it was the only thing they had to go on. They would hike from there, across the deep woodlands, and on to Ota village. Hopefully finding some trace of the bear on the way. Spending the night in Ota if they didn't.

Ashiya had driven over to a clearing used by loggers to pull their trucks over in, where Ogoto said the hunting party would meet up. She was right that Ryoji would be there. He wore purple designer ski wear. It had a gaudy gold tint to it as well. He ignored her—thankfully—and busied himself with his cigarette instead.

Officer Kawamoto was there. She was surprised, given the man's obvious fright the other day. Maybe they needed actual law enforcement along for the ride for supervision. He wore a black jacket and brown ski pants, but still had his white police sash wrapped around his right arm. His gaunt face highlighted his bony cheekbones and made his eyes look bigger than they were in reality. Everything about his body language screamed, *Let's hurry and get back home.* He kept asking Ryoji about the time. When they would get to Ota, when they would come back. Time was all the man seemed to care about.

Ogoto was there. A rarity to see the man up before noon. His beat-up military green jacket seemed too thin for the weather, but he seemed perfectly relaxed in the cold. He stood by someone she hadn't seen before, Taro she presumed, as the latter lifted a khaki nylon backpack from Ogoto's truck and strapped it to himself.

He wasn't very tall. The shortest man there, on par with her own height. But his shoulders were wide and his limbs thick. He had a bushy beard with bits of snow clinging to it. He had one of those faces where whatever they were thinking would elude you. A feature of nature like a rock formation more than a human face. She was surprised to see that his eyes had a slight blue grayness to them. Like a pale blue sky right before sunset.

Ogoto had vouched for her presence in the hunting party. Apparently Ryoji and Kawamoto had objected, but Taro said nothing either which way. Since he was some famous bear hunter or something, was necessary for the hunt, and didn't say no to her being there, she could stay.

Taro didn't speak to her at all. The men—Ogoto aside— tolerated her presence in the way one might a stray dog that followed at a distance. Nothing to worry about, but not something they wanted any closer.

Ashiya was last in the line, followed by Ogoto, Kawamoto, Ryoji, and Taro in the lead. She worried for Ogoto, but he promised her he had had nothing to drink that morning, and didn't bring any with him, anyway. Taro hadn't spoken a single word to anyone since she had arrived. And she doubted he was talking before then, either. In his inscrutable face, she sensed an annoyance at their presence, not just hers. Like the man would rather have been doing this alone and had been forced to let the others come along.

An atmosphere of anticipation filled the spaces between them. She listened for any crunch of snow, the snap of a branch, the rustle of leaves. All seemed normal out here.

Kawamoto was the most visibly shaken in the group. He jerked his head wildly when some snow fell off a branch. His finger twitched over the trigger of his rifle, even while at rest.

Ryoji stepped aside from the direction they were heading and let Kawamoto and Ogoto pass him. He waited until Ashiya caught up to him.

When she walked by, he resumed walking to keep pace next to her.

He smiled. "I feel like we got off on the wrong foot the other day. Since we're in this together and it is dangerous and all, how about we start over?"

He put out his hand for her to shake.

The way he spoke made her skin crawl. She could tell he wasn't sincere. The smile was too wide. *No lines by his eyes.* The kindness out of nowhere and forced. If he hadn't said those nasty things to her just yesterday, she might have fallen for it.

"Why are you being nice?"

His smile stayed plastered on his face, but his eyes winced for a fraction of a second. "Well, because I am nice. People from your country don't smile much, do they?"

Even in his façade of kindness, it seemed he couldn't help but let a jab out at her.

"Where is it you're from again? Mongolia?"

Irritation boiled under her skin. If she wasn't careful, she'd lose her temper at him.

And that's not why you're here.

She kept her mouth shut and looked ahead.

"Come on, I'm just messing with you. Lighten up." He made to pull ahead of her, but stopped and softly grabbed her arm by the elbow. He tugged her to a stop.

She pulled her arm back from him. "Do not touch me."

Ryoji's face showed some shock. Like the man wasn't used to being challenged like this. His faltering expression quickly morphed back to his steadfast smile.

"Okay, okay, don't overreact now. I'm just trying to get to know you. But I'm worried about you being out here, you know? The cold. The hiking that we still have to do. Your bag must be heavy. You know we might have to spend the night in Ota, right? And that will be at the end of a long day's hike in the snow. And that bear that's out here, this is a dangerous place. If you wanted to turn back now, nobody will think less of you. I mean, it's amazing what you've done already, all things considered."

"What things?"

"You know, you not being from around here. The language is probably very complex and I'm sure you feel isolated, yeah? And, well, you are a tiny person and this job is going to be tough."

He smiled his politician's smile while his eyes danced with glee. It had been years since she had been in a fight. The last—but not only—time was with Svetlana back in high school. Ashiya wasn't bullied too much back in those days. The few times it had happened, the bully instantly regretted their decision. She was walking home from class one day when Svetlana came running at her from behind. Pushed Ashiya down. Said something like *Stay away from my boyfriend.* Not that Ashiya had been doing anything with that guy, was just nice to him from time to time. Svetlana spit on Ashiya and said she was happy Alexei was dead, that sluts didn't deserve good men in their lives.

Red washed over her eyes. Ashiya stood up. Grabbed a metal trashcan from the side of the road. And smashed it into Svetlana's face. Mom was furious. Dad was proud and gave her a shot of vodka. Svetlana had a broken nose. And the police held Ashiya for two days.

But it felt good. As ashamed as she was to admit that she lost control, a part of her relished seeing Svetlana sprawled out on the street, blood gushing out of her nose, crying, mascara mixing with the tears and the blood.

That same feeling filled up the dam of her patience just now. Rage and shame.

She clenched her fist.

"Hey!" shouted Taro.

His arms swung at his sides wildly, and his eyes were wide. Ryoji actually flinched when Taro stopped so hard in his tracks that he sent up a spray of snow.

"What is all this talking about?" he whispered and hissed at them. "We are here to kill a Kesagake. That means you make a mistake, you are dead. I don't give a shit what beef you two have. I don't care if you're fucking. I don't care if you stab each other later. We are silent on this trail. If you speak again, or you cause problems with a member of this team again. I will drag you out of here myself."

Ryoji started to speak, but Taro grabbed the man's jacket collar. The mayor seemed to shrink in age just then and nodded his head. Taro released him and looked at Ashiya. He grunted in a way she took as being either disgust or annoyance.

Ryoji walked forward ahead of her, not looking back.

She was glad to be done with him. For now, at least. And the sooner they finished up here, the sooner she could get on with her life without having to face that prick again.

Taro's dismissal grated against her. But he wasn't being aggressive out of trying to antagonize her, at least. So she could stomach it.

And they should be quiet. A normal Ussuri bear was dangerous in its own right. And she wasn't even sure if that's what they were up against.

They walked on in silence for several more kilometers.

The only sound a soft *crunch crunch crunch.*

At least it grew colder, and the slush became less and less frequent. The snow became almost rock hard.

The white bark of the birches almost matched the landscape save for the dark brown and black spots and stripes. They walked through a frozen creek bed, using stones to hop across—not a simple task with snowshoes. They climbed a low hill and, for a moment, had a view of the forest ahead. Snow crested pine needles and fir leaves. An ocean of them. The forest was mostly flat, with a large nearest mountain a good twenty or so kilometers off in the distance. Some smaller hills to the right, near where the village of Ota was.

Wispy streaks of clouds snailed across the bright blue sky.

The cold made Ashiya feel alive, as it always did. For a moment she could forget the men in front of her, already descending into the forest valley. Ashiya had never ventured this far out into this forest. There was no need since the deer routinely came in close to her cabin. She could even forget the reason they were out here. The peace in that moment was short-lived. As she hiked down the hill, the trees grew closer together and their branches partially blotted out the light. Most of the branches were dead, thin, and gnarled.

The cold grew more intense as well. Beyond that brisk freshness that she craved and into the kind of cold that even sitting by a fire doesn't dispel you of.

The path ahead was dark, lonely, and above all, freezing.

CHAPTER 19

Everyone stopped moving. Taro had lifted his balled fist and brought them to a halt.

Ashiya listened to the forest.

Dark gray light filled the hollow spaces off the trail, almost as if under heavy rain. Further out, all looked as dark as night. The clouds were thick and almost black. The clouds had swallowed the blue sky.

"Something doesn't feel right," Taro said. "We're being watched."

"What are you talking about?" Ryoji said.

Taro said nothing more. He pointed the tip of his rifle ahead. The low light made it too difficult to see much further than a few meters into the trees.

Ashiya felt it. That slight rise of pressure building behind her temples. Her heart pulsed that rhythmic drum beat.

A roar.

The bear.

Crows took flight off to their left.

Kawamoto turned around and ran. Dropped his rifle in the snow and it disappeared in the powder. He blew past Ashiya and knocked her to the ground. She lay on her back and gasped for air.

"You idiot! Stop!" Ryoji yelled.

"It's coming!" Kawamoto yelled.

Ashiya felt her body rising. Given the force of Kawamoto running right into her, she thought she must have gotten a concussion. Then she looked up and saw Ogoto and Taro lifting her up by her hands and setting her back on her feet.

"Kawamoto, stop!" Ryoji yelled out again.

Kawamoto might have been trying to string a sentence together, might even have been stopping and about to turn around from what she could see.

He fell right through into the ground.

There one moment and gone the next.

He let out a quick, high-pitched yelp as the snow absorbed him.

If she had blinked, it would have seemed as if he had literally evaporated out of existence in an instant.

Ryoji and Ogoto ran over to where the hole had appeared in the snow, at the base of a tall pine.

Taro looked out into the forest, scanning. The roar didn't come again. Ashiya, still lightheaded from the tackle, walked over to the hole. Taro came from behind her.

She stumbled up to the hole, Ogoto and Ryoji down on their knees, peering into it and shouting. She took a flashlight out from a side pouch in her backpack and shined it into the darkness.

The light fell on Kawamoto. He was on his back and moving about three meters down. Groaning softly and in obvious pain, but alive. He was lying on a slick patch of ice at a forty-five degree angle. His left leg bent underneath him. A deep chasm below him that the flashlight couldn't pierce to the bottom of. A pine tree formed a pillar to his right. He had fallen into a tree well, with what looked like another hole in the ground, even beneath that. She had seen this before many times, but never one as deep as this. Branches could keep the snow from building at the base of a large tree, leaving the ground free of snow, thus forming a hole. This tree must have been growing near another hole in the ground as well, given the deep chasm below Kawamoto.

Because he was so close to the surface, he could have jumped and grabbed a hand if he hadn't been so dangerously positioned on the ice. Any wrong movement could send him flying into the dark. The walls surrounding the tree well were also ice. One of them could jump down there.

Sure. Land on ice. Slip. And then both of you fall to your deaths. Or *make the snow walls cave in and smother the man.*

"Are you okay?" Ogoto shouted out.

"Uhhh. I'm, yeah, I'm okay." He tried to sit up using his elbows, but the movement made him slip further into the deep. He flung out his arms and stopped his body from sliding. "H-help me!"

Taro stood up. Looked at his phone. "Anyone have service?"

They did not. Black clouds swirled above the canopy. Possibly messing with their reception.

He continued, "We have to go get help. If we try to get him out now, we'll make the snow collapse and bury him. Unless any of you have a ladder up your asses. Ota is close. You two, you stay with him." He flung his hand out towards the men. "Girl, you come with me."

"Can't we, I don't know, throw a rope down to him?" Ogoto asked.

Taro grunted. "Have any?"

He did not.

"I'll go back with you," Ryoji said. "Leave her here. I know the village and—"

"No."

"Why?"

"You scared to stay out here?"

"Fuck you."

But Ashiya saw it, the fear in his eyes. Despite all his boasting.

So he'd rather sacrifice me than have to face it. Good to know.

"He'll die if we leave him for long," Ashiya said.

"Then you'd better keep up," Taro replied.

"I know. You all stay with him and keep him warm and safe," Ashiya said. "I can run to Ota faster than any of you."

She fastened the straps on her bag and prepared herself to trek. She could do it faster without the bag, but if something happened to her as well, she'd need it. Running in snowshoes was not her idea of a good time. Maybe the snow would be hard enough for her to ditch them. She was light and could probably get away with it.

"No," Taro said. "I'll go with you. Too dangerous to be alone. Ogoto! You and pretty boy here, stay with him."

Ogoto nodded with a look of trepidation in his red eyes. Ryoji seemed to be on the verge of saying something, but one look from Taro silenced him into submission.

"He'll need water and a way to stay warm," Ashiya said. "Ogoto, keep him safe."

"You too, Anasootsjyah."

Taro and Ashiya headed out.

Snow started falling, lightly, but enough to fill in their footsteps.

"Do you know where we're going?" she asked.

"Eh."

They hiked up a hill, the icy air stinging her lungs. She doubted if she had the strength to actually make it, despite her earlier confidence, but she had to try. Taro looked like someone who would easily get winded on hikes. But he kept a pace she could hardly keep up with. She felt inferior next to the professional hunter and desperate to not appear as a burden.

But his silence annoyed her.

They walked for what must have been thirty minutes, though in the haze of exhaustion it could have been five. They came to the top of the hill. She looked back down into the forest but couldn't see where the other men were. The tops of the trees were now being frosted over by the snow. The valley looked like an arctic ocean more than it did something that belonged on land.

She felt the need to stop and catch her breath, but Taro kept on trudging forward.

"Hey, can we, just for—"

"No."

She said no more, took a drink of water from her pack, and forced herself to keep on walking. The rest of the way was downhill and then flat, at least. Ota was nearby but with all the tree cover she couldn't see the rooftops from here.

She walked next to Taro, but the man didn't look at her, nor did he seem interested in her presence at all.

But here was somebody she felt she could relate to. He was a hunter, something she had been striving to be all her life. He was the real deal, whereas the likes of Ryoji—and even Ogoto—were not.

"How long have you been doing this? Hunting I mean," she asked.

He stopped walking and turned his head so quickly she let out an embarrassing, but mercifully quiet, gasp.

"Let's get this straight. You're in the way, just like those fuckers down there. I don't give a shit that you're a woman. If it wasn't for that cop down there making me, I'd be free to do this on my own. I don't need you. Don't care about conversation or trading life stories. I only care about—"

"Kesagake."

He looked at her with what looked like surprise for a moment. "Yes."

"Me too. I want it dead for what it did to that boy."

"Animals don't deserve death. They do what they do. And so do I."

He turned away from her and began marching down the hill.

Asshole, she thought.

And for a moment, fear washed over her that she had said it out loud.

CHAPTER 20

The snow whipped around their faces, and the entire world was now a flurry of assaulting ice. Ashiya's face was beyond feeling numb. She wondered how long the men back at the tree well could hold out in this.

Taro was slightly in front of her and was the only reference point for her sight. She was literally blindly following him.

The snow was piling on top of her snowshoes and weighing them down. Her legs burned but gave her no warmth. She felt as useless as her legs trying to plow through the snow. She wanted to do something about Ren's death. Wanted to make a difference. Of course, that wouldn't bring peace to Hikari and Itsuki, but she could have at least brought them a sense of justice. And here she was having to go back into civilization because that dumb cop ran and might get himself killed because of it. Ashiya doubted she'd have the strength to go back out into the woods after getting to Ota. Her warm cabin, the local bathhouse and sauna, a bottle of hot sake, these were the things beckoning to her now. Comfort and warmth. She could almost feel the heat of the fire on her face.

But then what? She'd still see *their faces* at night, no matter how comfortable she could make her life. She felt in this moment that there was only one way to rid herself of their specters. And she was going the wrong way.

The answer was back in those woods. She heard the roar. They were close to it.

But she couldn't lie to herself and say she wasn't somewhat happy to be going back.

They walked on for minutes more. She couldn't see the trees or stones, only the faded silhouette of Taro.

The wind howled. Even more, she could hear rage in the storm. And what could have been laughter. Then came a thundering crack, like lightning from underground.

Taro stopped, and she almost ran into his back. He held out his hand as if to brace her for the impact.

"You hear that?" he asked.

"The wind?"

"Hmph. Not the wind."

The screeching wind carried what could have been laughter further away.

The storm lightened to a graceful fluttering of snowflakes. The wind died down to a standstill. Patches of blue sky pierced through the gray clouds. For now, at least.

The trees unveiled themselves, covered in snow, looking like freshly cut marble statues with multiple arms. They continued, but she kept her hand ready to grab her rifle at any moment. Minutes more passed and something off and to her left took shape. At first she thought it was a hole filled with snow and that's why it had a lower impression than the rest of the terrain. As she walked by it, she could clearly see what it was: tracks.

Taro saw it as well and diverted from their straight path to Ota. He bent down over the footprint.

"Bear. Big."

Ashiya walked around him and saw it more clearly: a single bear paw, no others near it. Just like by Ren's house. But it was big. At least the size of the upper half of her body.

"Can't be. It's way too big," she said.

"You're right. But it is a bear all the same."

"Then where are the other tracks?"

She felt hot shame at the nervousness she heard in her own voice.

Taro looked out at the forest, ice clinging to his beard, eyes matching the cold in the air. He got up and started walking towards Ota again.

"Hey, wait!"

He ignored her and kept walking.

Shit. He's just going to keep walking into it, *isn't he?*

She followed him.

The already quiet forest grew quieter still. Even their footsteps made little sound. They had just passed a wooden sign on a snow-buried hiking trail showing that Ota was a kilometer ahead. Every so often, they spotted another bear track, showing that they were going the right way. But, like the others, they were odd. Once they found all four paw prints near each other. Only once. Twice they found two sets of prints. Mostly, it was just the one. And what disturbed her the most was that the size kept changing. At times, suggesting something larger than even a polar bear. But there was also one set of prints that were much smaller, almost human sized. A different animal altogether?

As they drew closer to the village, the trees grew further and further apart. Soon she could see the sides of buildings. Homes.

What she couldn't see was any smoke coming out of the chimneys.

Taro looked at her, and she understood his intent without him having to speak: *be ready.*

He slung his rifle off his shoulder and steadied it in his hands. She did the same. Checked the safety. Checked the round.

The first house was on their left. A small wooden cabin done in a Western ski lodge style. Deer antlers hung on the wall in front of them. When they rounded the corner, she could see shattered wood in the snow leading away from the house. She looked at the wall and saw a hole in it, from floor to ceiling. Someone's voice—a woman's—came from inside.

"Hello?" she said.

The woman kept talking, though Ashiya couldn't understand what she was saying.

Taro led the way, and the two entered the home. The lights were off, but the daylight flooded both the hole and the four windows on the ceiling, the type used for stargazing. They found the owner of the voice quickly: a TV that had been left on showing some weight loss infomercial.

Something had flipped the sofa upside down and against the wall opposite the hole. Snow blowing in from the hole covered the shaggy red carpet.

Taro went up the stairs while Ashiya lingered downstairs. She went into the kitchen, the only room she could see that still had the lights on. Freshly cut pumpkin on the counter, the knife embedded halfway into it. A tea kettle on the stove, full of cold water. The microwave light was on. She opened its door. A soggy and lukewarm cup of instant noodles.

Footsteps coming down the stairs.

"No one here," Taro said.

"It looks like something attacked them while they were making dinner."

Taro growled and blew air out of his nose. Something Ashiya was coming to understand meant an affirmation of sorts.

"What do you think we should do?" she asked.

Taro left the house through the hole without a word.

Dick.

She followed him out in the blazing white light. The sun was reflecting off the snow and for a moment, she could see nothing but a blank canvas that stung her eyes. When her sight adjusted to the light, she saw Taro just as he was turning the corner of the house, down the front of the building that faced the rest of Ota.

She walked around the corner and came to the driveway, Taro standing at its head. He was looking down at something she couldn't quite see. A mailbox or a post of some kind. The house was on a hill and had an unobstructed view of the rest of Ota. It was a hamlet more than a village. She counted maybe a dozen homes. One street that ran down the center. A government funded botanical garden just outside the village itself, now buried in snow.

The tops of the homes were white with frost. The yards and gardens also white and untouched by human or animal trespass.

Amid the tranquil mountain village before her, several things stood out. She saw that someone had broken every door of every building into pieces. Most of the homes had holes gouged out of their sides, like the cabin she stood by.

And from the head of the driveway, right in front of Taro, leading down into the street, a bright red streak of blood. Flowing from every door and driveway to the street. Making a scarlet river through the village.

She was so distracted by the scene she didn't see it at first; the thing hanging to her left, from the rafters of the porch above the front door. When she saw it, she couldn't even scream. Instead, she sucked in a breath so hard it hurt.

A skinned body. Human, by the looks of it. Headless. Arms and legs stretched out and impaled to the bannisters of the front porch by fragments of wood, probably pieces of the home itself. And next to Taro in the driveway, the thing he had been looking at, a tree branch with the head of a man thrust upon it. His mouth opened in a silent scream of eternity.

CHAPTER 21

Fuck this.

Ryoji paced back and forth in front of the pit that idiot Kawamoto had fallen into. That foreign girl and Ainu Neanderthal left hours ago. Ryoji and Ogoto had gotten a fire going by the tree well, which provided some relief from the biting cold. They boiled some snow in a portable stove kit, filled two rubber bottles with the water, and tossed them down to Kawamoto to keep himself warm. Though Ryoji suspected the only way he'd escape frostbite would be by some miracle.

Ryoji scanned the trees with the scope of his rifle. Put the gun down to his side. Sighed.

"Ogoto, let's talk," he whispered.

Ogoto's eyes didn't look so red anymore. The man hadn't touched his flask the entire trip.

Fucking good for him.

Ryoji continued, "Kawamoto isn't going to last and your bear guy has been gone too long. Let's get out of here."

"Excuse my bluntness, but fuck off, mayor." He did not whisper. "I'm not leavin' nobody. You want to go so bad, you just do that."

Ryoji could do just that. He was a fit man, fitter than this asshole in front of him, fitter than the dumb cop in the hole. He was captain of his university's soccer team not too long ago and kept himself on a strict regimen of five-kilometer runs every morning in good weather, on the treadmill in bad. But to leave now would mean to go it alone. And that bear had just roared nearby, not over thirty minutes ago. He wasn't an idiot.

"You heard that bear. That motherfucker is huge. Do you think our guns are even going to do anything more than piss it off? It was a mistake coming out here. I'll make a call into Sapporo when we get back and I'll get the Defense Force to send some real fire power out here."

With me leading them, of course.

It pained Ryoji to admit defeat. He had wanted nothing more than to finish the bear himself. Kawamoto's insistence that Taro lead the hunt irritated Ryoji beyond measure. He was driven even more annoyed by the presence of the foreign woman and the town drunk. On this, his sacred mission. He planned on finding the bear first and killing it, despite this supposed professional and his skills. But then he heard that roar. Kawamoto falling into the hole was a minor inconvenience. If he died, well, that was his own fault. But that bear's roar, it was louder than any he'd ever heard before. More than any grizzly or polar bear or even tiger. He had his family's legacy to uphold, yes, but he also wasn't going to get himself killed over it. For now, the smart thing to do was to leave. Then come back better armed. He thought about the elephant gun in his office.

Ogoto's eyes glazed over. "Uh-huh. Then you'd leave Kawamoto to die."

The man in question let out a faint whimper from the dark hole, "Please don't leave me."

Ryoji could hear clacking down there. Might be the man's teeth chattering. Or ice falling further down into the abyss.

"I'm not leaving you, don't you worry about that," Ryoji said with a smile. The smile that never left his face, even when he wanted it to. Too many hours of practice to get it just right that it had etched itself into his muscle memory.

He turned to Ogoto. "We have to leave, and soon. The sun is going down in—," he looked at his Rolex, "two hours. You want to go get firewood in the dark with that bear out there?"

Ogoto squatted in the snow and lit up a cigarette from his jacket pocket. He tossed another one down to Kawamoto. The man had little to keep him warm, and the cigarette would do jack shit, but it was a distraction at least.

"I know it isn't smart to stay. But Taro and Anasootsjyah got it covered. They'll be bringing help soon. And I ain't leavin' him behind."

"Thanks for the reassurance," Kawamoto said. A slight hint of levity in his voice.

"You put too much trust in them. Taro, sure, he's a badass. But he's wild and disorganized. And that foreigner—"

"Anastasia," Ogoto said. That was the first time Ryoji had heard him use her proper name.

"Whatever. You told me she's never even shot anything before."

"She can hit any target better than the three of us can."

Ryoji scoffed. "Okay. But she's never hit a living thing before, a moving target, has she?"

Ogoto looked down at the snow. "Sure she will, when it counts. Just hasn't gotten 'round to it yet. But she will, I trust her."

Before Ryoji said another word, deep laughter rang out from the forest.

He and Ogoto stood straight up and shouldered their rifles.

The laughter cut short and gave way to the unmistakable growl of a bear.

"What the hell?" Ryoji said.

"What's going on guys!?" Kawamoto yelled up at them.

Out of the right corner of his eye, Ryoji saw snow fall from the branches of a tree. When he turned his head fully to look at it, the branches were swaying as if something had jumped off of them.

No, it's just snow that did it

More clumpy snow fell from a nearby tree. Then from the branches of another one. One by one, branches shook and snow fell. But he couldn't see what was causing it.

"What is going on!?" Kawamoto cried out again.

Ryoji's palms grew sweaty, and he feared he'd lose the grip on his rifle. His heart beat faster and harder than it ever did on any of his other big game hunts. Even that one in South Africa where he had to pay some hush money to local police to let him shoot rhinos on a preserve. This was different. He did not know what was coming for him.

Apelike laughter exploded from above him. He looked straight up in time for powder to fall on his face. He frantically patted it away with his gloved hands. Ogoto fired his rifle at the spot above them. The shot momentarily deafened Ryoji's hearing. But when Ryoji looked, there was nothing there, just the swaying of a few branches.

"What did you see!?" Ryoji barked at Ogoto.

Ogoto's lower lip trembled, and he stuttered, but he couldn't get a word out.

Then came the sound of something heavy falling in the snow behind him. A *thwump* that he felt in his spine, almost as if it whatever it was, was so heavy that it shifted the snow he stood upon. Ogoto was facing it, and his eyes opened wide. Tears were falling from them. Both lips quivered now. Ryoji could feel the heat of breath on the back of his neck.

A huff of air. Growling. A shadow that consumed his own and washed over Ogto's pale face and his shaking hands. Ogoto dropped his rifle.

Ryoji ran. Didn't dare look behind him. Sprinted forward with all his strength, despite the incumbrance of the snowshoes. He passed Ogoto and pushed the man over.

Not on purpose, but he was in the way, his fault, not mine.

Ogoto stumbled backwards, fell, slid down into the tree well, and disappeared.

Ryoji didn't hear the creature chasing after him. Maybe it was happy to have an easy meal. Two for one. Ryoji could laugh at the sick joke. Of course he could. He was alive. He was going to stay that way.

Now run faster, you lazy fuck!

He did run. Faster than he ever did before. Faster than he did at the prefectural championship when Ayumi was watching from the stadium, cheering him on. That was one of the few times he felt happy in making her smile. Her dazzling eyes pushed him beyond what he thought he was capable of. But terror was much more effective to get his feet moving than love.

He ran towards the village of Ota, following the half-filled in footprints of Taro and Ashiya. He wished he could take the snowshoes off, but that would only slow him down, cause him to sink down into the snow like quicksand.

Ryoji hazarded a look behind him. He saw it there, by the tree well.

A massive brown bear standing on its hind legs. It stood taller than any he had ever seen before. Maybe three or even four times his own height.

How could that thing have snuck up on us?

It stood straight up like a person, standing absolutely still, watching him flee. At the moment that Ryoi saw it, he could tell something was wrong with it. Not just in the way it stood motionless. He was too far away to be certain, but the bear appeared mauled. Its fur was bloody, dark red—almost black—against the white trees behind it. The thing that stuck the most in Ryoji's mind was its eyes. Black. Bright. *Darklight*, he thought. He felt their gaze penetrate his mind. As if the bear were pushing its consciousness into his own.

Words that were not words. Impressions full of meaning assaulted his thoughts.

Coward.

Failure.

Murderer.

Ryoji turned back to face the path ahead and ran.

CHAPTER 22

Someone positioned the skinless body the same way they had positioned the deer. Now that she thought about it, likely what would have happened to Ren had Hikari not found him when she did.

This was no bear that had done this. The deer was not some isolated incident created by some sick individual. The attacks and the ritualistic altars of flesh had to be done by the same person, the same *thing*. She doubted she had even seen a bear. Perhaps it was some psycho dressing as one, leaving behind false prints.

But no. As much as that would have been the preferable option to the doubt that was growing in her mind—*abaasy,* came Grandmother's voice—she knew this was not natural. Something otherworldly was happening, she felt it deep in her gut.

Ashiya walked down the single street of Ota. No fresh tire tracks or dirty snow to show that anyone had left since the snowfall from last night. That made the blood stand out all the more.

The red was almost fluorescent. Blood trails led out from every home and down into the street, and then on out of the village, and into the forest, in five or six different trails. But there were no bodies, aside from the one hanging from the porch. She and Taro checked each of the other homes. Nobody in any of them. Signs of struggle everywhere.

Overturned furniture. Broken windows. One pot must have had water in it at some point, but was now nothing more than dry molten metal on the still burning stove flame.

There were tracks from the people, some of them at least, just outside their homes. Boot prints. Some bare feet. Something had disturbed the snow in a way that suggested the flailing of arms as people tried to cling to something to keep from being dragged away.

The bear's tracks were much the same as in the forest. Massive but not evenly spaced apart. As if the thing could be where it wanted to be without having to walk. Stupid thought. But one that latched onto her mind like a leech, draining the reason out of her slowly, yet surely. The events of the past few days were reducing her mind to that of a child's, to one who believed in magic and monsters. What happened in this village was another step on that path. No bear, not even a polar bear, could wreak such havoc on a town like this. Not when people could have gotten away in their cars or had hid inside their sturdy homes. Some had big windows that could be broken into, but others did not. Their walls were thick and strong. Yet they, too, were ripped apart.

Taro came out from an outhouse just on the outskirts of the hamlet.

"What do you think?" she asked.

"Don't ask me."

He looked into the forest as he rubbed his hands together.

Something in his eyes, she wasn't sure what exactly, made her think he knew. At least partially.

"You know what's happening, don't you?"

The now familiar grunt.

"Doesn't matter," he said. "But we can't move anymore today. Sun's gonna set soon. We'll have to make camp here."

The sun was just above the horizon, over the trees. The sky was clear but turning a smoky gray in the twilight.

"Are you serious? We need to get out of here. Take a car."

"You know how to hot-wire a car? Did you find any keys in the homes?"

Ashiya said nothing.

"That's what I thought. If we find some keys, we can try to get out of here. But we need to secure a place for the night in case we can't, and I don't want to be searching in the dark."

She looked around. The thought of staying at a dead person's—and that's what she assumed everyone in this town to be—home unnerved her. But it was the smarter choice. Either that or pitch a tent out in the snow with the bear out there. Not that the homes seemed to provide much protection. But better than nothing.

"How about that one?" she asked as she pointed to the A-frame cabin nearest the forest, next to the one they found the skinned body at.

The cabin had a large window covering most of the wall, and its front door was splintered apart. Every single home had a hole ripped into it, but with this place, it was just the door. She reasoned the window wall could help them see what was coming, given that nothing would provide much protection, anyway. This home would require less boarding up of the holes as well.

"That'll do. Get a fire going. I'll fix the door."

She nodded and walked over to the wraparound deck of the cabin. They had already checked this house before and she remembered they had firewood out back and a wood fire stove inside.

She grabbed an arm full of wood by an overturned tractor of some sort, something with a long robot-like arm with a snowplow blade attached to it, and walked inside. Set her bag and the logs down on the floor, next to an acoustic guitar propped up against the wall. There was an axe above the fireplace and she used it to break off some kindling from the logs. She used the fire-starter hung next to the axe to light the fire. While she got the fire going, Taro pushed the sofa to the entrance and wedged it into the hole that used to be the door. He knocked over a lamp in the process and it shattered on the floor.

"Hey!" she shouted. "Just because these people might be, you know, doesn't mean you can just disrespect their home."

He glared at her as he walked across the living room. He yanked a bookshelf over to the sofa-door as dozens of volumes fell to the floor.

"This is not disrespect," he said. "I'm sure they wouldn't mind us using their home to protect ourselves."

He stomped on the lower shelf of the bookcase and broke it off. He shoved the pieces of the shelf into the gaps between the doorframe and the sofa left exposed.

"I agree, but you could show some care while you do it."

He kicked and stamped on the case until he obliterated it. After he finished using the pieces as duct tape, he took the pillows that had fallen from the sofa and shoved them into the gaps.

"There, as good as it'll get."

He smiled. The first time she saw the man make that expression. She had thought his face was incapable of any other emotion aside from "grimace."

It was short-lived. "You take watch now," he said. "I'm gonna sleep. And then I'll be up from midnight till morning." Without waiting for an answer, he set his pack on the ground, took out a sleeping bag, and got inside it with his straw shoes and outerwear still on. In seconds, he was snoring. Ashiya stood there dumbfounded at this specimen of what humanity used to be prior to civilization. She wanted to laugh at the sight, but held it in.

She looked out the only window of the cabin; the triangle shaped one that took up the entire wall. She imagined the bear crashing through it in the night, but this was the only cabin that still had its walls intact. And the cold could kill just as good as a bear. If not better.

The sun had dipped below the trees and the stars were coming to life in the now almost black sky.

She worried about Ogoto. She knew it was too late to go back for him and Kawamoto—she mentally blocked out Ryoji even being there. But this was the smart move for her and Taro to make for now. No wandering around in the dark.

Ogoto was a fool, but she had faith in his experience. He knew how to survive out in the wilds and they had the gear to do so. She was more concerned that they would have to spend the night inside a tent and not a cabin like her. And Kawamoto... she accepted it right then and there: that the man would be dead by morning. She couldn't see how it would be otherwise.

To take her mind off of the situation, she went upstairs to the loft to look around. The home still had power, and she kept the lights on. Taro didn't seem bothered by inconveniences such as bright lights while he slept. The man looked like he could sleep through war itself. Keep the lights on until it got too dark outside. Then the window would just reflect the living room back at her and she would lose her ability to see what could be approaching.

They hadn't checked the loft earlier. What was the point when they could see it from downstairs and had called up to anyone that could be in the house?

She climbed the ladder and saw a single bed draped in pink and black blankets. A stuffed skeleton sat by the pillow and Christmas lights hung in the corners. The throw rug in front of the bed was a shaggy pink.

A little girl's room. One who liked the cutesy and the macabre.

Ashiya's heart sank at the sight and what the deserted town and the blood on the snow implied about what had happened to the owner of this cozy nook.

She lifted herself up from the ladder and entered the loft. A faint vanilla scent lingered in the air. It all reminded Ashiya of her own childhood. Her home was not anywhere near as nice as this one. But she too, if rumors could be believed, loved pink and fluffy things, once upon a time. She decked out her own room like this one when she was in elementary school. Before boys and cigarettes and Alice in Chains led her heart to a different world.

She sat on the bed. Across the loft, she saw a writing desk with a drawing of skulls and roses on it. For a moment, she thought it wouldn't be so bad to just lie down and let the now warming up cabin swallow her whole. Go back in time to a world that was innocent and safe. When Alexei was still alive and her own mother still talked to her.

Ashiya looked at a wardrobe in the corner. A body-sized mirror built into the front door. To her surprise, she saw her own crying reflection. Hadn't even noticed it was happening. She wiped away the tears and stood up.

When she did, the wood beneath her feet creaked and groaned. But so did the floor from underneath the wardrobe. Something shuffled inside the closet and bumped against the door.

Her rifle was downstairs. She had her hunting knife strapped inside her breast jacket pocket. She placed her hand on it but didn't take it out of the sheath. Undid the button that held it in place.

It was a tiny wardrobe, it couldn't possibly be the bear.

She walked towards it. Another creak from behind the mirrored door and a soft *thump* of something falling.

She placed her hand on the door handle. Opened it, her other hand still on her knife.

Crouched behind hanging dresses and jackets was a little girl. She was shaking and her face was wet with tears. But she didn't make a sound. Didn't even look at Ashiya. Stared blankly ahead at nothing.

She removed her hand from the knife and extended it to the girl.

CHAPTER 23

"Hang in there. They'll be back for us," Ogoto said.

Kawamoto squirmed in pain on the slick ice shelf, which looked more like a slide angled as it was. Being down in the tree well with him, Ogoto could now see how perilous the man's position was. Kawamoto needed to keep himself propped up with both of his arms stretched out on the ice—though they couldn't grab anything—and his left foot dug into a cleft of hard snow for support, the right one bent behind his back. One wrong move and he'd go sliding down into the darkness.

Ogoto was on his own shelf across the width of the hole, the gap separating him from Kawamoto. His tailbone hurt from where he landed, but he didn't mind the pain too much. His shelf was icy but flat, he was free to stand and move around. The walls were another matter. Straight and slick. No ledges or clefts to grab onto. The opening above was maybe just out of reach of a good jump. But to risk that; if he missed he'd fall on the ice and possibly slide off into the void. To make it, he'd have to grab onto the edge of the opening and pull himself up. He lacked the strength to do that even if the opening had a handhold. As it was, it was nothing more than snow and loose soil.

Not to mention he'd probably just dislodge more snow from the walls if he tried.

Burying them.

There was no climbing out of here for him, doubly so for Kawamoto. There was no choice but to wait for help.

"You don't know that," Kawamoto said. "Ryoji left us. He pushed you down here. And for all we know, that thing out there already killed Taro and Anastasia."

Kawamoto groaned and leaned back. Even in the fading light of the hole, Ogoto could see the sweat on his forehead. He didn't want to admit it to himself, but Kawamoto's chances of getting out of this with all his fingers and toes were grim.

They hadn't heard the bear for what must have been at least an hour. But was it a bear? Bears can climb trees but don't travel across them as fast as this thing did. Ogoto refused to remember what he saw, standing behind Ryoji as it fell from the branches. But the image kept on pressing into the wall of his suppression. If he had a drink or five or ten, he could probably hold it back. Being sober meant he had no such defense. He couldn't remember many details, but he remembered the black eyes. The partially exposed skull. The giant body that blotted out the sun.

"Ah, come on, don't say things like that. Yeah, Ryoji is a bastard, but he doesn't want to go down for murder, does he? And Anasootsjyah and Taro are trustworthy. They won't leave us here."

He hoped his cheerfulness wouldn't just calm Kawamoto, but also distract himself from that horrible image of the bear's skull. How could the bear still be alive after an injury like that?

Kawamoto strained himself to look up. "Ryoji doesn't have to go down for murder if we die here, idiot. He can just say it was an accident and no one will look into it further. They might not even find our bodies if we fall down there."

Ogoto looked down at his feet and rubbed the back of his head. He went quiet. Felt like a child chastised by the teacher.

Kawamoto's expression softened. "Hey, I'm sorry. I don't think you're stupid. It's just this situation and the stress and our impending deaths looming over our heads. Small things really. Forgive me, yeah?"

"Nothing to forgive. I know I'm slow but... but I know that there are good people coming for us."

Kawamoto looked into the void below.

The distance to the bottom was impossible to tell unless they sacrificed gear and dropped it down. There were no rocks nearby for the task. Just smooth ice and the pine's trunk. Ogoto wondered if it went down to the center of the earth. Or maybe to Canada? He laughed at the thought. Wouldn't that be something? He couldn't wait to tell Anasootsjyah the joke.

Mama never approved of his schooling much, thought it was a waste of time. Did the government mandated years until middle school and then he was out in the working world. Followed his father in the hunting and fishing game. Wasn't much money in it, but damn if it wasn't the best thing in the world for him. Open air and freedom. No teachers looking down on him and calling him dumb.

He lost both of his parents when he was seventeen. They slipped driving on some black ice on a mountain pass and wrapped their truck around a tree. Ever since then, he took up the family business solo. Got married. Then lost her due to his careless flirting with Kaede. That's when the drinking started. He passed the lonely nights best he could; drunk off his ass. That way, he could keep from thinking about his wife. Keep from feeling the weight of the guilt. He found out she passed from an aneurysm a few years after they divorced. His drinking doubled after that.

In that hole, he wished he could talk to his Mama again. She had this way of making him feel better, no matter what. Like the time she found him crying in his room, saying a boy at school called him a retard. Sure, Mama never thought school was for him, but that didn't mean she thought he was stupid. She walked over to him, crying in his bed, and slapped him on the back of the head. Told him tears were not worth as much as effort and a good heart.

Some of these soft touchy feely types nowadays may have called that abuse. Ogoto called it love. Never really knew the difference between the two. But whatever, it worked and got him on his feet right away.

Just then, Kawamoto's body slipped a few centimeters down the slope. He yelped and slapped the ice with his palms. The man must have been beyond freezing but he couldn't afford to take his hands, gloved as they were, off of the ice.

"Hey, hey, hold on there, you hold on and be calm, okay? You got this," Ogoto commanded. A rare authority now present in his voice. It sounded like Mama to him and gave him some warmth in the tree well.

Kawamoto slid a little further. He started sobbing. "Please, don't let me..."

"I'm not letting you." Ogoto scanned the pit for something, anything, to help him out here. It was nothing but ice and darkness. With a dim pink haze of sunset above, lighting the area of the hole just above his head, but no further down. The leafless branches of the trees above thrashed about as a gust of wind lashed them. Snow dusted off of the trees and glittered in the sunlight as it misted across the opening.

Then a thought came to him. There was no way out of the tree well, but that didn't mean he couldn't try to get Kawamoto to his side of the hole. It would be better than his current situation, at least. The gap between his shelf and Kawamoto's was small. Too big to cross by simply stepping over it, but easy enough to jump it. To his left he saw, just barely in the dark, an outline of something sticking out of the tree's trunk, just beneath his shelf.

"Hey, you still got your flashlight?" he asked Kawamoto.

He had stopped crying now, more out of a desire to not move than any emotional stasis, and said, "Yeah, I think so." He moved his hand to his backpack, which was squished under his back. The outer pocket he reached into was poking out from under his body. He unzipped it and took out a hand-sized flashlight. "What do you want with it?"

"Shine it down the hole best you can, to your right."

He did so, and the light revealed a thick tree root poking out of the pine, disappearing into the wall of snow. It had the girth of a python.

"You reckon that root is strong enough to hold me?"

"What!?" Kawamoto's voice echoed sharply in the dark chamber.

"I'm gonna get you over to my side here so that way you are safer than you are now, okay? Just keep the light on the root."

Kawamoto protested, but Ogoto tiptoed to the edge of his shelf and reached out a leg and touched the root with his toes. It didn't budge.

"Be careful," Kawamoto said. But there was hope in his voice. Hope of success and also a frantic fear interwoven in his tone.

Ogoto pressed down harder on the root. It didn't bounce. It felt as solid as the ice shelf he stood on. He leaned his full weight onto that one leg, while trying to hold on to the slick wall for support.

He held his balance and moved his other leg to the root. Now he was fully standing on it. It didn't give way. Ogoto laughed like a little boy then. So did Kawamoto. Both men drunk on hope.

From the root, Ogoto could bend forwards and touch Kawamoto's slope. His plan was to grab Kawamoto's right hand, for the man to lift himself up—trusting in Ogoto for balance—and then he could pull back and both of them could jump back to the more secure shelf.

"Grab my hand," Ogoto said.

Kawamoto moved slowly but tried to sit up straight. He slid down the slope some more. Closer to falling off the edge, his left foot now dangling over the edge. But he was also closer to Ogoto's outstretched hand. Kawamoto reached forward and grabbed onto the hand. Ogoto dug his heels into the root and leaned back. Kawamoto could stand on his right foot in an awkward, crouching stance. But his stance wasn't stable. His single foot had no real traction on the ice. One wrong shift of his bodyweight would send him flying down the slope.

"We got this," Ogoto said.

Kawamoto laughed. "We do, we do." His voice was now almost hysterical with hope.

"You just gotta jump when I pull you back. You can make it to the other side."

"What about you?"

"I'm alright, I'll fall back into the root some. It'll hold me. Then you can help me over if I need it."

"Alright."

Kawamoto took a few rapid but deep breaths, like he was prepping himself to take a plunge into an icy lake.

Snow fell from above and landed on Kawamoto's shoulders. The little light pouring into the hole rolled into darkness, as if someone rolled a boulder over the opening.

Ogoto looked up. And then he saw it. The face that no drink could hold at bay. Dark though it was, the black eyes stood out even with the blotting out of the light. It was leaning over the hole, looking down at them.

"Jump!" Ogoto shouted.

But he was too late. The dark shape above reached down a massive paw and snatched Ogoto out of the hole. It flung him into the fading light of day. He landed on the powder just outside of the hole's opening. The snow was soft, but he landed so hard that he struggled to breathe. He felt something wet on his stomach, along with a burning pain. Ogoto squeezed his eyes shut and thought of Mama. For the first time in years, thought of his wife.

I'm so sorry.

He heard Kawamoto's screams. They were sharp and loud at first. But they kept getting smaller and more distant until he barely hear them at all. And then a sudden end to the screams and a heavy smack of something hitting a solid surface.

He opened his eyes and saw the bear's face right above him. It had broken through his need to forget. It was here, forcing him to look at it, and it looked like it was smiling.

CHAPTER 24

The fire was dancing high now. Ashiya had gone outside one more time to grab as much wood as she could carry. Taro held the sofa away from the hole so she could slip out.

She found some fresh vegetables in the kitchen and some eggs and put on a pot of water and boiled it. She was a shit cook if she was honest with herself, but she at least knew they all needed a meal, especially now that there was a child with them.

Taro sat in front of the fire with the girl, Saho, she called herself. Ashiya looked out from the kitchen in amazement. Taro was making a fool out of himself, telling some story about monkeys in the woods and making odd faces to try and make Saho laugh. But she looked like she was maybe eleven or twelve, and had already outgrown such things. But she laughed politely at Taro as he fell into a slapstick routine for her.

Taro may have been an asshole to the hunting party, to her as well, but children were the way to his heart.

He sat in front of the fire, trying to get Saho to open up. While behind him his rifle, rounds of ammunition, four large hunting knives, and even a bear trap stood against the wall; the other one he had on him was outside the cabin's front window right now. Primed to go off.

Darkness had fallen over the land hours ago. The only light was from the fire and a little lamp above the stove Ashiya was cooking on. Anymore than that would make it too hard to see outside. Saho went from mute to at least telling them her name, but not much more. Ashiya left the boiling pot and brought over some hot chocolate she found in a pantry and passed it to the two by the fire.

"Thank you," Taro said. Those may have been the kindest words he'd spoken to her all day.

"No problem," she said and turned to Saho. "Hey, how are you feeling?"

Saho looked at her knees in silence. She wore a pink ski jacket and blue pajamas underneath. Her long black hair fell to her waist. "Better." She took a sip of the cocoa as she stared deep into the flames.

"Do you know where your parents are?" Ashiya asked. She tried this an hour ago when Saho wasn't speaking at all and unsurprisingly got no answer then.

Taro looked at Ashiya like she had said something offensive.

Saho kicked her feet—which couldn't touch the ground from her sitting position on the chair—and said, "I was outside with Dad last night. Thought I heard something singing a song from the forest next to my house. I was scared, so I came inside and shut the door. But Dad was still out there working on the harvester. Then he started screaming..." Her eyes reflected the flames back at them.

"I... he stopped screaming. Mama woke up and ran outside. I told her not to. And then she was screaming. I didn't know what to do, so I hid upstairs in the closet. And then... everyone was screaming. Everyone in Ota. I heard glass breaking and people shouting. Dogs barking. A few gunshots went off. Then it was quiet, like five minutes later, it was so fast. Then something pounded on my door. I heard it break open. Something was walking around downstairs, and it was... still humming my song, the song I was humming outside before it all started. How could it know that? It was humming and stomping around. I even heard the ladder to my loft creak, and then it left."

The adults said nothing.

She said all of this matter of fact with no emotion. The detached analysis of the event scared Ashiya. Maybe the girl was in shock, because none of this sounded like the behavior of a bear. Then again, what about the last few days did?

Taro wiped his hand across his face. Was he crying? She couldn't see clearly with the firelight as the only source of illumination.

Ashiya placed her hand on Saho's shoulder. The girl didn't react. Barely registered her presence.

Taro stood up and walked over to the giant window that took up the entire wall. Ashiya left Saho and joined him. Some homes still had their inside lights on from the previous night, some were dark.

At least the darkness covered the bloodstains on the snow. And aside from the one body hung off the porch—with the head shoved onto a branch—, they couldn't find anybody else. Ashiya thought about tomorrow, about how she would guide Saho through the village without letting her see the blood. For all she knew, the skinned body could be her father's.

There was also Kawamoto and Ogoto and Ryoji—she allowed him a moment of empathy—still out there. The hunt for the bear, no, the creature, would have to be postponed. First, get the girl to safety, then take care of the men left behind, then rethink their plan of attack, if there was going to even be one.

"Taro, what is it? The thing that's out there. I know it's not a bear."

He stayed silent for a moment. "Kesagake."

"But that just means dangerous bear, like one that has a behavioral issue. This is not that."

"Do you know about the Ainu?"

"Not really."

"I am Ainu. The people who lived in Hokkaido before the Japanese came. We used to have a belief, and some of us still do, I still do, that every living thing has a soul, is a god in a sense. And bears are the chief among them."

He said no more.

"So, this is a god you're saying?"

He grunted. "No. The bears were the gods come to us in the flesh. And they were good. They helped to balance the world of people and nature. But sometimes even a god can become a demon if it suffers enough. Especially in winter. Around the solstice, the nights are the longest that they get. It lets things slip through from that other side."

She didn't want to believe this. But want to or not, she was coming to.

"abaasy," she said.

Taro raised an eyebrow. "What?"

"Nothing, it's just something—"

Screaming from outside the cabin. Saho jumped to her feet and ran to the ladder and began climbing it.

"Help me!"

Ashiya heard a man calling out from the street. She looked out the window with her hands cupped over her eyes to give her a better view. There was somebody out in the middle of the street, waving his arms and calling out. He had a flashlight in his hands and its light bounced around the village frantically. As it did so, Ashiya saw, for a split second, something large and furry, moving in front of a yard three houses away.

She went to pull the sofa from the doorway, and Taro helped her.

"Over here! Hurry, a bear is right behind you!" she yelled.

Taro aimed his rifle into the dark. He must have seen where the bear had been as well.

The man turned to her voice and ran to them.

"Be careful!" she said. "We have a bear trap in the yard."

The man ran up to the driveway, flashing his light in front of him. Floodlights from somewhere above the window turned on. Motion detectors. It revealed the bear trap, and the man jumped over it. He made it to the door.

It was Ryoji.

Taro kept his rifle aimed outside while Ryoji practically dove into the cabin. After he was inside, Taro pushed the sofa back into the doorframe.

Ashiya noticed Saho peeking out from the loft down at them. Her eyes wide and shiny in the dark.

"Where are Ogoto and Kawamoto?" Ashiya asked, a slight tinge of panic in her voice.

Ryoji's face was almost blue and he couldn't speak properly. Ashiya took his hand and led him to the fire. Taro took off his snowshoes and jacket. The snow had soaked his clothes. Ashiya went to the kitchen, wetted a few towels and microwaved them. Then she came back and applied them to his face and wrapped his now shirtless body in the hot towels.

"Saho," Ashiya said. The girl poked her head out from the loft. "It's okay, you can come down. Can you grab me some blankets and a sweater of your dad's?"

She threw down her own pink and black blankets from the loft and they fell next to Ryoji. She then scampered down the ladder and raced off to her parent's room.

Ashiya bundled Ryoji in the blankets.

Taro cupped Ryoji's face in his hands and looked over his body. "No deep cuts or anything. Don't look too bad. Let me see your hands and feet."

Ryoji couldn't move anymore. He had been running on pure adrenaline for hours. He was exhausted and cold. But after Taro took off his shoes and socks and gloves, he declared that frostbite wasn't a concern. Hypothermia maybe.

Saho came back into the room holding several sweaters and pajamas from her parents. She handed them to Ashiya and she and Taro helped to put them on Ryoji, whose limbs he could hardly move.

"Ryoji," Ashiya said. In a soft tone she never would have imagined using on him before. "What happened?"

He moved his eyes to hers. His facial features remained stiff. "Th-th-they're d-d-dead."

Before she could process what he said, another man began yelling from outside. It was Ogoto. Clear as day. Calling for help.

Ryoji's eyes bulged out of his blue face.

CHAPTER 25

Ashiya ran to the window and looked outside. Much the same as Ryoji had done minutes earlier, Ogoto was now walking down the middle of the street. Staggering and falling to his knees. She couldn't see his face given the lack of light, but she could tell by his gait and his voice that it was him.

He fell face first into the snow and stopped moving.

Just then a roar erupted from somewhere in the darkness. A bear's howl of rage. She could hear it clearly inside the cabin, as if it were right next to her. The window pane rattled.

How big was this thing?

The sound came from somewhere near the driveway of the A-frame but she couldn't see its source.

Then the floodlights turned on and she saw a tuft of fur dart away around the corner of the house to the right.

"We have to get him!" she cried out as she began pulling the sofa from the doorway.

Taro grabbed her from behind and pulled her away as she struggled against him.

"No. Not now."

She twisted her torso and turned to face Taro and beat her fists against his chest. "Let go!"

"No." He picked Ashiya up off the ground like she was a child and moved her to the other side of the cabin. "If we open the door now, we put everyone in danger. We must wait."

Ashiya quit her struggle. Taro released her.

She felt a weakness in her knees. Her hands shook. Her only friend, the only one in town who consistently accepted her as she was, was out there in the street, lying in the snow. Not moving. If the bear didn't kill him the cold would, if it wasn't already too late.

"It can't be him," Ryoji said, still wrapped in the pink blanket by the fire, some color having returned to his face.

"Why not?" Taro asked.

Ryoji gave no explanation and refused to meet anyone's eyes. "It just can't be. Don't open the door!"

"Okay, we won't open the door just yet. But we can't leave him out there much longer," Ashiya said.

The roar came crashing into their debate from the backside of the cabin now. It was circling them.

"Help!" Ogoto cried out. He began sobbing and wailing. It almost sounded like it came from behind the house as well.

Ashiya felt her heart shrivel up into itself. But no, they couldn't go outside, not now. She told Saho to go hide in her closet. If this bear was really as big as it seemed to be—and it could definitely rip through walls, let alone glass—she didn't want the girl exposed. Saho flew up the ladder again. Ashiya ran over to her rifle leaning against the wall and shouldered it. She picked up Ryoji's and tossed it to him. He could barely make the catch. He looked down at the gun with apprehension, like it was a snake.

Taro looked out the front window while Ashiya went to the kitchen and looked out the smaller window leading to the backyard. Taro yelled at Ryoji to cover the back door attached to the kitchen. He reluctantly went.

"Help me! Please!" Ogoto's desperate wail.

The thud of heavy paws broke into the snow to the left of the kitchen window, just out of sight. Something snorted and huffed. The bear let out a jaw-popping sound. The kind they do to let you know you were too close to them.

"I don't see Ogoto anymore," Taro called out from the living room.

A heavy *thump* struck the wall nearest the fire. The axe above the fireplace fell to the ground with a clatter. Ryoji let out a soft whimper. The bear grunted and puffed out air. It walked to the back of the cabin again, near the back door in the kitchen. Ryoji took a step back towards the living room. Ashiya replaced him by the door. Taro joined.

The bear grunted again. And then came a rhythmic puff of air that almost sounded like laughter. The bear struck the kitchen door, and it shook. Then the door handle turned as if it were trying to open the door. Thankfully, they had locked it. Another growl, one that spoke of something utterly massive, almost like a car engine revving up, just on the other side of the flimsy door. Ashiya could feel it in her stomach. And with it, the pressure in her head grew, just like before. Another strike against the door. The wood near the top split. If it could rip through heavy wooden walls, then this door would be nothing to it.

Then came a sound she didn't expect. Knocking at the back door. Three raps of a fist against the wood. Not of a giant paw, but sounding like a regular human fist banging on the door. Followed by the puffs that could be laughter. Then the heavy footsteps moved around the cabin to the front door.

All three of them moved back into the living room. Ryoji's face was wet with sweat. Taro's was stone.

The sofa wedged into the doorway wriggled. Laughter. That's what it was, not a random puff of air, it was clearly laughter. Though not human in origin. A scratching at the doorpost.

Then the thing hummed. It hummed with a human voice, a woman's voice, a rhythm of some song.

The floodlights turned on again.

Ashiya wanted to run to the window to see it, but didn't for fear of the thing bursting through the glass.

Pounding on the side of the wall. Starting from the ground floor and moving on up to the second. The ceiling creaked and groaned as the bear walked atop the roof. And moved over to the loft.

Saho.

Ashiya slung her rifle back over her shoulder and raced up the ladder, her hands slipping on a middle rung, almost sending her falling. There was a tiny window over Saho's bed. And in it, the bear's face, upside down, it was looking in from the top of the house. Ashiya climbed to the last wrung and stood in the loft, rifle aimed at the window. It was gone.

Pounding right above her. Scratching. Humming. Saho crying softly in the closet.

Then silence.

Followed shortly after by a final creak in the ceiling and a heavy *thwump* in the snow on the ground in front of the house.

The floodlights came back on in the driveway.

"Holy shit!" Ryoji yelled.

Ashiya looked down into the living room and saw it by the window. The bear lumbered close to the glass. Taro stood with his gun aimed at it. Ryoji had his gun in his hands, but they were shaking too much for him to take aim as well. Ashiya climbed back down the ladder and raced to the window.

And stopped.

Her heart sank into her stomach.

The bear stood in the driveway, near the glass. Before the floodlights died out she saw it. Took in every detail. Even on all fours, its shoulders reached the top of the window, meaning it could be as tall as the entire cabin on its hind legs, maybe even taller. The body was as big as a shuttle bus. Its matted and rust-colored fur glowed dimly. Dried blood covered it fully. Two ribs on its left side poked through its fur. The bones sticking out of the flesh like teeth. Half of its face was gone on the left side. Nothing but a skull with tattered flesh clinging to it. A white lightning pattern of fur streaked across the right eye.

And its eyes. Even as the floodlights went out, she could still see them. Two burning black orbs in the darkness. She stood there shaking, unable to look away. It was pitch-black outside, but still those eyes pierced the shadows. It shouldn't have been possible, but it was happening anyway.

The floodlights came to life again, and the bear was gone.

And beyond the light, a figure. Crawling from the street and then into the driveway. His face bloody.

"Help," Ogoto said. Lifted himself to his knees. And then collapsed into the snow.

CHAPTER 26

They waited, watching Ogoto's near-motionless body. He was breathing but not much more.

They waited five minutes for any sign of the bear. But that's not what it was, was it? It was too big. Its flesh was rotten and its bones were protruding out if it. Like it was already dead...

The moment they could convince themselves that the bear, the thing, was gone, Taro pulled the sofa away from the door, passed it off for Ryoji to hold up, and both he and Ashiya ran out. They picked up Ogoto by his arms and dragged him back to the cabin, skirting the bear trap that was never set off—despite the bear coming right up to it—and brought him inside. Ryoji pushed the sofa back into the gap. Though they knew it provided no protection. That thing could have broken inside if it so wished to.

Which birthed a disturbing question in Ashiya's mind: why didn't it just come in and kill them?

They laid Ogoto in front of the fire. He was unconscious now. His skin cold to the touch. His fingers were blue, almost black, causing a shudder to run throughout Ashiya's bones. He would have to have them amputated. There was no saving them. But maybe they could save him.

Ashiya and Taro rushed to take off his wet clothes and wrap him in blankets. Ashiya took gauze out of her first-aid kit and wrapped his black fingers in it, keeping them separate from one another. There were three gashes in his right shoulder. She could see the shoulder blade through the bloody mess. Black blood. That detail lodged itself in her mind. Was he infected with something? The thought passed, and she disinfected the wound with rubbing alcohol and cleaned it as best she could and then wrapped it in the gauze. By the end, the bandages had almost mummified the man.

His lips moved without making a sound. She lifted his head on her knees and caressed his frozen hair. There were no tears in her eyes, not yet at least. That would have to come later. For now, there was much to be done.

Ogoto started making a sound. She leaned close to his lips to hear what he was saying. "Thank you, Ana—" And then he went quiet. No strength left in him.

Ryoji, still holding onto his rifle, walked over. "No, no, no. I don't like this. Ogoto is dead!"

He lifted his rifle and aimed it at the man's face.

With a rush of animal ferocity, Taro flew across the room and grabbed the rifle. In a second, he ripped it away from Ryoji and pushed the man away. Saho was in the corner on the floor, hugging her knees.

Ryoji pushed Taro back, but the man barely budged.

"What is wrong with you!?" Ashiya shouted at Ryoji.

"He shouldn't be alive!"

"Calm down," she said. "You still haven't told us what happened out there. How do you know he shouldn't be alive? What the fuck happened?"

"He slipped. That monster attacked us and he slipped down into the hole with Kawamoto. There's no way he could have gotten out. And that thing was there. I had to run, I had no choice. You would've done the same thing I did if you were there!"

Taro placed his palm on Ryoji's chest. "My friend, we are all scared right now. I know I am. But if we are going to survive this, we must do it together. You are a good shot. That man lying there told me so. We need you to get your shit together, because if you don't, we are all dead."

Ryoji's wild eyes relaxed, and a semblance of calm washed over him. Somewhat. "I...I...you're right. You're right. Sorry everyone, I'm just, I don't know, this is a lot to handle." His characteristic smile broadened across his face again. But Ashiya could tell by his eyes that he wasn't just afraid, he was borderline mad.

Taro patted him on the shoulder. "Good." Then he went over to Saho and grabbed the girl's hands. He whispered something to her, and she nodded. She reached her arms up and embraced Taros' neck. He picked her up and carried her in his arms. She seemed to sob into Taro's chest as he pat her back.

Ashiya got a pillow and put it under Ogoto's head and then stood up.

She went to Ryoji. "I know this is all fucked. But we need to talk about this now." She spoke to Taro across the room. "That is not a bear. It might look like one, but it is too big, too smart, and we all saw it, didn't we? It looked dead." *And those eyes.* "Can't you all feel it? What did you say earlier, Taro? That some gods can become demons if they suffer enough? I don't know what I believe, but I know this thing isn't natural. In the morning, first thing, we need to get out of here and back to Kamuy-Kotan. Ryoji you need to get some serious help here to deal with it."

His eyes looked through her, but he did nod his head slowly. Like he was someone accustomed to doing so while other things occupied their minds. But he was not really listening. Ashiya ignored it for now.

Ogoto coughed and opened his eyes. He tried to sit up, but Ashiya bent over and gently pushed him back down. "Hey, don't try to move."

He looked up at her and smiled. "Didn't...think I'd...ever get to see you again. I had the most beautiful dream. The crystal waves crashing on the eternal shores."

Does he have a concussion?

"What happened to you? Where is Kawamoto?" Taro asked.

Ashiya looked at him with disapproval. "Give him a break."

"No, it's okay," Ogoto said. He pushed himself up, using the floor, and sat upright. He looked at everyone in the room and smiled. His eyes rested on Ryoji with a look that could have been fascination or even amorous desire. Ryoji looked away and intertwined his fingers nervously. Ogoto then looked at Saho, who was hiding behind Taro. "Why isn't she a little cutie." He stared at Saho for two seconds too long for comfort, then looked back at Ashiya. "The bear attacked us. It killed Kawamoto."

Silence filled the gaps in between the crackling of the fire.

"Ryoji said you fell into the hole," Taro said. His eyes studying Ogoto.

"Oh, I don't remember that. My head hurts, though. I need to rest some more." And with that, Ogoto laid back down and closed his eyes.

CHAPTER 27

Hours passed and the first light of dawn poked through the black sky, creating a deep purple and dark brown hue, giving the appearance of a swelling bruise. The fire continued to burn though they had no more wood to give it, unless they wanted to hazard a trip outside. Ryoji, Ogoto, and Saho were asleep in the living room. Ashiya had caught a few hours herself but was now fully awake, slightly exhausted but her mind was clear with purpose: get out of here. Taro stood by the window, gripping his rifle. He didn't sleep at all.

Ashiya crawled out from under her blankets, ones taken from Saho's parent's room, and put on her insulated pants and her down jacket. It was mostly warm in the cabin, aside from some cold seeping in through the cracks by the sofa, but she wanted to be ready to move. She looked down at Saho's face. A faint glimmer of tears in her closed eyes. Innocence wrapped up safely in a blanket. Ashiya wanted to keep her that way: innocent and safe.

Too much had happened in just the past few hours. No time to talk to Saho, not really. No time to interrogate Ryoji on what seemed incredibly suspicious—Ogoto falling into the hole. No time to ask Ogoto for the truth either. She checked her phone for reception. Again, no bars. The storm had lightened up but must still be messing with their signals.

She stood and walked over to Taro's side. "See anything?"

He grunted a no. He fixed his fierce eyes on the dissipating darkness. "It didn't leave any tracks."

"What?"

He pointed out to the driveway. The first rays of morning showed just enough of the front yard that they should have been able to see tracks, especially from a bear that big. But the snow was smooth. Aside from the human tracks they themselves made yesterday, there was nothing.

"What is going on?" she asked no one in particular. Maybe she was asking God to intervene and give an answer. She used to believe, back when she went to church with her Grandmother when she was Saho's age. But all faith died the moment she saw Alexei's teeth in the grass. Her religion couldn't survive seeing that, no matter how much it pained her family.

Saho groaned and stretched out her arms. "Good morning," she said. Some cheeriness in her voice. Something Ashiya hadn't heard from the girl yet. It gave her hope that the day could go well. She also feared losing that hope just as quickly.

"Morning," Ashiya said. "What do you want to eat?"

Ashiya was cooking for others again, less than ten hours after the last time. Something she hadn't done for anyone in years. It was one thing that she could control in this madness. Whatever that thing was outside, it didn't belong to the world of reason and order. But frying spam and eggs was something she could hold mastery over. There was even coffee in the house. She almost cried with joy that they were safe in here, not *out there.* Taro helped her. It was clear he knew little beyond the basics of "put food in pan—heat—eat." But she appreciated the effort. He caused a flame to spike up in the pan by adding too much oil, spilling it over the flame. Ashiya laughed as she swatted out the fire with towels.

Ryoji offered no help.

As Ashiya finished cooking the food, guilt pierced her heart for Kawamoto. She accepted his death even before Ogoto had come and told them plainly about it. But there would be time to honor the man, even if she didn't know nor like him much. Still, he deserved some basic respect.

Saho inhaled the food like a black hole. Taro ate his quietly and with a restraint that surprised her. Ogoto wasn't at full strength, but sipped his coffee by the fire. Ryoji was at the dining table with the rest of them, eating and drinking, with his eyes lost and wandering around the faded pink tile of the kitchen walls.

It was a silent meal. Ashiya was fine with that. But Saho's eyes darted nervously the whole time she devoured her food.

The adults—well, Ashiya and Taro, that is—had already discussed the day's plan. Wait until the sun had fully risen. Saho didn't know where her parents kept the keys to their truck in the drive and couldn't find them inside the home. The house across the street had a Jeep, a Hilux truck, and a smaller *kei*-car out front. There was bound to be a key inside for at least one of them. They had checked yesterday for survivors, but not thoroughly for something small, like keys. But first, wait until the full light of day. No sense in taking everyone outside, in the dark, while the bear could still be—no, most definitely was—nearby.

"Saho," Ashiya said. The girl looked up at her with some egg grease around her mouth. "You like Band-Maid, don't you?"

Her eyes lit up. "Yes! How did you know that?"

Ashiya smiled and pointed up to the loft. "I saw a poster of them above your bed. When I was a little older than you, I saw them live in Moscow."

Saho's eyes widened even more. "Did you meet Atsumi? She's so cool."

Ashiya laughed. "No, there were thousands of people. Hey, want to hear me play one of their songs?"

"You can do that?" Saho's eyes were now portals to another dimension of wonder.

Ashiya smirked and walked over to the fireplace, grabbed the guitar, and sat near Ogoto. "Come, sit and listen."

Saho sat cross-legged on the floor in front of the fire. Taro stared out the window, but she noticed he tilted his head slightly to listen. Even Ryoji joined, albeit at a distance and standing in the corner with his arms crossed, that same vacant look in his eyes. Ogoto stared into the fire, not registering her presence.

There was a thin layer of dust on the guitar. She tired out a few of the strings and they croaked out a sour note. Ashiya twisted the tuning key on the G chord to something that sounded right to her, matched the other keys to it, and strummed the strings with her thumb. It was still slightly out of tune, but good enough for a song.

She played and sang:

Even if I'm wrapped in kindness

I can't see any meaning to it

Every part of me, even down to my cells

Calls out to you

She stopped and set the guitar up against the wall. "And that's about that," she said. She hadn't played in almost a year and it felt good to do something creative. Not everything had to be solved by sake and isolation and vain attempts at hunting. She chose the band's most melancholic lyrics, not quite knowing why, they had just come out of her then.

Saho had tears in her eyes. She got up from the floor and bolted up the ladder. "Be right back!"

Taro grunted softly and smirked. He said nothing but Ashiya could tell he meant *Good job, kid,* or that's what she hoped he meant.

Ryoji turned his head away from them, but Ashiya saw a faint smile. One not forced, but real.

Ogoto said nothing. His eyes trained on the dance of flames. Ashiya thought he must still be in a mild form of shock from the attack and the cold exposure. His hands and feet looked good today. No trace of the onset of frostbite from last night.

"You good to go?" she asked him.

Ogoto cocked his head towards her, a little too quickly, and smiled. "Why wouldn't I be? Today is going to be so much fun, isn't it?"

Ashiya smiled with closed lips and gave him a double thumbs up. She rose and walked over to her pack and put on her outside gear. Ogoto seemed a little off. The way he spoke. Wasn't like him. It was cheerful like him, for sure, but not in that drunken fool kind of way. And was he speaking more clearly than usual? Without a trace of his thick dialect?

Whatever, he's just been through hell, of course he's a little off.

"Alright everybody, let's move out in five," Taro said from over by the window.

Golden light was cutting through the morning darkness and it hurt to look at it directly. Sunlight had finally come to give them a break and guide them back home.

Saho came scrabbling down the ladder with something tucked in her arms. She alighted and ran over to Ashiya, shoving a CD in her face. "Here, this is my favorite album of theirs. You should have it. Maybe we can listen to it together when we get to Kamuy-Kotan? I got this from my Dad—"

She froze mid-sentence. As if talking about the man brought into clear focus what must have happened to him. Her cheeks lost their color and tears crested her eyes.

Ashiya remembered to shield Saho's eyes from the skinned body as they left. The body hung outside the home to the left of Saho's, right next to the one with the cars they were going to check out.

Ashiya took the CD and smiled. "Sure, I'll let you blast this in my cabin if you want to."

Saho nodded and wiped at her eyes.

Poor kid.

Ashiya put the CD in a side pocket of her backpack and gave Saho a quick hug. The girl didn't seem used to affection like that and stiffened in her arms before finally relaxing into it a bit. Ashiya gently pushed her away and put her hands on Saho's shoulders. "Go get dressed in your best snow gear. We might have to be outside for a while."

Saho bounded away.

Ashiya turned to Taro. "So, go to the house over there and see if we can find keys. If not, we can check the other homes. Worst-case scenario, we have to hike back. But we can make it before nightfall."

"The bear attacked us in broad daylight," Ryoji said. No smile. No venom in his voice. Just plain, unadulterated fear.

"We might get lucky and we can drive the entire way. To safety," she said.

Ryoji nodded and met her eyes. Was this the first ounce of humanity she was seeing? His eyes spoke of fear, hope, trust, all at once. "Yeah. The roads shouldn't be too bad, it didn't snow *that* much," he said. "We can make it."

Ashiya also felt a surge of hope that this was going to be over soon. If the keys were in that first house, they could be driving back in minutes.

She remembered the road to Ota was a winding mountain pass that took an hour to Kamuy-Kotan back in the Autumn when there wasn't much snow on the road. She supposed it could take two or three hours if the conditions were bad. But it beat hiking back through the forest.

All that mattered now was getting back safely. Getting Saho somewhere safe. Getting Ogoto checked out by a doctor. And then getting the hell out of here and taking a flight back to Russia as soon as she could. She was done with this. Ashiya thought about hanging up her rifle for good and giving up this stupid quest to shoot and kill a deer.

What would it prove if I killed one, anyway? That I can shoot when it counts? Like that would make up for when I didn't?

All that mattered now was getting the fuck away from Ota and that bear. Getting everyone to safety.

"Everyone ready?" she asked.

Taro pulled the sofa away from the door.

The world outside was bright.

CHAPTER 28

The house was cold in the morning light. No matter how much sunlight filtered in, no matter how bright the rooms were, Hikari could feel nothing. The home was no longer a home. It was a tomb for both the dead and the living.

She sat on the sofa with her leg—in full cast—propped up on a chair. Itsuki was at work today. His boss gave him as much time as he needed to mourn his son and deal with the logistics of how to lay a body to rest. He stayed home for a few days, but he too felt the frigid death that had washed over the home. Even small talk with Hikari was lifeless, a pale ghost of what it used to be. Maybe going back to work was his way of not having to deal with it?

Hikari resented him for that. Ren's body was still on display in their living room. A custom she never thought about much before it became a reality to her. She remembered her grandmother passing when Hikari was just eight years old. Rara had to be kept in the home longer than the traditional one last night in her own futon. Back in those days, storage for the dead was even more scarce than they were today. Her family kept Rara in the home for three days—just like Ren. The blizzard had kept the mortician from being able to come into town to receive him—they kept him cool by dry ice until the local mortuary had enough manpower to do the cremation.

Hikari knew from her American criminal investigation TV shows she liked that embalming was common in many places around the world, but not in Japan. Even had they opted for that, the law required them to wait a full day from the official time of death before they could. That would have been just two days ago, but again, nobody in town to do it for them. Besides, the thought of removing Ren's organs and pumping his corpse full of chemicals sickened her.

But maybe Rara should have been embalmed. Because after three days, the smell cut through all her mother's attempts to conceal it. The sweet and rotten meat stench forced its way into the home. No incense, no dry ice, no fabric softener spray could keep it at bay. Just like Ren right now. She felt guilt over her impending joy at sending his body off today for cremation. To be rid of the smell. And the sight of him. She felt like she was going insane, alone in this house, wrapped in the cold—to aid with preservation—staring at her son's body.

Smelling him.

Hikari remembered the last night Rara was in the home. Hikari was asleep in her parent's room, snuggled up to her mother in the same futon, when she heard a metallic clang come from the living room. Nobody else heard it or got up. She thought it might have been the cat—Mr. Cat, her sister proudly named it—so she left the room to go get him. Rara's body was in the living room and if the cat was playing around in there, that was disrespectful to Rara. Maybe her sister left the door open?

Hikari walked down the dark halls of her home, careful to not wake anyone by turning on the lights. She came to the living room door. It was wide open. The smell of death choked her throat. It felt like she was chewing on it.

That stupid cat. Stupid sister. Am I the only responsible one here?

She stepped into the room to get Mr. Cat and froze in place. It was just for a moment, but she swore she saw Rara sitting upright in the middle of the room. Hikari screamed and ran for the lights and flipped them on. Rara was as she had been, lying on the futon, cold and dead.

As she looked at Ren's body now, at the head of the living room, dressed in his black kimono, skin as white as bone, she knew that this would be his last stay in their home. She almost wished that he would sit up right now, regardless of how much her heart would wrench and twist if he did so. The coffin lid was opened now. A black cloth was draped over his neck. A local surgeon volunteered to sew his head back on for his funeral, but she was too afraid to look at the stitches.

They would send Ren to the crematorium later today. After Itsuki got off work and came home around noon. Then they would have the ceremony and burn his body. Then they would pick up his charred bones with chopsticks and place them in the urn.

That spot above the fireplace looks good. It has a view of the front yard from there.

At this thought, the wall of unfeeling numbness burst open. She could no longer suppress her tears, sadness, and rage. Hikari let out a moan she never thought herself capable of.

"No, you were just..."

That was all she could say. She didn't know what more she was trying to say. She sobbed. The tears rushed down her face. She felt liquid pour from her nose. She choked on the sadness that was leaving her body, knowing full well that no cathartic cry would ever make her feel okay again. Hikari cried so hard that she felt as if someone had stabbed a freezing steel blade into her chest. The sternum broken and her lungs deflated by it.

Minutes passed, and the wave of grief left her momentarily. Hikari wiped her face with a pillow.

I can't stay here looking at him anymore. I just can't.

She grabbed the crutch by the sofa, rocked her body forward, and lifted herself up, using the crutch and the sofa for balance. A surge of pain shot up her leg and into her pelvis.

She grit her teeth and hobbled to her right to get out of the living room. Maybe she could just go to Itsuki's study and watch TV to get her mind off of things. To leave the room, she had to come closer to Ren's body to move around the coffee table. If she didn't need a crutch, she could have squeezed by it without getting closer to him, but as it was, she had no choice, unless she wanted to stay seated on the sofa, waiting for the smell of death to overpower her.

No matter what, I will not have that. I will not have my last memory of him be that toxic smell. He will not be like Rara.

But then what will be your last memory of him? Will you see his unmoving face, his stiffened and white skin, his rigid limbs, as they pass into the fire? And then as you look upon his bones and place them in the urn? Will that be the last memory you have of him?

"No," she said to herself.

She limped past the coffee table and right next to Ren's body. Hikari was going to turn right without looking at him, but couldn't. She stopped where she was and looked almost straight down on him.

He seemed at peace. No thoughts. No feelings. Just a deep and endless sleep. Black cloth wrapped around his neck.

"Why?" she said as she let out a dry squeal that only broke her heart even more. "Why did it do this to you? My beautiful boy. Did you know Nana came to the wake? I know you liked her. She said so many sweet things to me about you that you never told me. How you stood up for Ben when he was bullied by some older kids. How she noticed you blushing when she spoke to you. Why didn't you ever tell me these things? I wanted to know! I wanted...more...of you!"

Ren's face remained plastic and still as a calm lake. Freezing cold waters. Hiding the depths of a world she could never know. Not yet, at least.

She felt another surge of sadness and anger. She wanted to hold him and slap him and kiss him all at the same time. Hikari couldn't bear to look any longer. She turned and limped out of the living room and into the dark hallway towards the study.

She swung her crutch out and hopped down to the right outside the study door. She grabbed the door handle. Twisted it.

Something fell to the ground.

Something made of glass shattered.

From the living room.

The house was already cold despite the abundance of light. But Hikari didn't know what real cold was. Not before this moment. That was one of the things of that hidden world, buried under the freezing waters. The world Ren was now a part of. She didn't know, but she was starting to. She shivered so badly she almost dropped the crutch and let herself fall to the floor.

A shuffle of feet on the hardwood floor. The sound of fabric scratching along a rough surface.

A black cloth?

If she heard one more sound, she felt like she would die. She couldn't bear to hear another sound.

A footstep. Another one. The scratch of fabric being dragged across the floor.

Black cloth.

A table being bumped and scraping against the floor. Another footstep. Now in the hallway. Like raw meat slapping against a cold stone.

That cold she didn't know was even possible to feel wrapped its arms around her. Embraced her. Wanted to show her things.

But I can't turn around. I can't. Please, no, I don't want to see. I don't want to know.

A voice from right behind her.

"Mom?"

CHAPTER 29

"Okay, Ashiya, you cover us from here. Ryoji, you check the truck for keys first. I'll go with you. Then we'll go inside the house if we have to. Saho and Ogoto stay behind Ashiya and wait for us to bring the car around."

Taro was animated. Both the thrill of action and the concern for their wellbeing seemed to possess him.

"Make Ogoto go, why me!?" Ryoji complained.

“Because Ogoto is severely injured, dumbass,” Ashiya stated.

Ryoji's eyes flashed with both fear and hatred at her. Taro punched the wall by Ryoji's head. "Just. Do. It. I'll be with you, princess."

Taro didn't give him another chance to speak, but pushed Ryoji out of the house as he walked out.

Ashiya shouldered her rifle and scanned the village.

The morning sky was a pale blue with wisps of clouds streaked across it. The wind blew gentle, yet cold. Elms shook, but so slightly you could miss it if you weren't looking hard enough. But she was. She was absorbing every detail of the village. The fox that just darted back into the trees. The blood on the snow. Not as red as yesterday. Faded and soaked more thoroughly into the snow. But the whole place was painted in it. She'd have to cover Saho's eyes after they made it to the car.

The black Hilux truck Ryoji and Taro were now running towards. The tree line. Quiet and still. No other motion could she see.

Ryoji opened the car door after a moment of struggling against the ice that encased it and jumped inside. Taro stayed outside and swiveled around, looking around the village. The engine squealed as it turned over. The keys were in there!

Finally, a lucky break!

Two more turns and the engine revved to life. Taro brushed snow off of the front and rear windows with his gloves. The truck crawled out of the drive. Taro jogged alongside it, keeping watch.

"Okay, Saho, Ogoto, be ready to run to the car." Ashiya lowered her gun and took a deep breath.

"Ashiya," Saho said. "Ogoto is gone."

"What!?" She turned to face the girl. She looked back at the cabin. She saw the backdoor through the kitchen, wide open.

"He was stumbling around, holding his head like it hurt real bad."

"Get back inside!" Taro shouted.

Ashiya spun back around.

Ryoji slammed on the brakes, and the truck skidded a little before coming to a complete stop. Taro had to jump out of the way to avoid being clipped by the side mirror.

Right in the middle of the road, off to the right of Saho's cabin, not more than a block away from the truck, stood the bear on its hind legs. Ashiya clearly saw in broad daylight that it towered over the cabin. Her brain refused to comprehend its massive size. The legs were tree trunks. The body bigger than the lifted truck Ryoji was now frantically trying to back up, the tires spinning and losing traction in a muddy patch of snow.

The jaws could easily grab any of them and bite them in half.

It stood still. So motionless it looked more like a movie prop, a cardboard cutout, than an animal. So ridiculous were its dimensions that people would have easily written it off as not real, because how could it be?

Its eyes were black. Even in the daylight, there was an onyx glow to them. Staring at the beast must have taken all of five seconds. But in those moments, Ashiya saw everything. Her mind moved in slow motion. The more that her adrenaline laced mind took in, the more horrified she became. It wasn't just the size and the eyes that were off with the bear. Flaps of meat and fur hung off the exposed skull and ribs. Black blood poured from the wounds as if they were just made. But the amount of blood that flowed would surely have killed the animal. But it stood still. Motionless on two legs, staring at them, great forelegs raised above the dirty snow, claws the size of machetes hanging loose in the air, ready to strike.

The air around Ashiya grew heavy. Like the pressure of rising quickly on a rollercoaster. And the fearful anticipation of the fall. Her vision blurred. Her head pounded. Taro's shouting and Ryoji's cursing and the truck's tires spinning all became a muffled sound. A movie left on in the background. She felt tiny hands grip her jacket from behind.

The world was receding from Ashiya. Before her stood something that should not exist. That could not exist. And now it took a mighty step forward. It made no sound as it fell to all fours. Slowly, it stalked its way towards the truck. Ashiya saw it plainly. It walked on top of the snow. Its massive weight disturbed nothing. Its paws did not sink down.

Gunfire shot out. The deafening punch forced Ashiya fully awake from the noxious trance she had fallen into. Taro was firing at the thing.

Ashiya took hold of the hands holding onto her. "Stay inside!" she shouted at Saho. The girl faltered for a moment before she obeyed and went back in.

Ashiya turned back to the bear and saw that it was still walking towards them. Dark blood and rusted fur flew off of it as Taro's rounds found their marks across its face and chest. The bear flinched slightly with each shot, obviously feeling the pain, but kept pressing forward.

Ryoji kept rocking the truck to get out of its rut, but to no avail. She could see him screaming and crying through the windshield.

Ashiya ran out of the house and jumped over the front yard fence. She kneeled and pointed her rifle at the bear, the Kesagake, the demon.

She aimed her scope at its face and fired. No hesitation this time. The blowback absorbed into her right shoulder. There would be massive bruising there by the end of the day. If she made it that far.

Aim. Deep breath. Hold it. Pull the trigger. Fire! Kickback. Pull the bolt back. Case falls out.

Aim. Fire again. Pain hits the shoulder. Case flies out hot.

Aim. *Fire again damnit. Screw your feelings.* Can't even see the case fall out. Smoke fills vision. Fire again. And again.

You're out.

She needed to reload. Got to her feet and grabbed her rounds from her belt harness. She did all of this robotically. As practiced. Every one of her rounds hit the bear in the face and the chest. As did Taro's. But the bear was still walking towards them. It stood right next to the truck now. How small it made the vehicle look. All she could think to do was reload and hit it again.

The bear stood up on its hind legs. Taro fell backwards, grasping at his rounds in his satchel, reloading the rifle while on his back in the mud.

Ryoji looked up at the thing from behind the steering wheel.

The bear swiped at the truck. Its talons hit the passenger door and the entire vehicle flew up into the air and landed upside down, right next to Taro's feet, missing him by the length of one of his legs.

The bear hunched over Taro and unhinged its jaws like a snake. He reloaded his rifle and fired it into the gaping maw. The bear flinched but did not recoil. A deep purring growl emanated from its mouth. A black pit of nothingness. It could swallow him whole without having to bite down.

Ashiya got to her feet and ran out into the road, reloading her rifle as she went, and stood next to Taro.

She aimed the gun up high. Not into the mouth. But right at one of its glowing black eyes. She fired. The light in the eye went out in a puff of black blood and the bear backed away. It let out a distressed infantile scream and took several steps backwards. It clawed at its own face.

Ashiya hung her rifle over her shoulder and grabbed Taro's hand, helping him to his feet. He looked at her with wide eyes and nodded, slapping her shoulder once with his open palm.

"Get me the fuck out of here!" Ryoji screamed at them.

He was hanging upside down, saved from smashing his head into the roof of the car by his seatbelt.

Taro pried open the driver's door. The bear roared and thrashed its head from side to side.

"Hurry!" Taro shouted.

Ashiya bent down, crawled into the car, and undid Ryoji's seatbelt. He fell, twisting himself so as to not fall on his head, and came crashing down on his right shoulder. He cried out and Ashiya grabbed him from under his armpits and pulled him as he kicked his legs, propelling himself out of the car. Ashiya landed on her back, and Ryoji stumbled up to his feet.

He looked down at her, out of breath, and gave her his shaking hand. "Thanks."

She took his hand, and he helped her up.

The bear stopped moving wildly and let out a roar that shook Ashiya's ribcage. It felt like her heart skipped a beat or two.

The bear lowered its head. The left eye was bleeding profusely. A dark river of chunky blood like spoiled milk. The right eye burned with a dark malice.

The bear charged them at full speed.

CHAPTER 30

The bear ran right into the heart of them and dove forward. It was so fast none of them had time to run, only to fall to the side and out of the way. Snow sprayed up like the crashing of a great ocean wave. The entire world was white. The bear threw out a paw—the size of a person from the waist up—towards Ryoji and missed, maybe blinded by the snow it had just kicked up. Separated by the bear, Taro got up and fled back to Saho's cabin. Ryoji and Ashiya, together on the other side, ran straight for the house they got the now useless truck from. The bear chased after them.

Ryoji got to the door first and flung it open.

Thank God for trusting communities.

Ashiya was only a meter behind him.

He slammed the door shut on her and locked it before she could reach it. She slammed into the door and nearly fell over from the impact.

"You fucker!" Ashiya shouted and banged her fists on the door.

No time to think.

The bear rushed in from behind her. Ashiya turned left and dove off of the porch, landing in some frozen snow.

The bear crashed into the house. Front door blew open. Posts on the porch snapped like twigs and the porch roof collapsed. It roared and rammed into the front of the house, splitting open the doorframe and half of the wall itself. It looked right at Ashiya.

She got to her feet and ran around to the back of the house. Half expecting to hear its paws right behind her. Fear pushed her to run even faster into a small backyard that extended to the tree line behind it. The forest started up on a hill that was too steep for her to climb up. There was no fence and the only object in the yard was a small toolshed. She ran to the other side of it and crouched down.

The sound of smashing wood and glass. The bear hadn't followed her but opted to enter the home. With how easily it broke through the timber, she wondered why it didn't just do that last night. It also brought the horrifying realization that no building was safe from this bulldozer of a thing. It might even be strong enough to break through stone.

She heard Ryoji shouting from inside the house as the whirlwind of destruction continued. Ashiya wanted to run back to Saho's cabin, but fear kept her glued to the toolshed. If the bear saw her running, it could pounce on her in an instant. She saw Ryoji appear at the back window of the second story. Just for a moment as he ran across to the left side of the house. Glass broke. She saw him climb out of a window and hang himself off its side. He looked up, screamed, and fell to the ground below. Luckily for him, the blizzard had piled up soft snow that reached to the tops of the windows on the first floor.

"Fuck!" he cried out. Maybe not too soft of a landing.

Moments later, another face filled that second-story window. One glowing obsidian eye and the face of the bear passed by, going the same direction Ryoji had. Was it smaller now? From here it looked like a normally sized bear, walking through the house with no problem. Given its size, that should not have been possible.

A car engine started from near where Ryoji had fallen. The corner of the house made it so Ashiya couldn't see what was happening there. A car door slammed shut. Keeping her eyes on the window, Ashiya stood and ran to the other side of the home, pressed herself against the wall, and edged her way around the corner to look out at the street. A dirty green Jeep drove onto the road, skidded, and crashed into the fence of Saho's cabin.

Taro came out with Saho in his arms. Ryoji flung the door to the Jeep open. "Hurry the fuck up!"

Taro let Saho down, and she ran into the car. He was right behind her.

Wood exploded from above where Ashiya stood against the wall. She looked up and could see massive claws gripping the side panels of the house, piercing the wood like a knife sliding into a pillow. The bear leaned forward out of the window, watching the Jeep. It couldn't see Ashiya directly beneath it.

The car door slammed shut before Taro could get in.

"What are you doing!? Anastasia is still here!" Taro shouted. The car backed up onto the street, Saho inside, looking bewildered through the backseat window. Taro chased after it, slapping the side of the door, trying to get Ryoji to stop.

The bear jumped from its perch, momentarily blocked out the sun as it sailed over the front yard, and landed right next to the Jeep. It was not smaller as it looked through the window; it was the same unbelievable size it always was. Then how could it have moved through the house? Snow and mud splashed over the vehicle. It peered into the windows and Ashiya heard Ryoji shouting. Taro tried to open the door, but it was locked.

Ryoji rolled down the driver's window. Pointed a handgun out from it. And shot Taro in the leg. He fell to the ground, screaming in pain.

Ryoji took off down the street in the Jeep. The bear chased after him, despite having easy prey with Taro squirming on the ground. Ryoji hit a mailbox before correcting the car back onto the road. In seconds he was at the far end of the hamlet, driving onto the road, fishtailing as he went, with Saho in tow.

The bear ran after him until the end of the village. Stopped. And watched him leave.

Ashiya ran into the street to get to Taro.

When she glanced back at the bear, it was gone.

CHAPTER 31

Taro held his right ankle and grunted. Ashiya walked quickly out to him, rifle in hand, scanning the village.

Where was it now? The thing was too big to hide so easily. It disappeared in less than a second.

"Don't worry about me, girl. Get back inside the cabin." He tried to stand, but fell back down.

She knelt beside him and offered him her shoulder. He shook his head. She smacked him in the face. They understood each other without speaking.

Shut up and let me help you.

With her eyes darting all around, she helped Taro to his feet. He didn't cry out in pain and limped along as they struggled back to Saho's cabin. It wasn't a place of safety, but what else did they have?

Bandage his leg. Get Ogoto. Get out of here. Fast.

They entered the cabin. The first thing she noticed was that Ogoto was standing in the kitchen, leaning against the wall, hands over his face, groaning.

He must have hit his head hard. Or maybe the cold did more damage than I thought. I'll check on him next.

She helped Taro sit down by the now cold fireplace.

"Oh, that fucker is going to pay," Taro growled. "He shot me so the bear would go after me and let him pass. Piece of shit." He laughed. "And it didn't even work."

Ashiya took out her first aid kit from her bag and rolled up Taro's right pant leg. There was a bloody hole through his calf. There was no way to tell if the bullet was still lodged inside for sure, but it looked like it had gone cleanly through the leg. She splashed some rubbing alcohol on the wound and pressed down gauze on both sides of the bullet hole. She wrapped the rest of the wound tightly with bandages.

This would have to do, for now.

"Can you walk?" she asked.

"Of course I can."

He held onto the side of the fireplace and stood himself up. The sweat on his face and the strained grimace told her he was in pain. But he said nothing and held it all inside.

"We have to go now. We have to grab another car and get back before dark. No way we're surviving another night here. And Saho..."

Taro met her eyes and nodded. If Ryoji was willing to let others die so that he might live, then the girl might not be safe with him. Hopefully, he would just drive back to Kamuy-Kotan and alert the authorities. But Saho had seen him shoot another person. She was a witness.

A liability.

The implication of what could happen lit an icy fire in her gut. Urgency replaced fear for the moment.

"What do we do about—" Taro began and stopped short. A hand fell on Ashiya's shoulder from behind. She let out a surprised gasp.

It was Ogoto. Smiling. He pulled his brown beanie down low, almost over his eyes. He held his hand over his left eye. "My head still hurts. Can we get out of here?"

"Can you walk by yourself?" She felt like this would be a constant question she would need to keep on asking everyone.

"Sure, why wouldn't I be able?" He smiled and winked at her with his one exposed eye.

The three of them crouched behind Saho's broken fence. Ogoto took the news of the bear and of Ryoji lightly, almost like it was a joke. Despite the urgency in her voice, Ogoto brushed it all off.

He was a carefree guy, but this wasn't like him. As far as she knew him, Ogoto genuinely cared when the situation called for it. Maybe he really had a concussion?

Taro could walk. But every step looked like it caused him great pain. At least he wouldn't bleed out. Despite his pain, Taro took point and made the other two wait behind him. He stood and scanned the hamlet. He waited a full minute before waving them up to follow.

The wind moaned softly as it blew overhead. Like the souls of forgotten ghosts, calling out to the living. There was no other sound. Taro limped forward, refusing Ashiya's help to let him lean on her. Ogoto seemed fine on his own.

The house where the truck and Jeep came from was in ruins. They looked inside the kei-car but found no keys. The house itself looked like a hurricane had torn through it. Ryoji may have been able to find the Jeep's key hanging on a wall when he ran inside. But now, the wreckage of fallen beams and splintered walls and overturned furniture would make any more searching impossible.

They walked down the street and made it two blocks down to a one story home with a thatched roof, on to the next car they could see, a gray RAV4. Taro tried the doors. Locked.

"You guys stay here and rest a bit, I'll go." Ogoto smiled widely and walked to the front door, not taking his eyes off of them even as he turned his body to the home. "Besides, you two have the only guns now. You need to keep watch."

He pushed aside a broken plank and made his way through what used to be a front door.

Taro leaned forward, face bright red. Ashiya put her hand on his back. He brushed it off of him and stood back up, falteringly, on his own.

Ashiya left the man to his stubbornness and turned to face the rest of Ota. Tranquil. Nothing moving now. Not even the wind. Of course, the blood stained snow and the shattered doors of the homes stood testament to what happened. Aside from that, it was a ghost town now. But that bear must still be here, nearby. Why would it leave when it did?

Maybe it took off after the Jeep when I wasn't looking? No, that would be too fast. Then again, what the fuck do I know about it?

"Found 'em!" Ogoto called out, now reemerging from the home. He was holding up a pair of keys that reflected the sunlight. He jangled them and laughed. "Aren't we getting lucky today?"

He pressed the button on the key and the RAV4's doors unlocked. They piled their bags into the trunk. Ogoto got into the driver's seat, Ashiya beside him, Taro laid across the two back seats. The fuel gauge said full. Ogoto started the car and pulled out into the street and drove out of the hamlet.

As the few homes passed by, Ashiya wondered why all the cars were still here. Not a single person had driven out for help or escape. She hoped that Saho's parents somehow had gotten out. But, if they did, why not come back for their daughter?

She knew they had to be dead. They left their car at the cabin. If not killed by the bear, then by the elements.

Ogoto turned right towards the big wooden sign that welcomed people to the village. A bigger street ran parallel to the sign. Following it to the right would take them on the mountain road and down back to Kamuy-Kotan.

As soon as Ogoto turned the car onto the main road, he hit the brakes. Ashiya put her hands out instinctively and stopped her body from hitting the dashboard; she had forgotten her seatbelt. Taro's body hit the back of the two front seats. They weren't going too fast, and she was thankful for that. She looked up to see why Ogoto had stopped.

On both forested sides of the road, dozens of human bodies. Most of them were adult sized. Others... she couldn't bear to think about. Each one of them skinned, headless, their limbs splayed out and impaled on the trees they hung from. In front of each body, a human head stuck on a branch, jammed into the snow. The bodies lined the road back to town. There were fresh car tracks in the snow, Ryoji's.

Did Saho see this? Did she see her parent's heads?

That thought made her sicker than what she actually saw in front of her.

And right in front of their car, with evidence in the snow that Ryoji had swerved around it, nearly missing it, another body.

This one was also skinned and headless. A single tree held it up in the middle of the street. The tree looked as if something had ripped it from the forest and planted it in the road.

Ogoto turned off the car and got out.

"Hey! What are you doing?" she yelled out after him.

He ignored her and walked forward, right in front of the body in the road.

Taro looked on, legs still propped up on the seat, and watched.

Ashiya got out of the car.

"You need to see this," Ogoto said, his back to her.

"No, I don't. This is horrible, and these people will be laid to rest. But not now. Now we need to get out of here. Give me the keys."

"Keys," he said. He lifted them up and tossed them forward. They landed in the road before the headless body.

Maybe Ogoto suffered a serious head injury. In which case, all the more reason to leave as soon as they could.

Ashiya didn't bother reprimanding him. She walked past him to the where the keys had fallen. She bent down and brushed the snow out of the way to find them. The spot was right in front of the impaled head. She didn't want to look up into its dead eyes. Find the keys and go. But something inside her told her to look. It wasn't morbid curiosity; it was deeper than that.

She felt this many times while out on hunts with her father. Never shooting anything, of course, but helping him track. Sometimes it was nothing. As far as they knew. But occasionally, this intuition of hers prevented them from walking in front of a pissed off animal. Once, while farther north in Siberia, Ashiya just knew where the tiger was. It had been stalking them without their knowledge, following them. They heard no sounds, but Ashiya just felt it in her bones, exactly where the tiger was hiding. That saved them.

That same feeling was yelling at her to look.

Her hands grazed the keys, and she pocketed them. Then she looked up.

And there was Ogoto.

Looking back at her.

Head severed from his body.

Mouth open in a soundless scream. Skin blue and frozen. Blood turned to ice on the branch it rested upon. His body stretched out between the trees, skinned, a chunk of flesh missing from his midsection, lined by the jagged tears of a great mouth.

Behind her, the other Ogoto laughed deeply.

A heavy laugh.

Throaty.

Wheezing.

Like an animal puffing out air, imitating a human laugh.

CHAPTER 32

She couldn't turn around. Hunched over where she'd picked up the keys, she was stuck in that spot. Almost as if by staying still, whatever horror that was unfolding behind her would just up and go away like a bad dream. But for Ashiya, her dreams were a waking reality. And so was this.

The surrounding light dimmed. She didn't know if from feeling faint or if it was actually happening. The air somehow turned colder. As if something had blotted out the sun, plunging the area into deep night. Her headache returned.

"Ogoto" shuffled on his feet. But it was not him.

The man she knew was in front of her. Head impaled. Body skinned.

Then what...

The darkness grew thicker and emanated from behind her. As if it were a bonfire producing darkness and draft.

Taro began shouting at her from inside the car. She heard a car door click open but fall back and close, as he was probably struggling to get out.

Growly laughter from behind her. Deep and with an echo behind it. It turned almost ape-like. The breathing became heavier. She felt heat wash over her backside. She even started sweating. And with the heat, the smell of decaying flesh.

The laughter twisted and turned into something else. The groaning and growling of a bear.

She felt the darkness tower over her. For all she knew, the sun didn't exist anymore in this new darkness.

Gunfire from the car. Twice more. The rifle shots echoed throughout the forest. A clump of of snow fell from a branch as a hawk took flight.

Ashiya finally broke out of the trance and rolled forward. Twisted her body as she did, turning around on her back in the snow. No gun on her.

In front of her was Kesagake. But not fully. She saw a furred body, ripping through human clothes. She saw something that looked like a bear, but with the face of Ogoto, his left eye a mess of black blood, growing in size. It was skinny and malnourished. Its torso too long for a bear. She could see skin stretched too tightly over its ribs, making them look like an accordion's bellows. It grew taller. Muscles filled in its skeletal frame. The ribs ripped through the taut flesh like a knife through paper. Ogoto's one good eye turned black. The bloody left eye shimmered like air in a scorching desert. A fresh eye emerged from the wound. Its jaws and its snout elongated until the bear's face ripped through the human mask, the human skin falling to the snow. Half of the bear's face exposed bone and muscle. Eyes a hateful black fire.

Taro fired more rounds into its backside. Its body tremored at the shots but it didn't move away.

"Ashiya, run!"

Kesagake looked down at her and almost seemed to smile. Before her eyes, it took on another face. The bones cracked and soft flesh stretched over the skull. Black eyes lightened to hazel. Incisors became flat. Black hair sprouted over an oval face. A pretty face of an older, kind looking woman. A tiny face while the rest of the body was still as large and monstrous as before.

Kesagake twisted its neck fully around to stare down at Taro. The bones snapped as it did so.

The gunfire stopped.

"Maya," Taro said. "No..."

"Yes, my dear." Came the sweet voice out of that horrid body. "I'm here now. For you. Always."

One more burst of rifle fire and the creature stood straight up and howled. Ashiya saw dark blood pouring from its right eye, splashing over the snow. Taro had hit its eye, and the thing stumbled and fell to the ground.

"Run!" Taro bellowed out. Ashiya could hear his footsteps hobbling through the snow on the other side of the bear—no, the demon—but couldn't see him.

Ashiya crawled backwards, slipping on the snow. Until she hit her head on a tree that shouldn't be in the road. Ogoto's body strung upon it. She pushed her back into the trunk and stood up.

The creature was twisting its head back to her. No longer a woman's face, nor a bear's, but somewhere in-between. Black blood flowed from the eye like crawling magma, like thousands of ants spilling out.

Ashiya turned and fled into the forest down a hill. She raced down the slope, her body picking up momentum. She weaved in-between the trees as she flew past them.

She could hear wood cracking and breaking from up near the road. It soon followed her down the hill. The trees not too far behind were being pushed aside and felled.

She ran with dangerous velocity, knowing that at any moment she could fall and crash into a tree, break her leg, or get caught by what pursued her.

"Asya," came a young man's voice. Calling her by her Russian name. "Why do you run from me? Don't you want to see my face again? I have all my teeth now. Look!"

She dared not look back. She ran and ran and slid and flew down that hill.

Until she hit the ledge. Too fast to stop. Too fast to turn.

She really flew now. Over the ledge and into the open air. All around her sky. Beneath her, a far way down, the ground.

CHAPTER 33

Itsuki drove away from the office and headed home. The town passed him by in slow-motion, like he was in an underwater vessel exploring the deep sea. Signs meant nothing to him and the people on the street had no faces to him. While at work he couldn't focus on a single task. He sat there, in front of his computer, and didn't even turn it on. He just stared at the black screen. His eyes wandered to the left of the device, where there was a photo of him, Hikari, and Ren at Universal Studios Osaka.

Ren had on a Spider-Man shirt two sizes too big for him. He insisted on riding that attraction as much as they could that day. Which, given the masses of people there, tuned out to be only four times even with the fast pass.

Itsuki smiled bitterly at his desk. He was annoyed that day. Annoyed at the lines, annoyed that his son kept on pestering him, annoyed that Hikari kept on telling him to keep his cool.

He now regretted ever taking those moments for granted. What he wouldn't give to be back on that hot summer day standing in lines for hours. Because he actually was happy then. Happy but refused to admit it.

He knew he was leaving his wife alone at home while he tried to escape into work. He hated himself for doing that. But he couldn't bear to be in that house while his son's body lay there.

I'll be there for her tomorrow and every day after. Once it is done. I swear.

He pulled the car into his driveway and got out.

The plan was for the mortuary service van to meet them here in an hour. They would let the professionals deal with transporting their son's body. Meet them at the crematorium for the service. And say goodbye.

Somehow, the thought of Ren's body becoming ash in an urn was easier to deal with than what lie in that coffin inside at this moment. The urn was symbolic. There would be no direct emotional connection to ashes. But that pale, cold, expressionless face in the house. That was something he couldn't handle. That was a mockery of what his son used to be. It made him feel like an eel was trying to inch its way out through his esophagus.

He walked up the drive to the front door. He stopped. Someone had drawn the living room curtains. Hikari loved having them open and letting in natural light. After a moment's pause, he went inside his home.

All the lights were off. With the closed curtains, even though it was midday, the interior of the home was too dark to see much of anything.

"Hikari?" He flipped the light switch. Nothing happened. "Are you home?"

He took off his shoes and hung up his jacket on the coat rack.

He regretted doing that because the house was cold. He forgot the reason: *to keep your son's body preserved until he gets carted away.* That eel started wriggling again. And with it, panic seized him. She wouldn't have just left the house, would she? Her leg was broken and they had to be here to get ready for the service. No way she would just leave.

He took out his phone and called her. A faint buzzing came from the living room. It rattled the surface of the coffee table.

She is home.

"Hikari!?" He said in a louder voice.

No answer.

He walked down the hall leading to the living room, trying another light switch, and still nothing came on. He'd have to check out the fuse box later and see if that was the problem. If not, he'd have to call somebody in to have a look.

Fucking trouble keeps on piling up, doesn't it?

The living room was dark, with deep shadows in the recesses of the room. He could make out the white sofa nearest him. The coffin that Ren lay in was further in the room and shrouded in a deep gray-black haze. The windows were to the left.

He walked up to them and opened the curtains. The light momentarily stung his eyes.

He turned around and froze.

The coffin lid was open. Ren was not inside. Someone had folded his black kimono in half at the foot of the coffin. They rolled up the black sash that was around his neck and placed it on top of the kimono.

Did she already send his body over? Without me? Then why are the clothes still here?

He felt shame over the relief that swelled up in his breast at not having to be present at the burning of his son's remains.

But no, she wouldn't do that. Itsuki's parents and Hikari's were also coming to the service. It wasn't possible they'd have it without him.

He was about to call out for his wife again, but the words got caught in his throat. A sob almost escaped him. The thought of never seeing Ren's face again, even that cold and lifeless one, unblocked the dam of welling up emotion.

Itsuki fell to his knees, sobbing freely now.

No more Spider-Man rides. No more long lines. No more warm home. What did he have left? He couldn't even be present to help his injured wife while she was alone in this crypt.

He rose to his feet and wiped the tears with his sleeve. He looked outside the window at the forest and thought about walking in there, naked.

Strange thought. Why'd I think that?

...maybe just keep going out there, until what took my son takes me.

Hikari will leave me anyway. I'll lose my job. Maybe it wouldn't be so bad too...

"Itsuki, you're home?"

The voice was so out of place in the silent tomb of the living room that Itsuki jumped at it.

It was Hikari. She was standing in the hall, leaning out from the corner, peeking into the living room. Her face was pale yet bright, half hidden by the corner of the wall, the rest of her body hidden from view as well. Both of her hands gripped the hall's corner.

"Honey, I was. I don't know. You scared me. Where were you? What happened to the power?"

He walked over to her. Then he stopped.

In that moment, he thought things through. As if he were outside of his own body, looking down from the ceiling, observing it all, and able to give advice to his corporeal self.

"You're... walking?" he asked. A feeling of cold plunged his insides into the depths. The familiar wriggle again in his throat. Hikari's face peered out from a height that wasn't possible if she were in the wheelchair. Her hands on the corner meant she wasn't using a crutch.

She said nothing. Her brown eyes seemed to glow in the dark. To darken.

He took a step back, away from his wife.

"W-where's Ren's body?" he asked. His voice just above a whisper.

"Body?" she said with a voice that was her own, but devoid of what made it her own. A song sung with all the right words but none of the soul. There was no sarcastic mirth in that voice. There wasn't even the rage and sadness it held over the past few days. It was her voice, without the things that made it hers.

"There's no body, silly. Ren is alive. He was dead, of course. But now he's alive. Back from the land of the once dead and forgotten gods. But don't worry, he brought one back with him, just for you."

Hikari slithered away and went out of view down the hall. Her footsteps thumped down the hall to the left. They seemed to grow heavier as she went. Their bedroom door opened with a creak.

He feared her mind had snapped. He wanted to run to her then. Until he heard that voice.

"Daddy?" came the voice of his son. From inside the room Hikari just entered.

No, no, no. Get out. Get the fuck out, now. Why can't you move? Run! You fool, run!

To leave, he would have to go back into the hallway and run down to the front door to the right. That would put him in full view of whatever had just come out of his bedroom. Of whatever was now walking down that hallway in tandem with his wife's heavy footsteps.

Because that is not my son.

Not my wife.

Either that, or break the living room window and jump through it.

But he couldn't move.

The footsteps of two people came down the hall and stopped right before coming into view.

The little light that came in through the window seemed to dim to twilight. The darkness of the hall thickened to a tarry blackness.

Waist high, a face poked around the corner.

Ren's face. Half hidden behind the wall.

With shining black eyes. His pale skin glowing softly in the darkness.

Above Ren came his wife's face, now with black eyes of her own. She whispered something to the boy that Itsuki couldn't hear. Nor did he want to hear it.

They laughed.

"H-how," was all Itsuki could sputter out from his now bone dry throat.

"I'll show you Daddy. I'll show you the once dead gods. Want to see?"

Fear yanked at his spine, shouting at him to turn and hurl his body through the window and run.

Ren stepped out from behind the corner. Skin white as the moon on a clear winter's night. Naked. The stitches across his neck stood out like ugly black fractures along the smooth skin that otherwise looked healthy and alive. His head lopped to the side once, like he didn't have the spine to hold it up, and he propped it back up with his hands.

Hikari came out from the darkness. She was also naked. Blood ran down between her breasts from a small bite on the front of her throat. He could see bone in that red mess. The blood flowed down like a river. Reaching down to her toes.

"Want to see?" Hikari said in a voice that was not her own. It was a voice laden with the weight of history and the unfeeling coldness of oblivion.

Itsuki fell to his knees. Pain racked his head. A great pressure weighed him down. "Yes," he said. "I want to see."

He wanted those days back. If he couldn't get the mundane days of life back with his wife and son, he would take this, whatever it was.

Hikari and Ren smiled. Flashing serrated teeth that were much too big for their faces. Their eyes flashed black.

Itsuki gagged on the eel in his throat.

They fell upon him.

CHAPTER 34

The weight of the world crashed down on Ashiya's temples. It felt like someone had hammered railway spikes into them. Like the biblical story of Jael, which her Grandmother used to tell her.

Be a good woman. Don't be afraid to sleep with the enemy. Then spike the bastard in the head while he sleeps.

Grandma's smoke scarred voice rang in her throbbing head. She hadn't thought of this in years, but she could see her now, smoking her cheap cigarettes, rocking back and forth in her chair, spouting out mostly nonsense in her later years. Ashiya had all but forgotten the woman's ravings. But now the pain brought it all back.

She struggled to open her eyes. The pain in her head jolted down to her lower back, frying everything in between.

She finally opened her eyes, and the sunlight put a wrenching twist on the pain in her head. Ashiya could see the branches above, leafless, covered in snow, crisscrossing the blue sky. She needed to wait a minute for her eyes to adjust to the bright light. Her head felt like it was going to crack open, with her brains spilling out like porridge.

She was lying a small hole in the snow. The walls of powder rose around her, as if to consume her.

When a last surge of pain subsided and became tolerable, she sat up and lifted herself out of the hole.

Spike the bastard in the head.

Ashiya could almost laugh. Was her Grandmother reaching out now, beyond the grave, offering her help like a spirit guide? She couldn't think of a funnier image than that short woman, bent over at the waist, yelling at everybody and nobody at the same time.

As Ashiya rose to her feet, she felt a cracking in her spine.

Maybe I'm becoming like her now—invalid and brittle—is why.

She stood to her feet and brushed the snow off of her.

She left her backpack and rifle in the car. Back on the road. Back with *it.*

Suddenly, she remembered what she was running from. She almost fell over, turning around. Above her was a straight rock wall. Above it, the ledge she must have fallen off of.

It wasn't too far of a drop. Maybe the height of a three story home. But the snow she fell on was deep and soft. Didn't stop her body from groaning in pain though. She observed where she fell. Most of the area was full of trees and boulders. She had gotten lucky and missed all of them, hitting one of the few patches of pure snow. Leaving behind a vague human shaped hole like some cartoon character.

She looked up at the ledge. Nothing was there. No bear leaning off the edge to peer down at her.

Immediate realization smacked her in the face. Ogoto was dead. That creature was wearing his face. It was him, down to the minute details of his smile and even how he walked.

But it didn't speak like him, did it?

Tears stung her eyes, but she forced them at bay. This was not the time to grieve.

That monster wasn't just a massive bear. It could change into people. She saw the woman's face as it turned towards Taro. Ashiya assumed it must have been his wife. She saw it mid-transformation as it went from human to a twisted abomination of nature.

She heard that voice as she ran from it. She heard it use Alexei's voice as it hunted her down.

Look at my face. I have all my teeth now.

No matter what, she could not see that face. She would not. She would die before that happened. His face. Worn by that demon. She doubted she could keep her sanity if she saw it. A nightmare born out in the real world.

She had no supplies. No watch on her wrist. No phone. She left everything in the car. Looking at the sun in the sky, she estimated she had two to four hours tops before it went down. If night caught her out here with no way to stay warm, she could die.

If Kesagake were to run her down right now, with nowhere to go, she was also dead.

Not many good outcomes, are there?

She was in pain, but nothing that felt too serious. She gave herself a cursory once over and—though she was sure she was covered in cuts and bruises—nothing was broken or bleeding profusely.

The road was behind her and up the hill. Which meant that if she were to walk to her left, keeping the road in sight as best she could, she would move in the general direction of Kamuy-Kotan. General, that is. Not accounting for the twists and turns of the mountain road and the thick forest before her. She could easily get lost.

The sun sets far to the southwest, nearest the winter solstice.

She tracked its position in the sky and guessed its trajectory for sunset.

And Kamuy-Kotan is just south of Ota.

That means, if I walk with the hills to my left and go straight that way, I could more or less get there. And the moss on trees grows on the north side, just like those there.

She failed to inspire confidence in herself. She was right about where the sun would go down and where the town should be in relation to it, but she had no way of making sure she would walk in a straight path on the way. And Kamuy-Kotan was the only other settlement in the region, meaning, if she missed it, she could get further lost in the forest unless she happened upon a road.

She thought about climbing back up to the road she fled from. That would be an easier path to follow. Where she stood, she could only see a sheer cliff face, but it could lessen to a rolling hill at some point.

But Kesagake wasn't—as far as she knew—here with her now. Maybe it was waiting for her on the road.

Forest it is.

She put her hands on the tree nearest her. Bowed her head to it. Whispered a prayer to anyone who would hear her. And started walking.

CHAPTER 35

Ashiya walked for what must have been an hour. The sun was lowering to a point just above the trees off to her right-hand side.

Southwest.

Which means the way ahead of her must be to the south.

The mountains and what she assumed to be the road back to Kamuy-Kotan were to her left. She wanted to go back to the road, but she feared the bear would be up there, stalking the roads for her. A flat expanse of woodlands in front of her and to her right. A frozen creek bed ran beside her. Arching in and out of her path. She walked right through it, not wanting to deviate from her path in the slightest.

If she was lucky, she could reach the town an hour after nightfall. There was no way she'd make it while it was still light out. She could suffer the cold for that long. As a kid she played in -50 degrees Celsius in winter. The cold that freezes car batteries and keeps the city in a constant fog because of the heat from homes being unable to rise through the cold air.

Of course, even then, she'd have to run back inside often for her own safety. She assumed—if it was the same as yesterday when she had access to her digital thermometer, clipped to the outside of her pack—that it was 0 degrees right now. With the nights dropping to -10. Not good, but she could make it. As long as she wasn't out in it all night, she could survive. She might get frostbite if she misjudged the time it took for her to get to town, but she would not let the cold take her life.

She had worse things to worry about.

Kesagake.

What was it? Clearly not of this world. Not something that obeyed the laws of nature.

An abaasy.

A demon that stalks the wilderness.

Makes its home near graves.

What did Taro say? A god that suffers.

But none of that mattered right now. What did matter was getting back to town. Getting back to Saho. She hoped Ryoji would act like a rational and humane person. But given what he did, she feared for the girl's safety. Ashiya knew she might not get back to town in time to stop Ryoji from doing something to her, if that was what he was planning, but she had to try.

This was no longer about her need to forget the faces of the dead. This was about saving the living.

She hoped her feelings about Ryoji were wrong. That he just acted out of fear and self-preservation in a crazy moment, sure, but resorting to harming a child? Surely not, she hoped. But the fact of the matter was: Ryoji shot Taro. Saho was a witness. Ryoji proved to not be a good man. Whatever glimmers of humanity she saw in him, few though they were, they had given her hope. No longer.

She felt guilt for leaving Taro behind. But what was she to do for him? If she went back, she was dead. She was certain of that. And the bear had chased her down the hill, hadn't it? At least up to the ledge. That could have given Taro enough time to get back in the car and get away.

Her heart dropped. She felt in her jacket pockets. She still had the keys on her.

Fuck.

But he still could have found another car in the time that the bear chased her, right?

And if she had to choose between Taro and Saho, as horrible as a choice as that was, she had to choose Saho. Had to get back to town and warn everyone about what was out here.

The Saito family.

She held back tears as she thought about them. This monster was the one who took their son. It wasn't an animal acting on instinct. In that case, she would still condone killing the bear, but at least there would be no malice in her thoughts. That was nature.

This was not. Kesagake was a thing that enjoyed inflicting pain. She knew it the second it used *his* voice against her. It spent the entire night with them in the cabin, wearing Ogoto's face, pretending to be injured. Why?

To play with us. Make us hurt.

A bird squawked above her. She reached for her rifle on impulse and grabbed nothing but air. The bird knocked snow off the branch and it fell on her in clumps.

"Fucking bird." She wiped the snow off her face. The bird was gone. But she saw it, didn't she? Right before the snow hit her. The black eyes that glowed in its tiny skull.

The hairs on her arm stood tall.

If Kesagake could turn into a person... what else could it become?

But crows have black eyes, anyway.

Still...

Stop it, you're driving yourself crazy. Just move.

She picked up her pace.

She didn't have her snowshoes anymore. The snow was firm enough that her legs didn't get swallowed fully, but she still sank down mid-calf.

Her energy was spilling out of her like blood from a wound.

Ashiya couldn't keep this pace up. Not for much longer. Her stomach tightened. She felt faint.

The crow cawed again.

She ignored it and walked—trudged on—faster.

It's just a bird.

Laughter.

She stopped to listen. No more sounds.

Losing my mind?

The wind picked up and rose a lament. The cold sank down into her skin. Into her lungs. Into her bones.

She walked on to a hill. She climbed it. Each stride taking all of her effort. When she reached the top, she had a clear view of her surroundings. Dead ahead, maybe a few hours more of a hike, the rooftops of Kamuy-Kotan bathed in the fading light of sunset.

The sun was being swallowed by the black silhouettes of the trees. If she gave it her all, she could make it. Not before dark. But soon.

Before she descended on the other side of the hill, she saw a glint of light off to her left, at the base of the mountains. The setting sun was reflecting off of something metal, not too far away. A car. In the forest. She stared at it and saw a figure crawling out from the crashed vehicle.

Taro.

CHAPTER 36

Ashiya came upon the scene of the crash. Taro was on his back, breathing, but otherwise not moving. The RAV4 they had been in back on the road was now upside down, a few meters away from Taro. She approached cautiously. It looked like Taro. And the car being here in a bad way also showed her it was most likely him as well. But, how could she know? How could she be so sure that this was him and not *it*?

"You okay?" she asked as she stepped into the clearing, wishing she had her gun. Bullets didn't seem to slow Kesagake down at all. Save for the eyes. If she could attack the eyes, she could buy herself time. She drew her hunting knife from its sheath. Better than nothing. She hid the knife behind her back.

Taro rolled to his side. "Do I look okay?"

She walked over to him. Knife gripped and ready to go diving right into one of his eyes should he prove to not be himself.

He squinted at her. "You gonna stab me?"

"Can you blame me? How do I know you're not Kesagake?"

"Fuck me. I could ask you the same thing. But if you were the demon, I wouldn't be able to do anything about it. So if you are, then come on, get it over with."

He laid down on his back and spread his arms out wide. It would be easy to drive the knife down now, wouldn't it? Maybe one good stab through the eye and right into the brain could put it down?

But if I'm wrong?

"I believe you," she said as she put the knife back into its strap. "Only because you still act like you. Like a dick. When it was pretending to be Ogoto, he was acting weird the whole time. I thought it was because he hit his head, but maybe Kesagake can't, or just doesn't, copy people perfectly? And your eyes are fine. Ogoto's was bloody, right after I shot the bear in the same spot. It healed, but it looked like it took some time."

Taro grunted, eyes closed, face upturned at the failing light of the darkening winter sky.

She bent down and took hold of his arms. Pulled him over to a tree. He grunted in what could have been pain or annoyance. Propped him up in a sitting position against the trunk. "I am so very happy you decided not to kill me, girl." He smiled one of his rare smiles.

Ashiya smirked back. "Don't count yourself so lucky just yet."

Dried blood ran down his face from a wound on the top of his head. But it had stopped bleeding some time ago. She checked his ankle. A mass of purple flesh wrapped around his foot.

A flat and smooth surface of snow leading from the top of the hill down to where the car had crashed.

"What happened?" she asked him.

He groaned and laid his head back against the tree.

"After you ran, that demon chased after you down the hill. I went back to the car. There was another set of keys in the visor. I couldn't run after you. I'm sorry, but with my leg I would never have made it. Thought I could look for you along the road and if I saw you down in the valley, I could call out to you and you could hike up to the car. That, or just book it to town and bring in reinforcements. I made it most of the way when the demon appeared in the road, right in front of me. It rammed the car."

She looked up the hill. Nothing was there. Nothing moved to show that it was in pursuit.

But why? Twice now it could have finished them, but didn't. Was it herding them down here?

Because it enjoys causing pain. That's why it slept in the cabin with you all and waited for the right time to attack. To hurt you. To make you feel some hope, just for it to crush you in the end.

If it was up there now, there was nothing to stop it from attacking. Nothing she knew about, at least.

Sunlight had mostly disappeared from the forest. A few dull pink rays wrapped around the treetops. The rest a cold dark blue.

"We can't make it back to town tonight. Not with your leg like this, too risky. We need to stay here and build a fire," she said. "Do you think you can walk tomorrow?"

"I shouldn't be walking on this leg. But I guess I have to, huh? I don't think the bullet hit a bone or tore me up too badly. It'll hurt like a bitch, but I can make it. Couple hours in the morning and we'll be back."

She didn't respond. The wound was severe and would probably be infected by the time they got back. It was a miracle that the crash didn't bang him up any more than he already was. Still, she'd have to take the lead on everything from now.

If there was one stroke of luck, it was that all of their gear was still in the car. Their rifles. Food and water. Sleeping bags. Flares. And an emergency fire starter kit. It would be cold tonight, but with the gear and Taros' body heat, it wouldn't be suicide; not like being alone with no gear would have been.

Taro gave no complaint as Ashiya set about building the fire. The kit was a miracle bag. She took out a small axe and chopped off a low-hanging branch above Taro. Broke it into pieces. She struck the magnesium starter rods over a pile of petroleum soaked cotton balls. They lit up quick. Added some char cloth, and the flames grew. Put some of the broken branch onto the fire and it took after a few minutes of struggling against the wind and the wet wood. She cut off a few more branches and prepped them. Not enough to last all night, but better than nothing. As she worked, Taro held onto his rifle and stared up the hill.

She didn't want to think what would happen if it came for them in the night.

She fastened a tarp on the car's tires and a low-hanging branch on the tree supporting Taro. The fire grew hotter and a semblance of heat wrapped around them. She grabbed some tin cans of tuna from Taro's pack and opened them up. Gave one can to Taro, and he grunted in thanks. They ate out of the can with their fingers in silence. Wiping them in the snow when they finished.

The woods grew dark. The stars pierced the sky. She threw more wood onto the fire. Taro watched the hills. She sat across from him, watching the forest.

"We can't kill it, can we?" she asked.

"Our rounds did nothing. Save for the one you put in its eye. I did the same when—" his voice faltered. "When it took my Maya's face."

Darkness was now all about them. The crackle of the fire filled in the silence that followed.

"Was she your wife?"

"Yeah. Died three years back. Breast cancer."

A piece of wood popped in the fire and sent up a flurry of embers.

"We couldn't afford treatment. Hunting doesn't really bring in much, save for meat. She couldn't work because of clinical depression. Not for some ten years, at least. It's my fault she died. If I would have noticed something sooner, or made more money, maybe we could have gotten ahead of it. But..."

Firelight danced in his pale eyes.

"It's not your fault," she said after another moment's silence.

"You don't know that. You don't know what it was like."

"I lost my brother in a hunting accident when I was young. A little older than Saho is now." She felt his eyes on her, though she didn't look at him. "We were with our Dad out in the Steppe, tracking a herd of caribou. Dad sent us on ahead with Alexei, my brother, taking point. Dad wanted us to do it on our own. Alexei had shot and killed animals before. He was a few years older than me, but I hadn't been able to yet. Once I could have shot a rabbit but just couldn't do it. So Alexei and I crawl through the grass, downwind of the herd. The plan was to go around back behind them and pick off one the bucks from there, let the rest go stampede on ahead. But Alexei sees this big ol' buck out in front. Antlers so big you could probably swing off of them. He wanted it bad, so he goes on ahead, in front of the herd. Tells me to cover him.

I didn't know what I was doing but I say sure, go for it. He crawls down in front of them, hiding right in plain sight. But the buck must have got his scent because he got all agitated, stamping his hooves and whining. I could have—I should have—shot it right then and there, but I couldn't. I froze. The buck sees... sees Alexei. He jumps out and shoots it. The bullet must have just grazed off its chest because it charged him. Brought its hooves down on him and stamped him into the earth. I still couldn't shoot the fucker. I just watched it pummel my brother into the ground. The herd runs away and I come running down to him. But the first thing I see isn't his body. I see his teeth scattered across the grass. The buck smashed his head in so hard the teeth exploded out of his mouth."

She grabbed another piece of wood and threw it on the fire with force.

"That wasn't your fault, girl. You were a child. Your father shouldn't have put that on you. And your brother, I'm sorry to say it, was an idiot. How can you possibly be responsible for that?"

She stared at the bouncing flames as they writhed and twisted around each other.

"I know but—"

"But nothing. It wasn't. Your. Fault."

She looked into his eyes. The sincerity and intent in his gaze were true. He meant it. Her Dad and friends told her it wasn't her fault—Mom didn't even bother. But she saw it in their eyes, that moment's hesitation that betrayed what they all really thought; that she was a coward and could have done more. But not Taro. He spoke truth. Always.

"I dream about him every night. Most of the time I wake with these vague feelings that he was sitting by my bed. Other times, I remember his toothless smile, hanging over me like he's clinging to the ceiling. Mom told me he'd haunt me if I didn't look him in the face. I missed my chance at his funeral, so I'm paying for it now."

"For the first year after Maya's passing, I couldn't look at any of her pictures. Thought it would be too painful. When I got 'round to it, it was just that, fucking painful. But it helped. Helped to let it hurt, to let it stare me in the face. Still hurts, but in a good way."

Ashiya stored that away in her heart. Maybe it wouldn't be as awful as she thought it would be, to face him. Even in those nightmares, to not wake up screaming before that red sash fully fell from his face. But to look at him. To let it hurt. To be okay with that.

They stopped talking and looked at the fire together. The sky was an ocean of stars now. Each individual point of light coming together to create a tapestry of glory in the darkness.

She sat there, looking at the stars, the fire, and at Taro.

All of them were tiny lights in the void.

Surrounded by emptiness and oblivion.

But coming together, they made some beautiful in the dark.

CHAPTER 37

SNAP!

Ashiya woke and sat straight up. The fire was low but still gave off some heat and light. Taro was awake, taking the second watch after her, rifle pointed into the dark. The sun was coming up just over the horizon.

She got to her feet and grabbed her rifle.

"What is it?" she whispered.

He didn't answer for a moment. "Dunno. Something broke a branch."

She peered into the dark but could see nothing. She checked her rifle was loaded.

CRUNCH.

Something was walking in the snow.

The sound of footsteps came again, a few at a time, and then it stopped. It was bigger than a fox. Could be a deer. A person. Even a normal sized bear. Or something far worse.

Muttering. A man's voice. Like somebody talking to himself. Not too far away from their camp.

The low firelight gave their position away, but that didn't mean she had to make it easy to find her. She pointed up. Taro nodded. He gave her his shoulder as a step and she lifted herself up into the tree. She grabbed hold of the branches and pulled herself up. She was a tiny woman, usually something that bothered her, but it always meant she could hide well.

Ashiya climbed up a few meters and stopped. There was no foliage on the branches to cover her position, but maybe being high up could give her an advantage, regardless.

Beneath her, Taro got to his feet with a grunt of pain and pointed his rifle out.

"Who is it!?" he shouted. The fierceness in his voice scared her for a moment. It was the sound of a person capable of great violence.

"What's the time?" came the voice. "Can you please tell me the time?"

The voice was familiar.

Kawamoto.

Not possible. No way he could have survived a night out here alone. And how would he have gotten out of the hole? Has to be Kesagake.

"Officer Kawamoto, show yourself, slowly," Taro said.

"The time. Time is a precious thing. Don't you think? Especially when there is so little of it to go around. Can you please tell me the time?"

More shuffling in the snow. Ashiya, from her vantage point, saw a shadow drawing nearer. She aimed her gun at the head as best as she could.

Something cracked. Another snap. With every step forward, Kawamoto made a creaking and breaking sound. Not branches. Bones.

"It hurts. The fall hurt so much. But time... time heals all wounds. Time is all I have now. I have seen the place where the gods rot. I have seen the eternal shores of the metal city. Seen the amber waves rolling in. Would you like me to show you?"

The shadow came to the edge of the firelight. The flames lit up a pale white face and a pale body.

He was naked.

The head hung limp and off to the side. A sharp break in the neck, twisted completely around, revealed a piece of shoulder blade protruding from his skin. The legs were bent and broken in several places. It shouldn't have possible for the man to walk.

The horrible mangled thing of a man took a shambling step forward into the light, looking like he might fall over at any moment.

He lifted his head with his hands and looked at Taro. "The hunter! Oh, I am so glad to find you. Out in the cold and alone. Come, child. Let me bring you His warmth."

Kawamoto smiled. His teeth were sharp and several times too large for his head. It looked like someone shoved a bear trap into his mouth. His eyes were fiery yet black at the same time.

BAM!

Taro fired the rifle and hit Kawamoto in the face. Half of his head exploded in a crimson mist and a shower of bone and brain. He fell backwards.

Ashiya looked around the woods for a sign of any other movement. There was none she could see.

Taro reloaded his rifle.

Kawamoto's body twitched. The bones creaked and snapped as the body rose to its feet, not by use of its own legs, but as if pulled upward by an unseen string.

Half of his head was gone. What remained hung loose off the neck like a piece of clothing, barely connected. His left eye—his only eye left—burned with hate. His half smile lit up in glee. He charged Taro.

Taro pulled the trigger again. But the rest of the head was hard to hit. The remnants of the face flapped around. He missed.

Kawamoto shuffled quickly across the gap between him and Taro.

Ashiya aimed and fired. Hit him right in the chest and opened him up. Kawamoto was driven back into a tree and he collapsed into the snow once more.

And once more, he rose. He could hardly move now, but still pressed forward, arms swinging out wildly.

Ashiya fired one more shot just below his neck. The rest of the head fell off to the side of the body as it collapsed in the snow.

Ashiya lowered herself down the tree and jumped off, landing next to Kawamoto.

The body began moving again. Struggling to get to its feet. The half-head lay off to the side. Left eye still glowing black. The half smile leering up at her.

The head gargled words at her, "*Chime ith oll yoo haf.*"

Kawamoto's headless body stumbled forward. Taro opened fire into the chest again, blasting a hole right through it, and again, knocked it down. It twisted in the snow and grasped at the air.

Ashiya unstrapped her knife and plunged it into Kawamoto's remaining eye.

The black light went out.

The headless body fell back into the snow.

It did not get up again.

CHAPTER 38

"Is this Kesagake?" Taro asked as he kicked the body over.

"If it is, it's dead. Unless it's fucking with us again."

Taro picked up the ruined head and tossed it into the fire. He grunted. "No, this isn't it."

"How can you know that?"

"I think if it was Kesagake, it would have turned back into the bear after I shot it. It was too weak as a man. That would help it sneak into a group and catch you off guard, but would do it no favors in a fight. This is the actual body of the cop."

"So, what? It can possess the dead?"

Taro stared at the body.

"Taro, I know you don't know what this is, but are there any legends or myths you can think of that might explain what the fuck is happening?"

He looked at her in silence as if to say, How the fuck should I know?

"You called it a demon before. Said something about how a god can become an evil spirit."

"Yeah, sure. Stories is all. No way to know if they apply here."

"Well, I'd like to know. As much as you can tell me."

Taro sat back down by the fire. The flaming half-skull of Kawamoto peering out at him.

"The Ainu believed everything has a soul in it. The trees. You and me. And especially bears. They were the messengers of the gods. Like actual gods come in the flesh to guide the people. They gave us meat and fur from their bodies and we honored them back. Gave them back to the gods."

"What does that mean?"

"We don't do this anymore, but the Ainu used to practice *Iomante*. We took a bear cub from its mother, raised it like one of our own children, and after a year we did a ceremony where we sacrificed it."

"That's horrible. You took bear cubs from their mother and then killed them after raising it like a pet?"

"I took? Never did this, girl. No one I know ever has either. And why horrible? We need meat to survive. The bears gave it to us. And we honored them. Gave them a good life. By doing Iomante, we sent their souls back to the gods, where they would be reborn again as a bear. This was the way of things. This was balance."

“I mean, we're definitely handling something that looks like a bear. Mostly.”

Taro sucked in air through his teeth. "Shit, I'm not the expert here. But I know that if you disrespect something that has died. Like messing with their burial ground, that thing, human or animal, can come back as a demon—a *wen-kamuy*—after death. And some demons can take on different forms. Shapeshift and shit. But that's about all I remember. Just stories my grandmother used to tell us."

She smiled. "Mine did that too. Talked about the evil spirits that haunted graves. We had something like that too, the abaasy. The dead needed to be honored in their passing or they could also come back. The only way to send them back to the underworld was through blood sacrifice. But why now? If that's what Kesagake is, a dishonored spirt, surely other animals have been treated horribly, and we never heard about them coming back?"

He shrugged. "Shit if I know. Even if it is a wen-kamuy, that doesn't help us much in stopping it. We need a priest or somethin'."

"Would giving it a proper burial help?"

"Girl, you keep asking me questions like I fucking know. Stop it."

"I'm not really asking you, just processing this out loud." She walked over to the fire. "Kawamoto went down when I took out his eye after you shot the other one. So that's something, go for their eyes. Maybe for the demon itself, the bear, that could work too, if we get both of them, maybe not. It got hurt when we shot it in the eyes, but then it healed pretty quickly. But Kawamoto isn't getting back up... I hope. Maybe for the, wen-kamuy you called it? If we can appease it somehow it'll stop?"

"I don't know the first thing about how to do that."

"Yeah, me too. It's just a thought, anyway. What's happening might not even have anything to do with Iomante or wen-kamuy or anything. All we know for sure is shoot the eyes."

"Good enough place to start."

More sunlight crept into the dark hollows. It brought no warmth with it.

Ashiya looked up at the mountain road.

"How far would you say you had left till you reached town?"

"Ten-minute drive maybe."

"Can't be too far of a walk from now. Can you make it?"

Taro went over to Kawamoto's body and kicked it over with his wounded leg. He grimaced but didn't let out a sound. "Yeah, I can make it."

"Good. Let's head out."

CHAPTER 39

December 21st

"Fuck. Fuck. Fuuuuck!!"

Ryoji yelled as he fumbled around his desk, looking for the key. He knocked over a coffee mug Ayumi bought him last year in Guam and it shattered on the floor. He glanced over at it. Half of the phrase "Best Husband" could be made out on one shard, now spelling *st sband* instead.

She was still out on her vacation in Okinawa. Coming back tomorrow if the roads cleared up. He supposed he should be grateful for that, for her to not be present in the middle of this madness. To not have to explain himself to her—again. But what he really wanted in that moment was that fucking key. He shoved aside a pile of papers and they scattered around his office. The handgun he put on the desk skidded across it.

Saho sat hunched over in a chair in the corner. Crying softly.

Every sniffle and every whimper irked him to no end. Things were bad enough without having to deal with the kid, weren't they?

And how are you going to deal with her?

He pushed that thought out of his mind and focused instead on his growing anxiety over the key. The key that opened his special gun cabinet. The one beside the polar bear's head on the far side of his office.

And inside that metal case, the .950 JDJ rifle he got through his less than reputable connections.

He never used it before. Even the most experienced hunter could dislocate their shoulder if they fired it, even with a good stance. Despite his bravado, he was no idiot. That gun could break his arm. He got it more as a memento of his time in Africa than for any practical purpose.

But that fucking gun will take down anything. It will mow that fucking bear's head clean off. It's a rocket more than a gun.

That bear's face haunted his waking mind. He recognized that face. The white lightning mark across its right eye. He should remember it. It was the same fucking bear he shot last week. Shot and failed to kill.

But that bear was normal sized, not much bigger than a man. Gaunt because of waking up too early from hibernation. It was not the mammoth monstrosity he saw back in Ota. What had happened to it?

"Sir?" Saho said in a voice that was barely audible. "Can I-"

"No, you can't! Just, just shut up, okay? I need to think things through."

Her face went white, and she stiffened even more as he barked at her.

No good Ryoji, no good to scare her too much. You might need her for...

He took a deep breath and flashed on his diamond smile. "Hey honey, I didn't mean to yell just now. I'm sorry. But you know that monster is still out there, right? The phones and internet are out and nobody is at the police station. Nobody is anywhere in this fucking town!" *Anxiety growing, chill out.* "I need to make sure that we are safe. And what I really need from you is for you to be a big strong girl. Can you do that for me?"

Can you forget I shot Taro while you're at it? That would make this easier. She nodded her head, but the tears streamed down her face, regardless. That was okay. He didn't give a shit what she was actually feeling, so long as she stayed out of his way and did as she was told.

Coming back into town last night, he noticed nothing off at first. Aside from the phones being down, but that could have been because of the snow. A storm came in and started dumping snow over the town. This morning he went out to the station to check things out for himself—Saho locked in his study while he was gone—and not only was no one at the station, nobody was anywhere. No one at the twenty-four-hour convenience stores. Nobody at the gas station. The storm was explanation enough for why people weren't out and about. But the stores and the gas station and the police? They didn't take snow days.

The blizzard made it impossible to get out of town just yet. He could try it, but he knew damn well how many people careened off the mountain roads in storms just like this. He should have left last night, before the storm hit, when he had a chance.

But how could I have known things were this bad?

"Mr.?"

"Honey, please, not now," he said as he almost threw his shelves across the room he pulled them open so hard.

"There's someone..." her voice raised and then faltered.

"What!?" he shouted as he looked up at her.

Her eyes were wide, and her body shook. She looked like death itself. She was staring across the office at the door, which was off to his far right-hand side.

Ryoji followed her gaze, and he too found himself shaking.

In the open doorway was his assistant Rina.

Naked.

Her once tan skin was now a milky white. She stood with her arms out at her side, fingers stretched out at odd angles, almost as if she were in pain. Her pink and purple nails, normally long on any other day, were much longer now. They ended in pointed silver tips that broke through the polish.

Her head rested on her left shoulder, like a dog trying to understand what its master was saying. Someone had ripped out half her throat. There were at least a dozen other small bite marks on her body. On her arms, her chest, her thighs, even her stomach. Almost as if she we attacked by a school of human-sized piranha.

She flashed a smile full of sharp teeth, each one the size of a butcher's knife. The massive teeth pushed their way out of her face, as if a much larger animal were wearing her face as a mask. Her eyes were a deep well of blackness that seemed to glow above the purple bruises on her face.

"My love," Rina said in a voice that spoke of eons, of the death and rebirth of stars, looking at Ryoji. "My daughter," she said as she looked at Saho. "Come with me. To the everlasting shores of the dead gods."

Ryoji picked up his handgun and fired it three times at Rina. One shot hit the wall in the hallway and shattered a picture of him and his wife on their wedding day, normally turned the other way around when Rina was staying the night. One bullet struck her chest, splattering fresh but black blood across her white skin. One hit her in the forehead. She stumbled backwards, slammed into the wall, and slid down it to a sitting position in the hallway, a dark streak like an oil spill painted behind her.

Rina laughed. "Don't reject His gifts, my love. Come to me now, and we can fuck in His presence. Wouldn't you love that?"

She slid back up the wall.

Ryoji fired two more bullets into her chest, but it had no effect aside from causing her to flinch. His hands shook, and he dropped the gun onto the floor. Rina stumbled forward wildly, like she had no spinal cord holding her torso up.

Saho flew across the room and slammed the door shut. Locked it. Rina charged the door, and it shook. The wood was a heavy oak, not something easily broken. Rina hit the door two more times. She couldn't—or at least didn't—break through it.

"What the fuck?" Ryoji stammered.

He wanted to believe Rina had just lost it. Some female insanity about not being appreciated enough or some shit like that. But no, not with those teeth and those black eyes and those wounds that should have left her well on her way to her next life. Not with that look in her eyes. He had seen it before. He had seen it in the bear. The bear he had shot.

Was it back for revenge?

"My love," Rina's voice, her own yet strangely ancient. "Please open the door." Ryoji and Saho stayed quiet, and a minute passed. "We will find another way in. Maybe that window in your office, not too high off the ground. Or we could just burn this house down with you in it. It would be so much easier to just open the door. Saho, my dear, wouldn't you like to see your parents? They are here with us. They are waiting for you on the gray sands with open arms. They behold the amber light of the coming devastation."

Ryoji looked at the girl as if she were about to unlock the door, ready to restrain her if she did. She backed away instead and covered her ears.

Maybe this girl is useful after all?

He didn't want to admit that he was a coward. But he knew deep down that he was. That truth heated his anger all the more. But the girl saved him just now.

Maybe I should keep her around until I can get out of here? She could help. Or, at least, I have someone to stand between me and them if I need a shield.

He didn't like the idea of sacrificing the girl to Rina out in the hall. Who would? But he would do it in a heartbeat if it came down to it. Open the door. Push the girl out first. And while she was being ripped apart, make a run for his truck. But could he make it out in that storm? And what if he crashed or got overrun by them out in the streets? Here he was warm, he had ammo, and he had thick walls. He could cover the window Rina taunted him about with his desk. If they burned down the house? Shit, then he'd have to run.

But he also had an elephant gun.

So get to finding that damn key.

CHAPTER 40

Ashiya and Taro walked down 3-Chome Street. The blizzard intensified, obscuring the buildings lining the road. Ashiya was thankful that the storm seemed to be localized over the town, since they had no problems out in the woods last night. They had emerged from the forest line twenty minutes ago when the storm struck in earnest. They had seen no one out driving, but given the howling winds and the steadily growing snow drifts, that was understandable.

They passed the Saito's Market. Still shut down for the foreseeable future. They passed the Post Office, also dark, though it should have been open, even in the storm. Taro tried the door. Locked.

They walked further down the street. The wind screeched above their heads. The snow blinded them. But Ashiya could still feel the stare of many eyes on her. That instinctive animal sense of being watched. Just like that tiger in Siberia. But she could see nothing but the whiteout conditions. Could hear nothing but the cry of the wind. Could feel nothing but the icy prickle of numbness in her fingers and face and toes.

They passed the only 7-11 in town, usually open twenty-four hours, rain or shine or even blizzard. The lights were on, with two cars parked outside.

They walked inside. Immediate relief from the cold. Warm air greeted them as the chime of the automatic glass doors rang out. The doors shut behind them. No staff at the counter.

"Excuse me!" Taro shouted out as he stamped the snow off his boots and walked up to the register. "We need to use your phone. It's an emergency!"

No response.

Taro lifted the counter trap and walked behind the register towards the tiny kitchen area, calling out for the staff. Ashiya looked down the aisle to her left—one of the three in the store. At the end, a pile of potato chips from an opened bag, a shattered sake bottle, and a streak of blood on a glass door of the refrigerated section.

"Taro!" she shouted.

"Yeah?" He walked back out from behind the counter. She nodded at the blood down the aisle. He nodded back. They both readied their rifles, Taro walking down the furthest aisle to the left, Ashiya the furthest to the right. She walked past the frozen dessert fridge and the alcohol shelves. She could see Taro's head above the aisle, moving down as well.

They met up at the end of the store. Nobody home. She looked at the one place they hadn't checked, the door to the bathroom in front of her. She opened the door and immediately recoiled at the sight.

Above the toilet, the skinless body of a person, limbs attached to the walls via broken off pieces of wood from what might have been a table. The head was in the sink. A man in his early forties, wearing glasses. Someone had tossed his clothing into a corner of the bathroom; it was a green employee T-shirt.

Ashiya stumbled backwards and nearly vomited. Seeing the same scene in the forest had been horrific, but for some reason she didn't understand, seeing this inside a modern building upset her even more.

Maybe it was the Christmas music still playing on the speakers. Or the electric lights and the cheap and tasty food all around. The trappings and vestiges of modern life. Of what was supposed to be safe. Out there in the woods, anything could happen. Death could come at a moment. But here, in a fucking convenience store, in places like this, horror was not supposed to extend its decrepit hands.

But it did anyway. It reached into the bubble of modernity and comfort and ripped out the illusion of safety.

Ashiya regained her composure.

"It's here, isn't it?" she asked.

"Looks like it."

"What do we do?"

"First things first." Taro walked back to the counter. Grabbed the phone. Didn't work.

"Well, we can't stay here," she said. "These doors will not protect us. Our options are my cabin, which is out of town and has thick walls and a few windows. Or, we could try the Saito's house. It's closer and I want to check on them, anyway. We need somewhere to stay until the storm passes and we can get some help."

"They live far? 'Cuz I ain't walking much more than I have already. Plus, I don't think we'd survive much more outside in this."

Ashiya took a deep breath and opened the bathroom door. Doing her best to not look at the body, she picked up the bloody clothes in the corner. She heard a jangle in the pants pocket. Car keys. And only two options outside.

Ashiya drove the tiny Mitsubishi into the storm. The heater filled the car with enough warmth to make her never want to leave it. She didn't know where she was, but the man from the store also had an iPhone. There was no reception, but she could still load his maps app and see where she was in town, despite not being able to see any of the buildings.

She drove slowly to not lose control. Despite that feeling of being watched, as if hundreds of eyes were looking out their windows and through the storm at the lone car on the road, despite that feeling that if the town were full of those things, those undead things like Kawamoto, they might run the car down and flip it over, despite all of that, she drove slowly.

Cautiously.

"We have to assume that there are at least a few of the," w*hat do I call them?* She thought of their incisors, "Bear-teeth things in town. It could be the whole place, but that would mean thousands of people were changed in just a few days. I've been thinking about it. If Kesagake could just turn somebody, why didn't it turn any of us while we were in Ota? It only turned Kawamoto because, I think, he was already dead. So let's assume that this creature can turn you when you're dead. Like raising the dead or something. The good thing is that Japan cremates their dead, and I don't think we need to worry about ashes coming back, or at least I hope not. But some people aren't turned. They're used as sacrifices, or monuments, or whatever the fuck it is, the headless bodies. Ogoto was one of those. And what we saw wasn't him, but Kesagake taking his form. So, we have sacrifices—for some purpose—and we have the Bear-teeth, who we can stop if we destroy their eyes. And Kesagake has to be the cause of all of this and we know that hurting its eyes hurts it as well. Maybe that's how we stop it, destroy the eyes."

She stopped to catch her breath. She'd never ranted as much as she had just done before. But she was trying to solve the chaos of what was happening, to impose some rhyme and reason to the disorder.

"Our guns could get its eyes," Taro said. "But we'd have to get real close, like we were in Ota. If we run into it again, we might not be so lucky. I have a feeling the mayor has some pretty powerful shit. He was boasting about it before you showed up for the hunting party. You know where he lives? I'd like to thank him for his parting gift as well." He grinned and slapped the area of his leg just above the wound.

"I know. He lives on the same street as the Saito family."

"Shit. That's some good luck there. So, we swing by your friend's place and hole up. See if they're okay. Then we go to fuck-face's place and get his guns and get Saho back."

"Sounds like a plan."

Ashiya turned down what should be a residential street according to Google. Two streets away from the Saitos.

She slowed the car down as she entered. Taro and she exchanged looks. The street was red. Even in the fury of the snow flurries, she could see the scarlet stains. Some of it was in the street itself. Some were in people's yards and driveways. Like Ota. They passed an overturned truck. Smoke pouring out from the chassis. She turned right. To her left was the forest. In front of the trees, she could make out dim shadows. They looked like starfish out there, or part of a faded fence. But she knew what they were. Those not chosen to walk as the undead.

One more turn and she was on the street, just two blocks away from the Saito home.

She stopped the car. It slid to the left before stopping. Outside the house, the Saitos were standing there, naked, hands raised to the sky. All three of them.

CHAPTER 41

Arms raised to the thundering sky. Black eyes visible even in the storm. Itsuki, Hikari, and Ren. Their skin was almost as white as the snow that wrapped around their naked skin. No gooseflesh, no hairs standing on end. It was like they were made for this.

Their bear-trap smiles of sharp teeth clenched shut with their lips curled back.

Ashiya's blood went as cold as the frosted air outside. Hikari, her friend—or at least she was well on her way to be—was here standing naked in the snow. Dried blood frozen to her bare skin. Throat ripped out by a jaw bigger than a human's could be. Itsuki next to her. Dozens of bite marks riddled his body. His intestines were visible through the wounds in his abdomen. Like sausage meat prepped and ready to go in the frozen foods section.

And then there was Ren. The smallest of them, yet his smile spoke of a greater evil than what had possessed his parents. Like he was a fine wine, aged to perfection in the vat of whatever force held his body captive to its will.

Ashiya hit reverse and floored the gas. The tires spun too fast and couldn't find traction on the road. She stopped, took a breath, eased on and off the gas until the tires found their groove. The Saitos stood vigil and watched them. The back of the car hit a snow berm and jolted its passengers. Ashiya switched to drive and turned the car back the way they came.

And stopped.

A tall skinny man stood in the road. Naked and black eyed like the rest of them. Behind him, a boy of no more than nine, squatting down, staring directly into Ashiya's eyes.

On the roofs of the three houses down the lane, a dozen of *them*, standing erect on the shingles, peering out at the car. Sentries in the storm. From the woods to her right, the movement of something larger than a person, walking on all fours.

In the rearview mirror, Hikari flashed her steel smile, lit up red by the brake lights. Ashiya hit reverse and slammed her foot on the pedal. The bumper hit Hikari's waist, and the tires pulled her under. Ashiya felt the sickening bump of the car as it climbed over her body. She felt the car's elevation dip suddenly as what was under the tires gave way to the tonnage of pressure.

She was sure the sequence of sounds would haunt her forever.

Smack. Bump. Crunch.

But that was a demon to wrestle with later.

Ashiya pushed the car to fifty kilometers an hour, driving in reverse. Itsuki and Ren ducked out of the way of the car.

She saw Ryoji's mansion. The gate was open.

A great roar ripped through the howl of the wind.

Kesagake.

Close.

The bear, veiled in the storm's fury, stepped out onto the road behind the car. At one end of the street, an army of the dead. At the other, the bear.

Ashiya veered the car backwards and down Ryoji's drive. It spun, slipped on the ice, whipping around once before crashing into the front door. The car split open a large crack in the top half of the door, the car's front hood blocked the bottom half. She and Taro got out. Ashiya jumped on the hood and extended a hand to Taro. He took it and climbed up to the gap in the front door. It was just big enough for Ashiya to squeeze in, but not for Taro. She forced her body through the opening and fell inside onto the hardwood floor.

The lights were on, and the heater was working. Somebody's home.

She scrambled to her feet. Taro grabbed a broken piece of the door and yanked on it. Ashiya kicked it from the other side. But it was too high for her to give it any genuine force.

The roar erupted from somewhere in Ryoji's front yard. Taro turned around.

"Hurry! Help me get this fucking door open!"

She hadn't heard him so scared before. He yanked harder at the planks and tried pushing his body through it, to no avail. Ashiya ran into the house and found herself in the living room. High ceilings complete with a chandelier. Leather sofa and a leather armchair. Black bear skin rug laid out in front of the massive fireplace—nothing burning at the moment—adorned with deer antlers. And beside the fireplace, an axe. She grabbed it and ran back to the front door.

"Back up!" she yelled.

She didn't wait to see if he was out of the way before she started swinging. The roar was louder now. And it was taking on a human voice. A woman's voice. Ashiya swung the axe down into the plank that looked the weakest. If she could just remove that one, he can get inside.

One strike. The axe wedged itself into the wood. She put her foot on the door and pulled it out. Swing two. The plank almost came off. Taro grasped it and pulled until it started splitting, but not good enough. One last swing, just like Dad taught her to, and *crack!* It came off clean.

Taro ripped out the plank and dove into the house, landing on his face. She dropped the axe and helped him up to his feet.

"Taro, don't leave me out here in the cold," said the woman's face that appeared in the fractured doorway. Her face was kind and lovely, attached to a body that was far too large for her. Attached to a furry neck that extended down into the gap like a snake's.

Taro whipped out his rifle and aimed it at his late wife's stolen face. Right at the eyes. The creature must have learned from their last encounter. It retracted its gangly yet uncomfortably muscular neck and disappeared back outside.

"Come on," Ashiya said as she tugged at his jacket. "We can't stay here."

He followed silently.

In moments, Kesagake could rip its way into the house. The walls were thick, but she had seen what it could do back at Ota. If it couldn't tear down a wall, it could always change its form and squeeze through the hole. Or, as she came to realize with increasing horror, enter through any of the massive windows on the first floor.

Even if they outran the bear, the Bear-teeth surrounded the house, and beyond them, the blizzard.

They were fucked.

"We have to see if Ryoji has any other guns and hole up somewhere upstairs," Ashiya said. "Barricade the stairway and force them to come at us in a bottleneck. I'm sure we can shoot our way through them." *Through your friends.*

Taro nodded his head, but his eyes were light years away.

"Did you hear me?" she asked.

"What? Oh, yeah, bottleneck, got it."

"You stay and shoot anything that comes at the gap in the door."

She didn't want to leave him at the entrance to guard it, but she couldn't trust that he was all there right now. He didn't seem capable of searching the house. Hopefully, he could at least shoot whatever came through the door while she looked. Taro's face was drained of all its vitality. He looked decades older in the weariness that consumed him. Something about that last encounter must have sapped him. That and the pain and possible infection ravaging his leg.

Ashiya ran through the first floor of the home. None of the rooms were locked. And there were no guns in any of them, none that she could see, anyway.

Gunfire.

She ran out of the bedroom she had just gone in and back to the front door. Just in time to see a pale body fall away from the door. Taro stood in a shooting stance. The barrel of the rifle smoking. The smell of nail polish and sulfur in the air. That action alone seemed to bring some youth back into him.

"Come on, upstairs," she said and tugged at him.

They went down the hall and found the stairway and ascended it. The landing opened up to a wide hall with six rooms, three to the left and three to the right.

Crashing from downstairs. The sound of wood splitting apart. Followed shortly by the sound of breaking glass.

"Ryoji!" she called out. "Are you here?"

Not waiting for an answer, she pushed Taro to the right as she checked the doors on the left. First locked. Second opened to a bathroom. Third to a bedroom with satin blankets covering a bed the size of her first apartment.

"Help!" came the muffled voice of a girl, down the hall where Taro stood.

Ashiya ran down the hall. At the end of it was a large reddish door that had several dents in it, with a streak of dark blood and a shattered wedding picture on the hall wall across from it.

"Saho!" Taro shouted.

Something covered Saho's mouth, cutting off her voice.

"Go away!" came Ryoji's voice. Shrill and panicky. "You are not taking me!"

"Open the door, you little fuck!" Taro growled as he kicked at the wood.

A voice from downstairs.

Hikari's.

"Taroooo." The voice sang out slowly, toying with them. "Anassstaaaaasssia. We are coming."

Taro pointed his rifle towards the landing as Ashiya banged her hand on the door. "Please! Let us in! We can fight them better if we're together!"

A heavy thud, the sound almost of a hoof coming down on the hardwood. Ashiya turned back to the landing. Pale feet crept into the hall. Sounding much heavier than they looked. The rest of Hikari's body followed. The car must have destroyed her spine, because she couldn't keep her torso up properly. It tilted to the side as if she were about to fall over. A single tire mark ran down the center of her body. The impact split and crushed the skull. Brains, like a dry gray sponge, poked out through the shattered bone. The left eye was gone. This amalgamation of a human body stumbled its way into the hall.

Ren followed her. Saying nothing. Smiling and peering at them with his black eyes. Staying behind his mother as if he were too shy to step out in front.

"Anastasia. I know what you see in the dark," Hikari gurgled out. "The teeth in the grass. The bloody face of dear Alexei. Come, let Him wash it all away. Come, child. Let me kiss you and then you will know peace."

Ashiya tried to aim her gun, but it suddenly became heavy. Burdened with the weight of having to shoot her friend.

Taro fired his instead. Hit what remained of Hikari's face. It exploded and Ashiya shut her eyes to the scene. Hikari's body fell limp to the ground. It did not move again. Ren stepped over her. Unaffected by the loss. Behind him, three more people Ashiya didn't know came into the hall. Ren jumped up with surprising strength and clung to the ceiling. He crawled forward, upside down.

Enough.

Ashiya forced her rifle up. She screamed as he she aimed and fired it at Ren. Taro fired his at the others in the hall. The barrage of gunshots replaced all sound. The lightning of rapid fire. The boy fell from the ceiling and rolled back up to his feet.

They fired again and again, and the things in the hall fell with the shots. And got back up. Ren sprinted down the hall, huge mouth opened and gleaming in the hall's light.

Ashiya aimed. Fired. Hit him right between his eyes. The head—the eyes—became a distant memory, replaced by nothing but a quick spurt of black blood, and then his body collapsed in a heap.

The sound of the red door unlocking.

Saho threw it open.

"Get in!"

CHAPTER 42

Ryoji jumped out of the open window and landed on the roof of the garage. He saw those things squirming their way through his front door below. He crouched down and waited until the last one, an elderly woman whose face he recognized as a regular from Saito's market, had forced her way through the fractured door.

He hoped Ashiya and pals could survive just long enough to keep those things busy and off his back. Beyond that, didn't matter. Would do him a favor if they all died up there. No need to explain his actions then.

He scanned the neighborhood.

Where is the bear?

Couldn't see it. Banging and crashing resounded from inside his home. But outside, all was still and calm. The snow continued to pour down heavily.

He jogged down the garage roof and jumped onto the bed of his truck that was parked in the drive. He looked down at the tires. Slashed.

He leapt from his truck and ran down the street, snow up to his shins. Nobody in sight. The snow was still blowing in hard and he hoped it would hide him from their gaze.

Where am I going? I need a car.

His truck was a no go. But he had the keys to the city hall on him and they had snowplows he could access. Not ideal, but better than nothing.

And when he got out of here? Well, if there are no survivors, there's nobody to say what actually went on, is there?

Just me and what I want the narrative to be.

He heard more gunfire from his home. If he was lucky, they'd take down as many of them as they could before being killed themselves.

Ryoji stopped running. A shadow off in the distance, down the street. Features hidden under the veil of snow. Vaguely human in shape.

He heard her voice clearly despite the roar of the wind.

"My love. Come with me to the eternal shores. Come and see the writhing things in the dark waters."

Rina's black eyes cut through the snow.

"Fuck off!" Ryoji yelled.

He took out his handgun and fired a shot in her general direction. He saw the black eyes jolt as if the body received a hit. But she did not go down. Ryoji turned around to run the other way. A constellation of black eyes met him. Perhaps a dozen of them, standing there, about a block away.

A whisper in his ear. Something Rina had done many times on early Sunday mornings while his wife was away at yoga class. Her foul breath caressed the inside of his ear. He felt the tiny hairs on his lobe move in the wind of her breath.

He yelled and flung his right elbow behind him to hit her. It connected with her jaw and drove her back a step. She righted herself and moved her jaws up and down. He could hear her long teeth clank against each other. A slow and steady rhythm of tooth on tooth. Like she was chattering. Or getting ready to use them.

He ran into the forest. The snow was as high as his waist off the road. He waded through it more than ran.

Rina giggled behind him. An absurd, almost blasphemous sound. So innocent, coming from a mouth so sharp and so wide. So ready to bite down on his flesh.

He pushed his body through the snow. Threw his arm behind him without looking and fired off a shot from the gun. He knew it was useless. Bullets were raindrops to them. As he ran, he caught sight of something above him in the trees.

Them.

Pale bodies hunched over the branches like birds of prey waiting for their meal to fall over and die. They didn't leap upon him. They just watched him flee beneath their gaze.

Without a sound, without the slightest hint that she had been running through the snow after him, Rina's voice, at his ear, again. Again, her sour breath wrapped around his neck. Ryoji whipped the gun around to shoot her. Before he could shoot, she pushed him forward, and he fell face first into the snow.

"Aaahhh!" he screamed in both rage and terror as he fought his way through the snow and back to his feet. Firing his last three shots blindly. At nothing.

Rina wasn't there.

"My love." Right at his ear. And with it, a bite at his shoulder. He felt sharp knives latch onto his skin and tear off something that should have remained attached. He saw her face right next to his now, sinking her jaws into his flesh. He took the gun in his right hand and slammed the handle into her forehead. She didn't let go. Again and again, he hit her. She refused to budge, like a pit bull clamping down on a rabbit. Hot blood warmed up his arm as it washed down to his wrists. He hit her again, the handle's edge striking her right eye.

She released him. Hissed. Shrunk back into the curtain of snow. But did not vanish from sight. Her silhouette remained visible in the fog-like snow. Waiting on the outskirts. Watching him.

The eyes. I hit her eye and she let go.

The realization that they had a weakness made him drunk with joy. He could have cried.

Ryoji backed up, keeping his gaze fixed on Rina's shadow. As he moved further into the forest, she followed at the same distance, just out of full sight, but not leaving him. Looking up, he did not see anymore of *them* in the trees.

I just might get out of this. Don't take your fucking eyes off of her. If she gets close, put hers out.

He knew these woods. Knew that if he went south, just off to his left, he'd avoid going further into the forest and end up in a cul-de-sac near his buddy Ryota's house. Could find the bastard's keys and take his car and get the fuck out of here.

A deep growl from behind him.

A sound that shattered all hope.

Hot breath. The smell of decaying fish. It poured over him. The smell that would attract hoards of flies if it weren't so cold out. Maggots flashed before his mind. Squirming their way into rancid meat. Wriggling through the holes they bore into the dead and graying flesh. He saw his own face in his mind. Covered in those maggots.

"Isn't it beautiful?" came the voice of his wife, Ayumi.

Hands clasped his shoulders from behind. The one on his left dug flashy pink nails into his bite wound. He cried out and tried to move, but those tiny hands possessed incredible strength and held him there.

"Ryoji, do not struggle," the thing that wore his wife's face said. "Do not fear. I will not turn you. You will instead be a testament to all who pass by. They will weep and gnash their teeth at the sight of you. At the sight of the little ones making their home in your flesh."

Rina appeared in front of him. She walked up to Ryoji and bowed her face down into the snow.

The pink nails of Ayumi's hands split open, and rough talons emerged. They sunk deep into both of his shoulders. His wife's voice turned deep and became a growl. "Let it begin."

The talons sunk down to his bone. They even scratched against his shoulder blades as they cracked apart.

Ryoji howled in pain. White hot lightning pain consumed his vision. Tears streamed down his face. He tried to twist his way out of the grasp but failed. Ayumi's hands grew fur. Grew to the size of paws bigger than his upper body. Those paws—matted with blood—shoved him down into the snow, face first. The paws batted him to the side, and he rolled until a tree stopped him. The air knocked out of his lungs.

He looked up and saw the bear. The last remnants of his wife's face dissolved behind the exposed skull of the creature. Behind the white lightning mark of its face. He saw hate. Saw vengeance. Saw jubilation behind its black eyes.

The bear pressed his body down into the snow again with its paw. The claws shredded his chest. Deep gashes across his stomach. Ryoji howled all the more. The bear brought its claws down again. Stripping off his skin. First the chest. Then the arms. Then the legs. It didn't kill him outright. It could have ripped him in half with its claws but chose instead to rake them across his body, surgically. It savored its bloody work. More slashes. More skin ripped off in mighty swipes.

Ryoji's vision became blurry and his sense of the world became numb. Perhaps his mind was trying to shield him from the horror and the pain. What happened next shattered that shield. The bear's fur writhed and rippled. Like tiny rodents moving under a blanket. Black and tarry tendrils burst out of the bear. From its back, its chest, its arms, its legs. Spider-like but with no leg joints. The tendrils whipped out and took hold of Ryoji's bloody limbs. They lifted him up and slammed his now nearly skinned body against a tree. Every nerve in his body exploded with such pain that he felt his mind would rip apart. That he would die then and there. But he didn't. He lingered on. The inky tendrils—maybe a dozen or more—dripping with a tar that caused the snow beneath them to steam, broke branches off of the tree. They shoved the splintered wood into Ryoji's hands and feet. Nailing him into place to the tree.

Now, near the point of total catatonic shock and death, Ryoji looked down at his red and wet body. The tendrils retracted back into the bear, though they still undulated just under its skin. The bear opened its jaws wide. All Ryoji could see was a black hole of nothingness. As the teeth clamped around his neck.

He thought of Ayumi at that moment. Of how much he actually loved her. Of how much pain he had caused her. He wished he could take it all back. Start over.

Dear God, I'd do it right if you gave me a chance!

Ayumi faded from his mind. The only image left was of the maggots that would feast on his face. He somehow knew, in that moment, that they were waiting for him. Those—what did Rina say?—those writhing things in the dark. And that, somehow, he would be awake to experience it all.

His wife's voice came to him one last time, from deep down in the bear's throat: *Isn't it beautiful?*

Then it bit down.

CHAPTER 43

Saho shut and locked the door. She was becoming a pro at this.

She ran up to Ashiya and embraced her, weeping. Ashiya hugged her back. Saho ran up to Taro and held onto him. The man looked both embarrassed and happy all at once. He didn't hug her back, but patted her on the head. Ashiya thought she saw tears in his eyes.

Pounding at the door.

Where do we go? Out the window like Ryoji did?

Ashiya looked outside and saw more of the Bear-teeth in the street. She saw Ryoji flee into the woods before the snow obscured him from sight. The dead didn't pursue him. Instead, they turned and looked up at her.

More pounding at the door. The sound of wood splitting.

Ashiya checked her rounds. Two left. She asked Taro how many he had. One.

This was it. Even if she got lucky and shot the things' eyes, there were dozens, maybe hundreds, fuck it, a thousand more. They spoke in the hall. Promising Taro and Saho reunion with their loved ones. Promising Ashiya an end to her nightmares.

Ashiya looked at Taro. She saw in the depth of his blue-gray eyes that he understood. He looked down at Saho, who had buried her face in his chest. In moments, those things would be in the room and take them. But at least she could spare Saho the terror of being ripped apart. Or of being used as a sacrifice, pinned to the trees. Maybe Saho wouldn't exist in her new body; black eyed and pale skinned. Maybe her soul would find peace elsewhere. But Ashiya didn't know that. What if you still went on as your body was taken over? What if you had to see through those dark eyes and taste blood through their enlarged mouths?

Ashiya loaded her gun. She imagined herself lifting the barrel and shooting Saho right in the back of the head. Then Taro. Then herself with Taro's last round. Her legs quaked and almost sent her to the ground. Stomach felt like it dropped into her knees. Vision blurred. She lifted the gun as Saho looked away towards the door.

A roar erupted from just outside the open window. The trees across the street swayed and snow fell from their branches. One fell over.

"Taro," Saho said as she pushed herself away from him. Ashiya lowered the gun before the girl could see it. "That man was looking for some kind of gun. He called it an elephant gun. But he couldn't find the keys for it." She nodded at the metal case beneath a polar bear's mounted head. She took a key from out her pocket. "I think this might be it. I saw it on the floor because he knocked it down by accident. Didn't want to give it to him because I thought he was going to hurt me."

The door split down the middle. Shiny black eyes and large teeth filled the tiny gap that was now widening. A shadow filled the room from the window. Deep guttural breathing and a moist heat that came with a stench of burring garbage to it. Without looking at the window, Ashiya grabbed the key, tossed Taro her rifle, and ran to the case.

A pale head forced its way into the room through the door. Taro fired a round, and that head was no more. The body jammed the door, preventing the others from entering. Small mercies. Ashiya unlocked the case and saw the gun. A massive, gold plated, bazooka of a thing.

Ashiya glanced up and saw the bear's horrid face at the window. Jaws agape and painted with fresh blood.

Taro picked up Ashiya's rifle and fired it twice at the bear, who had now pushed its muzzle into the room. The bear quickly retreated, turned its head to the side, and let the rounds hit in the neck instead of its eyes.

The blast opened craters in its hide but did little more.

Something moved under its fur. Pulsating.

Ashiya pulled the gun from its mantle. She could barely hold it up. Taro should be the one lifting it, not her, but he was busy now. Taking his hunting knife out and slashing at pale arms pushing their way through the door. She cracked open the chamber and grabbed a round from the case. The round was twice as long as her hand and half the width.

She loaded the gun.

Taro yelled. Ashiya could see he was pushing back at the arms at the doorway. He had a deep gash on his right cheek and a tiny head of a child was biting at his knee. Saho grabbed a letter opener from the desk and rushed over to him.

"Don't you dare!" he yelled at her. "Stay back!"

She froze in the middle of the room. And behind her, Kesagake's half destroyed face came in again through the window. It reached a paw into the room and grasped the wall to the side of the window. In one movement, it ripped out the wood and widened its entry point. The other paw did the same to the other side. It started climbing into the room.

Ashiya lifted the elephant gun. She had to squat down and jerk it up like a barbell. Her knees shook and her biceps burned. No way she could hold this thing up for long.

Another pale face bit at Taro's stomach. He drove the knife into its eye and it retreated. More arms clawed at him and held him in place. He couldn't move. Saho broke free from her daze and ran to Taro. She swiped the letter opener at the hands that were now digging into Taro's legs and chest. They didn't let go.

The bear lifted its upper half into the room. All light from the outside world blocked by its girth.

Ashiya raised the gun with all the strength left in her. She felt something in her shoulder tear. A grinding pain in her lower spine. The gun was so heavy she couldn't aim it properly. Just point it in the general direction and...

BOOM!

The blast from the gun was a rocket launch. A blinding flash followed by the ringing of tinnitus and the smell of acrid smoke. The blast flung Ashiya off her feet and into the wall behind her. Gun fell to the wayside. The force ripped her right arm backward, and she felt a crunch followed by electric pain shooting through her arm.

The round hit the bear directly in the face.

The impact and searing pain, which shot up her tailbone to her neck, left her momentarily unable to comprehend the aftermath. All she was aware of was that the bear slumped down on the floor, its lower half still outside the room.

There was a buzz in her ears and the world around her moved in slow-motion. She saw Saho crawling on the floor towards Taro—who was rushing to pick her up, his clothes soaked in blood. There were no pale arms pushing their way into the room anymore. She tried to lift herself up, but the pain in her right arm was too great. Fell down on top of her right arm, rolled to her left side, and got to her knees. She finally looked at the bear; it had no head. The bloodstains on Ryoji's desk, the wall, and the mounted animals revealed what remained of the head. A medley of bone and fur and meat. The polar bear, in particular, highlighted Kesagake's blood. It was nearly black and tar-like, clumpy, and smelled of rotten meat. The blood of an animal that had been dead for a week or more. Bone fragments and sharp teeth littered the floor.

No blood spurted from the gaping wound in the neck, the cavern where the head used to be. She could see the spinal column poking out of the dark flesh. Being so close to the bear, without the immediate fear of death, she understood: this is the body of an animal long dead. She could see the bloated flesh through spaces in the fur; purple and black.

The body slid backwards as the animal's corpse fell to the ground outside.

Ashiya grabbed the wall with her left hand and stood up. She hobbled over to the jagged hole in the wall and looked down. The bear was a pile of dark matter on the white snow. It didn't move. She turned back to the red door. The gap was wide enough for any of the things in the hall to force their way in now. But they were gone.

She saw Saho crying and Taro coming over to her, saying something she couldn't hear. In fact, she couldn't hear anything. Her eardrums ached as much as her right shoulder. She could still move her arm, so it wasn't broken or dislocated at least. But her hearing...

Taro's voice grew slightly louder. Up to a murmur, as if underwater. She pointed to her ears and said, "I think the gun damaged my hearing." Or at least she hoped that's what came out of her mouth.

Taro's hard face softened. A look of concern washed over him. He moved her head from side to side and inspected her ears. Looked at her shoulder. He patted her on the head and smiled. Ashiya saw a slice on his cheek. Tears in his clothing from neck to shin. She tried to look at his wounds, but he softly batted her hand away.

Saho dove into Ashiya, nearly knocking her over. She felt the girl's chest heave as she cried into her.

"It's okay, I killed it," she maybe said.

Taro gave her a thumbs up and waved his hand over to the door. She followed him over.

Taro—with his hunting knife raised high—looked out into the hall. From his lips Ashiya thought he said, "They're gone."

She hoped that was true.

She hoped it was over.

CHAPTER 44

Ashiya watched as the flames grew higher. The great black shape in the fire's heart gave off a putrid smell. She imagined this is what Vikings of old may have smelled as they set their dead on the pyres. The world's worst barbeque.

They had poured several containers of propane from Ryoji's storage on the bear's carcass and lit it on fire. It hadn't moved since she blew its head off.

Best to annihilate it fully, just in case.

The three of them stood outside, watching the thing burn. Hoping this was the end. At least of the bear, the most dangerous of the horrors they had to face.

The Bear-teeth were nowhere to be seen. She was sure they were still around. It made little sense that they'd just vanish. They must have gone into hiding once Kesagake was dead. They were probably in the homes or in the woods, watching them, or perhaps they were inactive now that the demon was dead. It was still good to be on guard. She and Taro found Ryoji's stash of ammo in his study, hidden behind the polar bear's head, and stocked up. They even had Saho wear a backpack full of ammunition, water, food, and a space blanket they found in Ryoji's house. The man had prepared himself.

The elephant gun itself only had one round, now zero, so they left it behind.

Ashiya's hearing was still mostly gone. It had gotten better. As far as she could tell, she could at least hear the approximation of sound. She knew when Taro spoke versus Saho, but not at all what they were saying. She couldn't hear the crunch of the snow beneath her feet or the sound of the wind.

At least the blizzard had subsided. The sky was gray and murky and it was still cold, but they could see their surroundings. There was enough snow to have covered all their tracks—both feet and tire—that they had made on their way to Ryoji's front door.

She didn't spare a thought for the man. He shot Taro, kidnapped Saho, and then left them all to die in his study. Still, she imagined him meeting his end, chased by the demons into the forest. He was now one of the undead, or someone had made him a sacrifice—neither fate she'd wish on an enemy, even Ryoji.

The fire from the bear's cremation spread to Ryoji's garage. Soon, the fire would consume the entire house, and maybe even the entire block, because of the proximity of the homes. If any of the dead were hiding inside, that was a good thing.

"Taro," she said. Sure that it came out as Daro instead. "We can hike to my cabin. Find a car if we can on the way. If we can't, it's only an hour's walk from here. My car is there, we can take it as soon as the road is clear, or holdup there for as long as we need to."

Taro squinched his face and leaned his ear towards her. She hoped she was making sense to him.

His mouth moved and the underwater mumbling came through. She thought he said, "Let's move." Fuck it, assume he did.

She led the way down the street, Saho glued to her side, Taro taking up the rear.

They walked through near knee-high snow. The woods would be faster to the cabin, but there was no way Ashiya was going back in there soon. She might opt for city living from now on because of this experience. They came out of the neighborhood with no incident. She thought she saw a curtain close quickly on one house. In another, she definitely saw a pale body move back into the darkness through a window. So they were still there. Watching. But they weren't attacking, at least. She assumed there had to be more survivors in the town. No way everyone could have been taken. But now was not the time for door-to-door wellness checks. Leave that for people with more firepower. Now was the time for them to get to safety and leave as soon as possible.

They made it to the town center. Most of the shops were closed. Lights off. Doors locked. A few had their lights on. But from the outside, Ashiya could see no movement inside the bakery. No one was in the Coco Curry, despite the three cars in the parking lot. They checked the doors. All locked. They were not risking going inside the buildings to look for keys or survivors. Get themselves cornered indoors.

They passed the police station. A patrol car was out front. Locked with no keys in it. Taro went closer to the station and shouted something. Nobody came outside. He threw a chunk of ice at the window and the pane shook. Still, nobody came out.

They walked on, toes becoming numb and legs getting tired. They came to the lake on the way to her cabin. The waters frozen over and buried under snow. They saw a single figure out in the middle of the lake. Reminding her of seeing Ogoto out there on his lawn chair just a few days ago. Waving that stupid fish. Now, a white body with its arms at its side, staring down into the depths. It didn't move. Didn't lift its head as they walked by. Ashiya thought about shooting its head off while they had the chance. Thought better of disturbing whatever peace it was at.

They walked down the forested road to her cabin and shortly came upon it.

It was as she left it, aside from the solid meter of snow that now covered everything. Her car was a white mound, only the bottom of the tires and a patch of windshield visible. Ashiya wiped snow off of a tire. Imaging taking off then and there. Despite her reticence to drive on icy roads, she would have risked it then. But given how much snow was on the roads, even in town, her Jimny would never make it. If it was this bad in town, it was even worse on the mountain roads. They'd have to wait for help to come to them.

Taro handed a small handgun to Saho. She looked terrified to hold the thing. He pointed towards the woods and positioned her body that way. Ashiya set her rifle down and picked up her shovel that was on the side of the cabin, having avoided being buried because of the overhang. She went to work at uncovering her front door. Taro dove in with his hands and helped to dig it out. Saho nervously held the gun and looked out at the forest to keep watch while the adults dug out the way in.

Nothing moved within the forest.

All was quiet.

All was still.

CHAPTER 45

The fire was roaring. The windows barricaded on the outside by snow. It cut off the line of sight into the surroundings, but it was least an obstacle to anything that wanted to get inside. The only way in or out was through the front door.

Saho picked up Ashiya's busted up guitar and was murdering the strings over by the fire. Ashiya could, of all things, hear that. Taro sat in front of the door, lying against a stack of pillows, injured leg propped up on a box, rifle aimed forward. Ashiya had some rubbing alcohol and bandages in her bathroom and used them to patch him up as best she could. Most of the wounds were superficial. The gouge in his belly and the one near his clavicle were not. The bleeding had stopped, and she wrapped the gauze around him, reminding her of a time when Alexei used the same material to dress up as a mummy for Halloween. She didn't think the wounds were life threatening, but they were deep and she worried about infection. Taro grunted and said he was fine. Stop worrying. But she saw him wincing even as he said this.

His leg was a deep purple and bloated. A miracle he could have walked as far as he did. But she was sure he could do so no longer. The only way he was getting out of here was in a car. Until the roads cleared, that was not happening.

Her hearing had come back some more. She could hear what people said, but her hearing remained blunted. Hoped it would continue to get better. Feared that this was as good as it was going to get. The only constant sound she could trust was a high-pitched and ever-present hum. At least it helped to drown out Saho's guitar playing. A little.

She checked her body in the bathroom mirror. The right shoulder was a canvas of purple and black blotches. It looked like a bruised piece of fruit. More bruises lined her right side, down to her hip. She had a black right eye. Various cuts decorated her. But she was standing. She'd be fine. Or so she thought as she nearly sobbed, putting back on her thermal underwear, her ribs feeling like broken glass. Too bad she didn't have any painkillers. And this was not the time to get drunk.

Ashiya sat by Saho on the wooden bench by the fire. "Hey kid, how you holding up?" She wasn't sure if she was yelling at her or compensating too much and whispering. But the girl got it.

"Good." She stared into the fire, no authentic emotion in those eyes. Ashiya could somewhat hear what she said, but sensed the rest from her lips. "I've been thinking. Haven't seen Mom or Dad yet. I should be happy if that means they weren't... changed. But, when Ryoji drove me out of Ota, I saw... I saw bodies in the trees. I think that's where they are."

Saho said this with no inflection in her voice. As if she were reading a report on patterns of migratory birds.

Ashiya frowned and put a hand on the girl's shoulder. "Maybe you don't need to hear it, but I know what it's like to lose someone you love."

"You do?"

"Yeah. His name was Alexei, my brother."

"What happened to him? Was it a monster?"

"No. Just an animal doing what it does. It was an accident. And I've been blaming myself for years over it when it wasn't my fault. I was just a little older than you are now when it happened. But life moves on, whether or not you want it to. But the pain doesn't. It gets numb and goes quiet sometimes, but it's always there. And that's okay. The pain reminds us of their love, you know? Like it wouldn't hurt so bad if there wasn't something good there first. Sorry, I don't mean to push this on you or get you to open up or anything. Just know I'm here for you. Always."

"Even if it comes back?"

"The bear? It's dead. And the other things, they're asleep now. They didn't mess with us the whole walk out here, did they? Even if they come, we can handle them. This place is safe."

"I know you don't mean that. But, thank you."

"Okay, real shit here, kid. Maybe it's not safe. But we do got it covered. We'll wait until the roads clear. Somebody's got to notice something is wrong soon. They'll clear the roads and we'll get out of here. I promise you, even if those things come back tonight, I will let nothing happen to you." She took Saho's hands in her own and led her eyes away from the fire and onto her own. "I swear, even if I have to die to do it."

Tears fell from Saho's eyes and she hugged Ashiya.

From over Saho's shoulder, she saw Taro wipe something from his eye.

It was dark out by now, though with no clear windows or phones or watches, they had to guess. The only sound from then on was the crackle of the fire in the dark room. The infrequent strumming of Saho on the guitar until she fell asleep holding it. Ashiya caught her in time, laid her down on the mattress she had brought in from her bedroom—they would not be sleeping separately. Soon snoring came from Taro's pillow post. It was warm. Dark. Inviting.

Ashiya wanted to succumb to sleep. Exhaustion overwhelmed her. She feared that her body ached too much for her to ever fall asleep again. And her mind was on fire with anticipation. She refused to let her guard down until they were out of this town. She and Taro had already dug out her car in preparation. Hopefully, someone would clear the roads soon. She'd go up tomorrow, by herself, drive as far as she could, check the roads, and come back for them. Either to take them out of here or hunker down for another night.

It had to end soon.

She paced the room to keep awake. It wasn't too hard. The pain shooting through her body was better than caffeine. As long as she didn't sit down.

Taro's snores ripped like a chainsaw.

Good, let him sleep while he can. He needs to recover. I can stay awake.

She checked to see if her rifle was loaded. Did the same with Taro's. Also checked Saho's handgun—a parting gift from Ryoji. It had his initials R. T. emblazoned in gold on the handle. She felt bad that Saho had to carry it, but it was a necessity. She went through bags and double checked the water and the food and the clothing.

Three times over.

It must have been close to midnight by now, or at least that's how it felt to her. Ashiya kept glancing over at the two sleeping humans on her cabin floor. An immense need to protect them was swelling up in her with each passing second. And with that need, the sting of potential loss. She imagined hoards of the undead breaking into the cabin and ripping them apart.

Of the bear and its open jaws.

Even if it was nothing but ashes now, she knew nothing about what it was. Nothing about what rules governed its behavior or abilities.

And that's why I have to stay awake.

She put another log on the fire, sitting on the floor to do so. Then that was it for her. All it took was her ass touching the floor just once. Exhaustion took her.

CHAPTER 46

Red sash falling off a face with no teeth.

The blue curled smile of a little boy with black eyes.

Ogoto's head on a stick, with frozen blood forming icicles that touched the floor.

All three faces staring at her from the ceiling.

A cold draft caressed her face. It felt soothing in the cabin that had become too hot in the night. Wind danced on her cheeks. Ruffled her hair.

Wind?

Ashiya's eyes shot open. She saw the dying red embers of the fire. Felt the heat they gave off, but also felt the cold blowing in from the other side of the room. It was dark in the cabin, but there was a strange light pouring in from the doorway.

The open door.

"Taro!" she yelled as she got to her feet.

"What?" came his groggy and sleep battered voice.

"The door is open!"

Ashiya looked for Saho. She was there, by the guitar. Sleeping on her back with her arms crossed over her chest.

Taro got up on his knees, looked outside, and then pushed the door closed. Locked it.

Again.

Ashiya had checked that lock repeatedly before she went to sleep.

She flipped on a lamp. The glare momentarily blinded her. When her eyes focused, she saw Saho stretching out her arms and waking up.

Ashiya took a knee by the girl. "Hey, are you okay?"

"Mm-hmm. What's up?"

"We might be in danger. Get dressed."

Ashiya walked over to Taro, who was inspecting the floor in front of the door. Ashiya grabbed her rifle and kicked open her bedroom door—aside from the bathroom, the only other room in the cabin. Nobody was inside the closet or hiding under the bed. The windows still buried under snow.

She went to the bathroom. Nobody there either. She came back out into the main living area.

"What do you see?" she asked Taro.

"Lock wasn't broken. No scratches on the other side of the door or on the floor. Wasn't forced open."

The shock of the moment distracted Ashiya from realizing that she could hear him. The ringing was still there, a pestering fly that would probably never leave. But fuck, she could hear.

"That doesn't make sense," she said. "If it were those things, wouldn't they just break down the door? And even if they got in somehow, why didn't they attack?"

She walked over to the door. The gap between the door and threshold was lit up with a waving light from outside. It flashed blue, turquoise, green, purple.

Taro saw her looking at it. "Winter lights. Aurora Borealis. Saw it when I shut the door. But they're strange. We don't get them too often and not like this."

She wanted to ask him what he meant, but there was a more pressing matter to solve: who opened the door and why?

The door looked fine, not broken into, like Taro said. She noticed a wet sheen on the floor, just in front of the door, but going no further into the cabin.

"Look here," she said to Taro and bent down. "Somebody was standing here from outside. The size of the puddle is about the same as a person's foot. Somebody—something—was in here."

As she said these words, a sinking feeling took hold of her stomach. She shivered involuntarily. Not at the thought that one of the dead had been here. If so, it did nothing and was gone now. Unnerving as that thought was, they were fine.

Did whoever enter take just one step inside? Or did the fire dry out any other trace further in?

But... Kesagake could take the form of people—maybe other animals as well. It was dead, though. She shot its fucking head off and they burned the body.

But was it? What did she know about it? For all that she knew, it was more spirit than a physical thing.

Was it in here right now?

Taro.

Saho.

She looked Taro in the eyes. He must have had the same thought. Or, was pretending to.

They both glanced at Saho. She returned their gaze with glassy innocence.

Fuck.

"I'll just say what you're thinking," Taro let out. "One of us could be Kesagake, right?"

"Could be. Could not be."

"What are you saying?" Saho asked. A tremor coming into her voice.

Was there a way to tell? Or was she blowing this out of proportion? Maybe they were all normal, semi-functioning human beings.

But then, why was the door open?

Fuck and fuck.

Asking personal information was useless. The bear knew about Alexei and Taro's wife. It knew about Ashiya seeing the teeth in the grass.

She gripped the butt of her rifle tightly. Taro also had a weapon. Saho had a gun near her feet.

Triple fuck.

"Let's keep our heads," Ashiya said. "We don't know for sure that Kesagake is even alive or came in here. Even if it did, I will not let us turn on each other. If it is here," she turned a steely gaze on Taro and then onto Saho. The girl flinched at the intensity of Ashiya's eyes. "Then it will show itself."

"Help me!" came the scream of a young girl from outside the cabin. "Ashiya! Taro! Please!"

Saho's voice.

From somewhere beyond the front door.

Sobbing broke out. It faded away into the forest but was still audible.

The Saho in the room's knees trembled. Tears welled up in her eyes. She tried to speak but her words came out in sputters: "Not... m-m... not... me."

At least that narrows it down.

Fuck fuck and fuck.

"Saho, we need to be sure and we need to be safe," Ashiya said. "Move to the corner." She raised her rifle at the girl.

Taro pushed her gun down with force. "What the fuck are you doing!?"

"You think I want to!? All I know is that Saho is right in front of us and that is also her voice outside. So that means Kesagake is still alive, mimicking her. At least it means it's not you or me. But it could be in here with us while Saho is out there right now, needing our help."

"Doesn't mean you get to point a gun at her."

"What would you like me to do, huh? How can we be sure?"

Taro stepped in-between Ashiya and Saho—who was by now in full on meltdown, face bright red and wet, almost falling to the ground because she was shaking so badly.

Ashiya remembered Ogoto's wound and his eye. The black blood. The same color that the bear's body bled.

She felt bile rise in her throat. She was going to have to say—and do—something horrible.

"We need to... we need to cut her," Ashiya said. "If it's red and normal, she's fine. If it's black and coagulated, then we know. But we need to move fast!"

"You want to hurt me?" Saho asked. The sound of her fear pierced Ashiya's heart.

"No, honey, I don't want to hurt you. But we have to know. Just a little cut." Ashiya slipped her knife from her belt. "I promise it won't hurt."

She took a step forward, but Taro blocked her with his chest. "No."

The screaming came in again from outside.

"What if that's her!?" Ashiya screamed back. "Move!"

"No. That's not her out there. You said yourself that Kesagake doesn't imitate perfectly, that it doesn't nail down how a person acts. Does she look like she's acting weird? It's messing with us. Look at her! Don't you see you're scaring her?"

Yes, she did. And yes, she hated herself for what had to be done. But it *had* to be done. And quick.

"I know you care about her, so do I. But if you're wrong, then she is alone and in trouble right now, outside. If I'm wrong, yeah, it sucks, but it's a passing thing."

Taro's hard stare softened a bit. That look she was getting accustomed to. The stone face relaxing into something approaching a fatherly one. It looked like he was understanding what had to be done. He opened his mouth to speak when Saho hugged him from behind. He laughed at the surprise of it and placed his gloved hand on hers.

"Don't worry, little one," he said. "We must do this, but I'll make sure it's done right. Done small."

He tried to turn around and face her, but he couldn't. She held him in place.

"Done right?' Saho whispered.

As ink filled her eyes.

As she bit into Taro's ribs with a mouth too large for her head.

He yelled out in pain, but couldn't break himself from her grasp. Her tiny fingers bent in half and extended.

Ashiya didn't wait for the transformation to continue. She raised her rifle and took aim.

Saho pivoted on her feet and used Taro as a shield, still holding onto his side with her teeth. She backed up into the now cool wood-fire stove and knocked a kettle to the floor.

Taro thrust his elbows back to strike her, but she was too short for him to make contact. And too strong for him to break free.

Saho flung Taro back and forth to block Ashiya's shot at her head.

So she aimed at the feet. Clad in pink fluffy socks. She fired and blew off her left foot. Saho let go of Taro and he fell forward, motionless.

Saho fell back into the wall and slid to the ground, laughing, face still bright red—not with tears now—but with fresh blood ringed around her large mouth.

Her body convulsed, and her tiny arms flailed. Ashiya fired another round into her head. Taking half of it off. Saho flung her body facedown on the floor and quickly changed. In seconds, her spine elongated. Fur burst out of her clothing. Muscles came out of nothing. What remained of her head fell off and dissolved into wet ash. The bear emerged out of the body of the little girl.

It was headless, as Ashiya had left it. Nothing but a black pit, lined with shattered bone, remained. Smoke filled the cabin. Most of the flesh of the bear was gone. What was left was blackened and smoking fur, disintegrated muscles, and bone. It was beheaded and burned. It did not regenerate, yet it lived.

Ashiya fired two more rounds into where its heart should have been, but was now an open ribcage with sooty flesh underneath. The shots did nothing.

The body grew until its shoulders reached the ceiling and its backside shattered a window, letting in a rush of snow.

Saho's voice called out from the abyss of its throat. "Child, I am the Eater of the Dead. Eater of the Gods. Death has no hold on me. Tonight, you all shall see the eternal shores. I shall bring them to you."

Fire erupted from within the bear's hollowed out body, consuming it whole, yet it did not burn. Something white began forcing its way out from the hole in its neck. A skull emerged from the hollows of its wounds. It was like a bear's but ridged with horns along its brow and even its jaws. Fire filled the hollow skull and poured out of its eyes. A shrill cry escaped the bear's throat. But it wasn't the fierce roar nor the disturbing growl she had heard from it before. It sounded desperate and afraid. She had heard sounds like this before: animals caught in her father's traps. Legs bleeding. Crying out for life as they died slowly.

It was as if the bear itself—the original bear, not the demon—were crying out. For the briefest of moments.

The fire from its body leapt to the cabin walls and ceiling.

Ashiya kicked open the front door and threw her rifle out. Grabbed Taro by his limp hands and pulled him. It was like dragging a bag of sand. One that left behind a red trail. She was sure if it wasn't for the adrenaline of the moment, firing through her nervous system, that she would never have been able to get him out the burning house. But she did. She yanked at his arms until they both fell into the snow.

The roof collapsed, and the bear rose on its hind legs from within the cabin. A flaming demon. It crawled out of the burning wreckage and into the snow. Steam erupted all around where it stepped.

Then the bear collapsed. The fire inside it went out. Its spine rose and fell as if it were breathing, though she doubted it needed to. Moments before, the creature surged with power. Now, it was lying in a heap on the snow. *Was the body finally giving way, breaking down?*

A tar-like tendril unfurled from its open mouth. It slowly made its way over to Ashiya like a worm inching its way forward. She picked up her rifle and fired at it. The snake-like thing recoiled and latched itself onto a nearby tree.

Saho's screams for help in the woods. The creature lifted its head—its monstrous skull—towards the sound. More tendrils burst out of its corpse and took hold of tree trunks. They pulled the body of the bear away and into the woods. Slowly. Soon after, the screams faded. Soon the bear was out of sight.

The sky was alive with color. It might have been beautiful. She didn't care or take stock of it. She flipped Taro over onto his back. The sounds of the bear dragging its body through the snow grew faint.

Taro flitted his eyes towards hers. He tried to raise his left arm but let it drop loosely into the snow.

The bite exposed his left ribs. The bones broken in half by the bite. She saw a fleshy movement inside his body, pulsating. It might have been his lungs, failing. Blood flooded out of the wound. Staining the snow red. It joined the colors of the Northern Lights above. It was almost beautiful. And she still didn't care.

"I'm so sorry," she said as she held his head up onto her knees, stroking his face.

A gargled sputter escaped his mouth.

"T-th...gr..l."

He smiled. It still didn't suit him, but she thought it was okay. He flashed his teeth at her.

"Ma...Ma...Maya.."

And then he stopped. His eyes open wide, looking up at the dancing colors of red and blue streaking across the night sky, lighting up his face.

He was beautiful. And she finally cared.

CHAPTER 47

She left Taro's body in the snow aside the burning cabin.

She couldn't hear Saho screaming anymore. If she was even there in the first place. If she was even alive anymore, that is.

Ashiya looked up at the sky. Blue fire danced with red waves. The colors changed and unfurled across the sky. They even bled down to just above the treetops, lighting the tips of the branches. The lights were everywhere. They lit up the forest in their kaleidoscopic glory. But she didn't feel warmth or hope in these lights. She felt the arrival of something horrible. As if the lights were a herald of something worse than the bear.

The bear wasn't the true danger, was it? It was what lived inside the bear. She heard it in the animal's cry as it burned. The bear itself was not a demon. This was an animal infected by something else. By the Eater of the Dead, the Eater of the Gods. By something that was not from this world. Something that had taken the bear's body for its own. A parasite.

She didn't know what this meant, but couldn't think of what to do. She imagined herself lying in the snow next to Taro. The fire from the cabin would keep her warm enough until she fell asleep. And then she could just stay there. Let the cold claim her body.

She thought about the damage she had done to Kesagake. Blew its head clean off, burned its body, and still it rose. Guns and fire did nothing but prolong the inevitable.

This Eater of the Gods and of the Dead was something beyond—not just comprehension—but outside her ability to do anything about it. As the bear rose from the burning cabin, it collapsed and escaped. It could have killed her. She didn't believe that it was toying with her this time. The bear's body reached its breaking point and could no longer move. Except for the stringy black tentacles that shot out of it.

She watched her cabin burn. Embers danced up into the sky and joined an amber wave of light that flashed out of the sky like a flare.

The air was not only freezing; she could feel a pressure building around her. Like a quick rise in elevation. The familiar headache—the sign that *it* was near, she was sure—returned and intensified beyond what it ever was before. She cradled her face in her hands and rocked back and forth.

"All so fucking worthless."

She tried so hard. To stay alive and keep others alive. To protect Saho. To forget her brother's face and the teeth that lay in the grass. Add to that Hikari's head getting blown off by the rifle and now Taro's quivering lungs.

And Saho's screams.

But no matter what she did, the horrors only multiplied. Caring only made it hurt more.

She looked at her gun. It had one shot left in it. Taro's gun, and all the ammo, plus all her supplies, were left in the burning cabin.

Quicker than waiting for the cold to take her.

And why shouldn't she?

There was nobody left. The demon was still out there. The lights in the sky and her pounding head spoke of something terrible to come. Even if she had more guns, at best she could mow down the human puppets. But what could she do against this God-Eater? Something that was beyond the touch of death, or so it said.

And there was no cabin left to go to. Hers would be ashes soon. The night was well below zero. Even if Saho was alive out there, it would only be a matter of hours before both of them would join the ranks of the naked and pale forms that walked in the snow.

Just use my last round. Put it in my mouth and bam, all gone.

She put the barrel into her mouth.

The cold steel made her wince and the taste of pennies made her sick.

She closed her eyes.

Finger on the trigger.

I'm so sorry Alexei, I couldn't hold on. I'm not strong enough. See you soon.

Her index finger curled around the trigger. She thought of how good it would be to be done with it all. Not just the insanity of demon bears and the undead. But of life. No more bad dreams. No more guilt over what she should have done. She told Saho she didn't blame herself anymore, but that was not entirely true. There still was—would always be—that clinging despair wrapped around her throat like an anchor threatening to drown her in the sea of her "should have dones."

Saho's face flashed in her mind. Her fear. Her laughter. She might still be out there.

Even so, what the fuck can I do about it?

Her finger pressed the trigger down halfway. She felt the click, and then she relaxed her grip. Pulled the gun out of her mouth. Let it fall in the snow.

She couldn't do it. As much as she welcomed death, she just couldn't. Not like this, at least.

She stood up, looked down at Taro's stiff body, eyes opened up to the spectacular light show of the heavens, his gray eyes reflecting a bright emerald shine.

Ashiya walked past his stiff corpse and away from the warmth of the burning cabin. Some flames were now lighting a nearby tree on fire. She entered the surrounding forest, to a clearing covered by branches holding up heavy loads of snow. The lights in the sky didn't shine as much here.

She laid down on her back in the snow.

Closed her eyes.

And waited for a cold death to take her.

CHAPTER 48

She stayed like that for what must have been half an hour. Her face, fingers, ass, and toes were numb.

Good, it's starting.

The winter lights flared up above her. For a moment, their light brightened her dark hovel as if it were day. She opened her eyes. The lights were red and orange. Dancing amongst the treetops in wavy patterns. The trees by the cabin—five at least—were now on fire despite the cold.

It was difficult for her to keep her train of thought. She was drowsy. Already falling victim to hypothermia. But as the lights flared up, she felt the air freeze over even more. A sudden drop in what was already a deathly cold. She felt someone near her. She sat up and looked around. Nobody there. She heard a faint whistle of wind, or it could have been the beginnings of a whisper.

In the hollow, as crimson light cascaded down, she almost saw a person standing before her. As the light surged, it became clearer. As the light diminished, so did the figure.

Another drop in temperature. And with it a sudden feeling of terror. Of being chased through the woods. Of watching a friend die. Of the anxiety and stress of having quit drinking. The desire to save loved ones. But these were not her feelings. They belonged to another. They enveloped her like a wet, cold blanket.

Taro's words, back in Saho's cabin, came back to her. Something about the solstice being the time when things slip through from that other side. And wasn't the solstice tonight? Ashiya assumed, if it were true, that only dark and evil things would creep through in the dark. But what if *others* could as well?

She stood up. So cold her teeth chattered against her will.

A red shadow of a man flashed in front of her before dissipating.

"Ogoto?"

His face materialized in the lights. For only a moment. But she saw his foolish smile beam out at her.

Tears stung her eyes.

"Can you hear me?"

He was gone. As were the feelings that had assaulted her.

Another image appeared, further away, near Taro's body. The lights above changed to a blueish green. She walked over to his corpse. Standing above it, she could see a faint mirage of a short and broad-shouldered man. He swiveled his face towards her and disappeared.

Warmth filled her bones. The cozy wrappings of love. Tinged with the sorrow of loss. She couldn't see him anymore, but she felt Taro's presence near her. Then came the terror. A feeling of drowning. Of something cold and black seizing the throat. Of water filling the lungs. Screaming with none to hear.

Looking down, she could see Taro's skin turning white. Not just from the shutting down of his vital organs. His gray-blue eyes were darkening. Like ink clouding up a glass of water. The feelings of love were being squeezed out by something else.

She thought she could hear a voice. A man saying, *Please.* Only a wisp in the wind.

Taro's hands convulsed. The black filled his eyes completely. His teeth cracked as something larger started protruding out from within them.

Embers from the cabin floated over his pale face. Like falling stars.

"Please, do it."

She heard Taro's voice in the falling fire. His body twitched. In moments, he would rise.

She unsheathed her knife. Bent over his body as his head slowly turned to watch her.

"I'm sorry," she said as she drove the knife down and released him.

She didn't have the strength to bury him. The best she could do was cover Taro's body in the snow. She grabbed a nearby soccer ball sized rock and put it near his head.

Despite being raised Orthodox, she never believed in God. She didn't know what Taro believed in. But she couldn't let this moment pass without saying something.

The sparks from the cabin and the trees danced around her like fireflies. More trees had caught fire. Soon she would either have to leave or let the smoke take her.

She looked up at the swirling of light above.

"Taro, I hope you find peace. I hope you find Maya. Somewhere out there."

There were no more voices or borrowed feelings from him. She hoped that, by destroying the thing that took over his body, that he was at rest now. That by honoring his death, his kamuy would find its way home.

"Anastasia."

The voice was clear. And loud. And right next to her face.

She screamed and backed up. She could see no one. But the feeling that latched onto her was one she hadn't known for years. It was laughter under a blue sky. It was sarcasm behind a smile. It was the love of a brother.

"Alexei.." her voice trembled, and she nearly fell to her knees.

Through the flurry of embers, she saw his face. Terror seized her. Fear that she would see *that* face. Red sash removed. Forever haunting her. For a moment, she saw her brother walking in the fire under the Northern Lights. He was smiling. A full smile. With all his teeth intact.

"Anastasia, hold on."

Those were the only words he said. But deep down, she knew it was him. Those words and that smile hooked her heart and tore something open. Something that had been locked away most of her life. He wasn't angry at her. He wasn't dangling from the dark ceiling of her cabin; toothless. Skull crushed. He was smiling. And she felt the love he had for her.

She looked at him. Truly let herself look at him. He wasn't the ghoul that had plagued her nightmares all these years. He was just as he was before that day he left this world. Her heart split with grief even then; yet there was something sweet about it as well. It was a beautiful sadness that filled her.

Alexei faded away in a wash of blue light.

That light shone down from the sky to the snow by her feet. She felt lightheaded. For a moment like she was flying. In the light, she saw a bear walking through the forest. A regular every day bear, awake too soon, looking for food. She saw a man crouching behind the bear, a man with a large smile, Ryoji. He shot the bear in the neck and the bear ran from him. The light flickered and took her to a den in the snow where the bear curled up, waiting to die from its injury. She felt the pain and the fear and the loneliness that it did. Then the bear died choking on its own blood. Then she felt *it.* She felt a cold blackness latch onto the bear. Something that came from deep within the soil. It wormed its way into the bear's flesh.

Something that came from the other side. Something that ruled and ate the dead. Something that was let in by... what? She felt that this was the key to understanding this Eater of the Gods.

The image of the bear faded and bled into the surrounding light.

A great roar arose from somewhere deep in the woods. A rush of whispers like the bubbling of a brook crashed into the clearing.

Just beyond the cabin, she could see them. Dozens of shining black eyes, reflecting the fire. They rushed around the clearing, skirting her peripherals, and moved on, deeper into the woods, towards the sound of their master's call.

She watched as the undead ran through the forest, away from the fire, leaving her behind. They didn't want her. They were running to the bear.

The roar came again. No longer desperate and full of pain. It was a victory cry. Stronger than it had at the cabin. It sounded... bigger.

Ashiya didn't know if Saho was still alive. But even if she wasn't, Ashiya couldn't let this thing win. It wouldn't stop here at Kamuy-Kotan, would it? It controlled the dead and ate their souls. She imagined it spreading throughout Hokkaido and the rest of Japan. Even beyond that? She imagined all the death and the pain that was in store for those that the bear set its sights on.

"Alexei, Taro, Ogoto, Hikari, Itsuki, Ren. Help me, please."

She repeated the chant of their names over and over again. Each time she did, she felt a rush of heat fill her veins. The numbness in her body melted away. She felt a fire kindled from within. Their names became a drumbeat that lifted her dead spirit from its icy grave.

Her hands felt hot.

One of the undead, the last one who had skirted the clearing and hadn't gone out of sight yet, stopped in its tracks and turned to face her. As if sensing the new heat she felt coursing through her veins. Its pale face reflected the yellow lights in the sky, but the eyes stayed the same; endless pits of dark night. It flashed its teeth at her. It rushed out from the forest and across the clearing at her. She didn't know who it had been before; the man running at her at full speed, but she felt pity for him.

"I'm sorry this happened to you," she said calmly, as she picked up and raised her rifle, knowing she had one round left. She pulled the trigger, and the shot rang out, hitting the man directly in the face, obliterating it entirely. Pieces of his skull flew across the clearing in misty crimson streaks. His body collapsed into the snow.

No pounding heart. No regrets. She was master of herself in that moment.

They are with me.

She felt the pressing of many hands enfolding her own. It was warm. It was powerful. She wanted to cry. Wanted to laugh.

They are with me.

Ashiya went back to the cabin to her makeshift archery range. Found her bow and five arrows in a quiver under the hay barrel. A heavy branch above spared it from being buried under the snow. She slung her bow and quiver over her shoulders. She kept the names of the dead on her lips, believing that they would walk with her into the darkness.

And into the darkness, she walked.

CHAPTER 49

She walked into the forest, away from the now destroyed cabin. The fire was spreading from tree to tree, almost chasing after her. The path ahead led deep into the woods, where she first saw the mutilated deer before all this started, the herald of what was to come.

She should have been freezing cold, but the fire within kept her from feeling it. She didn't know if that was what was actually happening—if *they* were with her—or if she was losing her mind because of hypothermia, but she knew she was walking forward to end this.

Somehow.

Embers from the burning trees fell like lightly falling snow. The winter lights danced in their now crimson glow. They had been red ever since she left the cabin. The world was afire with the blood-red shade of a fresh kill.

Alexei. Taro. Ogoto. Hikari. Itsuki. Ren.

Saho.

Their names drove her on into the woods. Their names drove the pounding pain of her headache away.

A pattering of feet in the snow. Somebody running. Behind her.

She spun around and saw a woman sprinting towards her. Running atop the snow. Feet not sinking down into it. Smiling her sharp bear trap teeth. Naked and yet not cold.

Ashiya nocked the arrow, drew the bowstring, and fired. Didn't even give herself time to aim for the head. The arrow hit the woman in the neck—where it lodged itself—and the woman fell face forward into the snow. Ashiya didn't give her time to rise. She ran over to the woman and pushed her body over with a kick. The woman was momentarily stunned. Black blood bubbled up from her throat in cadence with her breath. Ashiya plunged her knife into one eye, then the next. The woman's feet twitched. The blood stopped bubbling. She stopped moving.

Ashiya wiped the knife on her pant legs and sheathed it. Her arrow broke in the woman's neck and was useless. She got up and moved forward, scanning her sides. Looking for tracks of any kind. All she had to go on was where she thought she heard the roar come from. But given the recent attack, she felt like she must be on the right path.

She crossed over a frozen brook. Almost slipped on the ice but caught her balance. Climbed the banks on hands and knees.

Then she found the first set of tracks. Deer tracks leading from the brook in a straight line ahead of her. Puddles of water filed every track when it should have been too cold for that to happen. Wherever the deer stepped, melted snow.

The red lights in the sky reflected off the trees and made it hard to see what was in front of her. The fire from the cabin raced ahead to her left, far away enough to not be an immediate concern, but too close to ignore it. She feared it would circle around her and leave her cut off from escape. The smell of smoke was strong, but not enough to make her cough. Not yet.

Ahead of her, framed by the red light, a shadow stepped into view. As it moved forward, she could see its pale skin. Its black eyes. Its great antlers stretching as wide as a man is tall.

The deer stepped forward. The closer that it got, she could see that most of the flesh was gone. Hundreds of bite marks pocked the animal until it was mostly bone and ragged muscle. Its intestines trailed out of its midsection as it dragged them across the snow. Fire burned inside the rib cage and melted the snow at its feet. It flashed the large and sharp teeth of a predator.

So, it doesn't just resurrect humans. Fantastic.

The deer lifted its bulk onto its hind legs and stood there like that, like a person. Its spine extended and its forelegs cracked and lengthened. Its midsection was a waste of a thing; hardly there at all. Its ribs frayed out to the sides, exposing the flaming innards; a line of fire trailed the organs that draped down to the snow. Its obsidian eyes shone in the darkness, reflecting no light.

The deer-thing towered over her and reached up to the tops of the trees. A nightmare of shadow and flame.

The behemoth struck out a gnarled limb towards her. The twisted hoof formed a hook. She shot an arrow at the head. The arrow struck an antler and split in half.

Fuck.

Ashiya threw her body back as the claw swiped above her head. She landed in the snow and rolled herself to the side just as another hoof came crashing down where she had fallen. She got up and scrambled away from the thing. It lunged forward. She turned and ran. She dove between two close-growing trees, too narrow for the deer to follow. The deer-thing crashed into the trees and the snow on the branches shook loose. She got to her feet. Turned around. Strung her bow. A spidery limb wrapped around the side of a tree and was followed by the tips of an antler. Ashiya ran the other way, to the other side of the tree. The deer bent its head backwards in a way it should not have been able to and met her eyes with its own. Ashiya fired an arrow. Right into the left eye.

It howled and kicked out a hoof at her. Hit her in the chest and she flew backwards. All the air knocked out of her as she coughed and struggled to breathe. In seconds, the deer-thing was on her. Pinned her down by her shoulders with its forelegs. The hooves dug into her shoulders with searing pain. Black ooze poured from the left eye—the arrow still in it. It unhinged its jaw and made to clamp down on her head.

The only weapon in reach was the arrow in its eye. But its hooves held both of her arms in place. In moments, the deer-thing would shut its jaws on her head. Ending her instantly. The hooves tore her flesh, and she felt a hot fault line growing from shoulder to elbow. If she moved her arm, it could tear even more. But if she didn't, she'd be dead. Not a hard decision.

She screamed and pulled her left arm from under the hoof. The jagged hoof cut across her shoulder. Ripped the flesh down to her triceps. Ashiya never knew she could experience something so painful. The undoing of tendons like string to a flame. But she pulled her arm and let the hoof carve out her muscle. Freed her arm just as its head lowered down to her own. Grabbed the arrow. Snapped the shaft off—the head stayed in the eye. And drove the splintered wood into its other eye.

The deer-thing collapsed on her immediately and became immobile. It was mostly bone and not very heavy. But the flames from its ribcage lapped at her feet. She crawled out from under it and rolled onto her back.

She looked up at the sky. Waves of green light rolled over the cool blackness of space and the diamond stars.

"Alexei, please help me."

The pain shot up into her neck and then her face and even her sides. Like someone was cutting into her nerves with a box cutter.

She passed out.

CHAPTER 50

Saho sat in the corner of a dark janitor's closet with her arms wrapped over her knees.

She lost track of how many times her knees slapped against each other. The shivering was uncontrollable at this point. Her feet were blocks of ice, her socks thoroughly soaked, her shoes nowhere in sight. She had only known cold this bad once before in her life. When she was six, her Mom let her play in the backyard during the New Year's holiday at her grandmother's house. Grandmother had a big Akita dog back then. A fluffy monster named Cookie. She chained him up to a post and even though he snarled at the neighbors and the delivery guys, and even at Dad, he was a big softie around Saho. On that day, she ran up to him and hugged him, burying her face in his ocean of white and tan fur. The snow swallowed her up to her waist, but she was wearing snow-proof pants, so it was alright.

Cookie got a little too happy to see her, though. Jumped on top of her and pushed her down into the snow. He only meant to say hi she was sure, but in that moment his affection could have killed her. He jumped on her and pressed her down into the snow so far that she could see walls of ice towering above her. They collapsed and fell on top of her, along with the dog's paws.

She couldn't breathe. She thrashed her arms, but the snow was too heavy. And Cookie just didn't understand what he was doing. He eventually calmed down enough for her to pull her face, but not her whole head, out of the snow.

She screamed for Mom but later found out she was engrossed in some stupid TV show and couldn't hear her. And this was even before all the drinking started. Grandmother was asleep too. So, Saho was stuck like that, buried up to her neck in snow, for twenty minutes, screaming until her throat felt like gravel. No amount of snow-proof pants could keep her dry then. It was a wet freeze that seeped down through her skin and into her bones.

That was how she felt now. Frozen down to her core. Suffocating under the weight of something she couldn't move. Alone and forgotten.

She blamed herself for her situation. If she would have just ignored that voice! She was sleeping nice and warm in the cabin with Ashiya and Taro when she heard Dad's voice. She could swear she even heard Cookie bark, although he's been dead for two years now. Dad called her Bean, and, despite knowing it was impossible, a desperate need to see him overwhelmed her. Mom's voice was there, too. Never mind all the times Saho tried to convince herself that she hated the woman, deep deep down, in the places she didn't know existed, there was still love laced in that hate.

She got up and opened that door. There was no room for rational thought. Something compelled her to do it. Like someone was pulling at her feet with a fishing line.

Stupid stupid stupid.

A not-so-small part of her believed it had to be her parents. She never saw their bodies, did she? She never saw them with those scary black eyes and those knife-like teeth, did she?

As she opened the door, something instantly pulled her out. All she could remember was flying, the ice-wind slamming into her face. Didn't even have time to scream. Then she landed with a thud on the hard snow. Flung out like trash into the bin. She got up and was fine and all—physically, at least—but she did not know where she was. Whatever had taken her was long gone.

She called out for Taro and Ashiya and ran blindly into the woods until she found this big abandoned warehouse looking place. It was unlocked. The inside was dark and scary and smelled like Grandmother's nightgown, but it was some safety at least. Inside was big, dark, and full of large machinery and piles of logs. Some chains clanked overhead. It was too dark to see anything properly.

Saho was going to stay here until sunrise, walking in circles, rubbing her arms for warmth. She wondered if she should take off her socks. The wet fabric was hard and frozen now. But would the granite floor be any better? Then she heard the roar. And soon after, the sound of hundreds of feet running through the snow, just outside the building.

That's when she hid in the closet. And that's when the suffocating darkness and the wet cold brought back the memories of Cookie on New Year's day. She just then realized that Taro reminded her of that dog and that must have been why she liked him so much. Big and fluffy and strong. She couldn't wait to see him again. Couldn't wait to see Ashiya. Then she'd feel safe.

Strange lights filtered into the closet through cracks and gaps in the warped wood of the ceiling. Blues and greens and even reds. Somehow, the lights made her feel more cold and alone than she already was. They looked like a Disneyland Christmas show. But something inside her told her to not let them touch her. So she tried to shrink even more into the corner of that closet.

She hid her face behind a mildew-smelling coat that hung inside it. The only article of clothing there. It was in shredded strips and she was sure if it were summer, there'd be spiders and cockroaches living inside it. Maybe even snakes.

The roar came again. From the monstrous bear that took her family. It sounded like it was right outside the building.

A heavy *scrunch* of snow outside. Another one. Big footsteps of the thing as it came near the wall of the closet. The skittering of much smaller feet—dozens or even hundreds of them—some distance further away. Saho covered her mouth and held her breath. She remembered one time Mari came over and showed her a Taiwanese ghost game. You had to keep yourself from breathing when they passed by because that's how they saw you. She didn't sleep properly for weeks after that, and Dad didn't let Mari spend the night again. Saho was kind of sad about that. But she was glad she didn't have to play those games anymore. Only, she'd given anything now for this to be a stupid game.

The heavy footsteps stopped near her, on the other side of the flimsy wall—so thin and brittle even she could probably break through it.

She shook as she held onto her breath. It felt like her head was going to explode. The footsteps picked up again and moved away from the wall.

She let out a breath as if she had just come up for air from underneath that pit of snow and Cookie's paws.

The outside world grew quiet and she couldn't hear the bear anymore. But the lights still danced through the gaps in the wall. A ray of light filtered down from a hole in the ceiling; a pinkish light that looked like bubble gum, and landed on her left foot. She pulled her foot back into her butt as if the light were a fire.

"Saho," came a voice from the other side of the wall. From outside.

She didn't gasp. Didn't even cry. She sucked in another breath and held it. She knew that voice. If she heard it one more time, her mind might snap.

"Hello Bean," came Dad's voice. Soft and tender, yet distant and cold all at once. "What are you doing in there? All alone in that nasty place."

The same feeling that had compelled her to open the cabin door welled up in her again. That fishing line wrapped itself around her feet once more. But she knew better now. As much as she wanted to believe that Dad was okay, she knew he wasn't. It was his voice, but did not speak how he spoke. It was using the right words, but with none of the levity of her Father.

A scratching at the wall. "Darling, why don't you come out of there? I can show you the everlasting shores. No more cold. No more monsters—"

"You are a monster!" Saho cried out. Surprised that a shout like that could even come out of her. "I will never come with you!"

Dad stopped talking but kept scratching at the wall.

A full minute passed. Saho stopped trying to hold her breath.

"Hmm. You see Bean, we need you to say yes. Will you say that for me? My friend needs a new body. He's just a cuddly old bear but His flesh has failed. And He is so close to entering this world. Then He won't need a body at all! Just come on out and I will make all the scary things go away. Or... make me come in there and get you and then you'll see my face. My true face." His voice deepened, and he growled and snarled as he spoke. "Then I will take you to where the gods rot and force you to watch as I devour their sacred flesh. You can be a vessel or an offering. Which is it?"

Saho shook, and the tears washed over her face. *Those would freeze over later*, she thought. *If there was a later.*

In a shaking voice, she said, "No."

The scratching at the wall stopped.

And then the boards burst inwards like a truck had rammed into the wall.

A pale face—one she knew all too well—with black eyes that hid all of Dad's kindness, forced its way through the splintered wood.

It smiled as its clawed hands took hold of her sleeve.

And then she screamed.

CHAPTER 51

High-pitched screams cut through the gray land of Ashiya's dreams. They were familiar screams. They were Saho's.

Ashiya forced her eyes opened and pushed her body off of the snow. As she did so, pain ripped across her torn flesh and she fell back down into the snow. Saho screamed again. From somewhere not too far away.

Come on you bitch, get up. This is nothing.

She clenched her jaws tight and pushed her body up again. Lightning crackled in her brain and her exposed muscle tissue felt like someone had dumped a bucket of salt on them. She got to her knees. Sweating. Heart beating against her ribcage. She brought one knee to standing and forced her body to her feet. Her arms and chest were in searing pain. Fresh blood leaked down from her wounds and into the snow.

Blood and snow. Death and life. Light and dark.

She laughed like a madwoman. Was this it? No beauty without ugliness? No joy without pain? Warmth filled her again. The pain subsided a little. Still there, aching and sharp, but not as intense. She knew that somehow the spirits of those whom she loved were with her. Keeping her held together. It should have been amazing; this miracle. Her wounds should have kept her immobile. But it felt like duct tape holding together a submarine. She felt she would not survive this much longer.

The entire forest behind her was ablaze with fire. The winter lights were a deep red, almost a purple, now. Like an ocean of blood writhing in the sky.

All snow now covered anew in blood. All good things buried under death.

Something is coming.

Those didn't feel like her thoughts. But she knew they were true.

Ashiya stumbled into the dark towards the sound of the screams.

The arrow flew through the chill air and pierced the man's right eye, spinning him around. His face slammed into a tree stump—with a crack—and his lower back twitched. He rose, placing his bony hands onto the stump, and pushing himself back up.

Before he—*it*—even had a chance to react, the hunting blade swung from the dark and into its left eye and it fell down dead.

Ashiya pulled her knife and the arrow out of the thing's head. Trying her best to not notice his—its!—face. It was good old Gray Beard. She felt no joy in taking out the man that had almost blown her head off during the search party. She felt great pity for the thing that now lay at her feet.

Ashiya nocked the arrow, ready to let it loose again. The pain in her arms lashed out just as the warmth that came from nowhere fought it back. She felt lightheaded, no telling which side would win: mortal wounds or whatever this power surging through her was. Yet she knew that this was only possible because of the solstice. While the barrier between worlds was at its thinnest.

Come the morning... well, let's not think about that.

Ashiya crouched as she moved through the forest. She couldn't see any other of the dead, advanced with caution, looking up into the trees, just in case. The forest thinned out to a sudden descent.

In front of her, a porcelain-like corpse stood with its back to her. Looking down the hill. She stopped walking. To go any further would surely alert it to the sound of her footsteps in the snow. She heard whispering and the low moan of the bear, just down the hill.

Have to kill this thing without it being able to make sound.

She aimed her bow. Steadied her breath. Pull back the string. Her lacerated muscles screamed out for her to stop. The gashes in her arms felt like they were about to rip open like a tear in a shirt. The warmth filled her like a drug and pushed the pain down. She let the arrow fly. Right into the back of the corpse's neck and out the center of its throat. It fell to its knees, but quickly grabbed for the arrow and began yanking it out. A gurgled yawning sound escaped its throat as it tried to yell but couldn't. Ashiya raced across the distance between them, readied another arrow, and fired it at the face. It raised its hand in time to block the arrow and it pierced right through the hand, sticking it to the forehead. Before it could rip the arrow out, Ashiya was on it.

Knife ready.

Down the hill Ashiya saw it all. The lumber yard and mill that Ogoto pointed out to her all those months ago. Piles of wood buried under the snow. The derelict tractors. The rickety warehouse. The clearing it all stood in.

Ringed around the entire snowy meadow were hundreds of white bodies with black eyes. Some were in the trees, hunched over and looking into the clearing. Most were standing atop the snow as if they weighed nothing. Their onyx eyes somehow glittered like vacant stars. They swayed and lifted their wasted arms. A low humming, something discordant and unsettling, groaned to life from their dead throats.

Saho was being pinned down in the snow by the corpse of a man in the center of the clearing.

Near them was Kesagake. It lay in the snow. Seemingly incapable of much movement. The body pulsed as tendrils flailed out of it. The skull looked more alien than something that belonged on any terrestrial animal. Almost as if some new organism was emerging from the husk of the bear. Nearly all of its flesh was gone. Just tatters of blackened meat and fur clung to it. Fire burned from within its ribcage, same as the deer's.

Ashiya could rush in and—do what? They would immediately swarm her. Then they would kill her and turn her into one of them. Or—she shivered at the thought—skin her alive as an offering. But if she didn't act, Saho was dead. Or worse. The creature—the God-Eater—said that tonight it would bring the eternal shores, whatever the fuck that meant. The sky raged in its crimson display. She knew beyond any doubt that something new was about to show itself.

The bear suffered for days because of the wound Ryoji opened up in its neck. It died alone and in great pain. And that's what attracted the God-Eater. That's what let it in. And what had Saho experienced, if not great suffering, these past few days? By the looks of it, Saho was not being killed or skinned. It looked like a ritual was about to take place. The horrid humming coming from the dead was like some infernal chorus.

So, after all this lovely analysis, what the fuck are you going to do?

She let out a prayer through the clouded air, escaping her lips. "Alexei, please help me, like you did before. Taro. Ogoto. Hikari. Itskui. Ren. I need you all now."

On a night like this, anything seemed possible. The very heavens were bleeding down into the valley in hellish glory. All while an army of the undead led by a demonic bear held vigil below. The barrier was weak. Why can't this work? "Please, I need you all. I need your help."

The temperature plummeted around her. The gashes in her arms—instead of being relieved by the cold—felt like they were being torn apart by it. She clenched her teeth as tears filled her eyes. She felt like passing out again. Blue light from above, like fire, lit up the snow at her feet.

A day-long hangover. The smell of bleach in a hospital waiting room. Stew with too much salt in it. A video game being played with a friend. And her brother's smile. All these sensations flooded her. They were with her; she was sure of it. Just as they had been before, picking her up, numbing her body to the effects of the cold and the searing pain in her flesh.

"Please, draw them away."

The feelings left her. Like water evaporated in the fire. She felt empty. But the blue light was still at her feet. It moved away from her. It washed down the hill and across the clearing. Passing over the heads of the damned. It raced to the tree line on the other side of the valley, lighting up the trees like St. Elmo's fire. From her distance, she could barely see it. But there was a person standing in that azure fire. Arms waving wildly overhead. She thought she heard him yell something.

And so did the hoard of the dead.

As one, they let out a screech that destroyed any beauty in the lights. A sound that scarred the soul. She was sure—if she survived this—that it would be a sound to haunt her sleepless nights for years to come. They rushed across the clearing towards the figure in the blue fire light. They leapt from their tree branches and flew across the now red snow, lit up the lights in the sky. The figure disappeared deeper into the woods until she could no longer see the glow of its presence.

The man pinning Saho down and the bear stayed where they were. Watching as the rest of the dead fled in pursuit.

Ashiya stood quickly and fired her arrow at the man. It soared through the crimson haze, but missed his eyes. It struck him in the cheek and knocked him off of Saho. Rising to her feet, the girl ran toward the mill's large warehouse. The man thrashed around in the snow. The bear watched as the girl sprinted into the decrepit building. Then it turned its gaze towards the hill.

Ashiya ran down the hill towards the bear, nearly stumbling over herself. The bear rose from the ground and stood on its hind legs. Somehow still able to hold its body erect. Fire poured out of its empty eye sockets. She knew behind them lay an eternal darkness. The skull wrenched open its jaws and it let out a roar. Tendrils twitched and curled around it.

Ashiya ran headlong towards the thing.

CHAPTER 52

Saho squeezed through a hole in the mill's side. The edges of the hole were jagged and rusted over. Her shirt got tore up, but it missed touching her skin. She found herself in a near total darkness. Saho got on her feet and ran, immediately bumping into something large and metal. Her knees hurt.

A sound of something soft ripping. She looked behind her. The hole lit up red by the strange lights in the sky; and saw Dad, naked, forcing his way through the hole, the jagged edges ripping off strips of his back. His smile and his eyes flashed in the dark. Making it somehow even darker.

Saho held back a scream and turned around. Walking quickly—not running—with her hands out in front of her. She brushed her hands against a chain and nearly peed herself.

"Saho, come back. Let us embrace you."

Saho saw the faint image of what might be a staircase to her left and ran to it. She nearly tripped on the first step, but quickly found her footing and ran to the top. Behind her, she heard Dad's foot make landfall on the first step. She tried to open the only door she could find on the landing: locked. No windows to break. She looked to her left. Nothing but an open space and a drop into a void.

Dad was halfway up the stairs now.

The only thing visible was his smile and his eyes. Like a hollowed out crescent moon, the teeth reflected crimson light. The black eyes glistened.

Ashiya shot an arrow. Missed. It got lodged in the bear's chest. She ran forward and fired her last arrow at the bear. It drove itself straight into one of its flaming eyes. The creature howled. She flung her bow to the side and took out her knife. The bear towered over her, flaming, like something out of nightmarish myth. She ran and dove in-between its legs. Somersaulted to the other side. Thrust out her knife and slashed at its Achilles tendon on the left leg. Despite there being some muscle still attached to the bone, the attack did nothing.

The bear spun around with a speed that didn't fit its size. Its flaming leg smacked into Ashiya and sent her flying into the snow. Air left her lungs without so much as a goodbye. She gasped and coughed and struggled to her feet.

Blinding pain. A firestorm in her brain. She saw purple blotches even with her eyes open. The bear rushed her and snapped its jaws around her right ankle. It lifted her off the ground; she swayed upside down like a fish on a hook. She looked up and flung her knife at the bear's other eye. Missed. The knife fell uselessly to the ground. She felt something snapping in her ankle. The fire in the bear's mouth burned her skin. The teeth closed around her ankle and sank in deep. It released her and Ashiya fell to the ground on her head. Without letting up, the bear's great skeletal paw swatted her, and she went flying into the side of the mill.

"Come and give us a kiss," Dad said. Standing not even a meter away from Saho. The bear roared outside as if in pain. Shortly after, the tin walls rattled.

Dad stepped closer. Saho could see the torn flesh. Multiple bite marks had created a hole in his chest, revealing his heart. It didn't beat. The frozen blood all over his skin. It gleamed in the little light that stole its way through the gaps in the roof.

Dad reached forward with his arms outstretched as if to embrace Saho.

Saho turned and jumped into the darkness.

Arms outstretched.

Even turning her head felt like an ice pick was being driven into her brain through her eyes. Her skull felt like it could fall into pieces at any moment. Soon, the heat from the bear's open maw washed over her. The beast leaned over her. Placed one paw on her chest and pushed her down. Her spine felt ready to break.

It may have been out of pure spite for taking its head earlier, or maybe it got some sick joy from torturing others, but the bear didn't end her right away. The paw on her chest grew smaller, but lost none of its strength to hold her down. Charred fur receded into human skin. Claws into human fingers. Human skin covered the mangled flesh and flaming skeleton. It wore a human smile. Her brother's smile.

The thing wearing Alexei's face bent close to her own. The hazel eyes. The crooked smile. The short and messy black hair.

"Child," it said. "What did you hope to accomplish here?"

That voice coming out of that face wrung her heart. She tried to stand and lash out at it, but even so small, it had more than enough power to hold her down with just one hand.

"I am eternal. Older than death itself." It looked down at her ankle, the blood pouring out from the wound, sure to cause her unconsciousness soon. "Why not?" it said to itself. "You have suffered much, and this body is nearly at its end. I shall take yours instead."

It smiled at her until the teeth cracked in its mouth. The broken enamel fell out of its face and onto hers. A deluge of broken teeth showered her. She held her face away from the downpour and screamed and kicked her legs out. Alexei's teeth washed over her face. No way to ignore them now.

"Child, look at me. Look at what awaits you."

She couldn't. She knew, she just knew, that it was no longer Alexei's face. It had changed into something else. Something that, if she were to gaze upon it for even a second, her mind would break.

It released its hand from her chest. Her skin burned.

Her body floated up into the sky, raised by unseen hands.

She couldn't move.

She refused to see its face.

All the warmth left her. The pain came in devastatingly powerful waves.

She screamed until her voice left her.

Saho landed hard on the metallic surface, narrowly avoiding hitting her head on what she could see—so close up—was a chainsaw as long as a car.

Images of her Dad running a machine just like this flashed in her mind. She was on the roof of a tree harvester, its giant arm curled up towards the cab, the chainsaw angled up towards the windshield. Slightly different from Dad's, but the same basic model. Without thinking, she slid off the roof to her right and reached for the window. It was open. She swung her body through it and landed in the driver's seat.

A thud on the roof above her.

Saho shot out her hands—unable to see clearly—and fumbled for the controls. She knew that the chances the keys were in the ignition were slim. But as Dad used to say, *the folks up here are a trusting kind. Never lock the doors to their homes even when gone for a week.*

Her hands touched everything. Flipped on every switch. Groped for anything they could grasp.

Thud.

Dad landed on the hood of the harvester. Stared at her through the windshield. Smiled his shark smile. He was about to say something when Saho's hand gripped the dangling keys still in the ignition—*trusting folk they are*—and turned the machine on. The machine jolted to life. Enough to make him fall backwards off the hood, onto the immobile chainsaw blades. He tried to pull himself up, but had fallen at an awkward downward angle.

Saho flipped more switches. Lights blazed forth. The radio crackled to static life. Some jazzy tune played that Saho thought Dad would've liked. The chainsaw revved up.

The teeth sped up and ripped into his back. He howled his unearthly howl. His arms reached for Saho and clawed at the air for support, but there was none. Almost as if he were reaching out for one last hug. Then the blades sawed through his chest, splitting him open from neck to hips. Even so, he growled and clawed at the air. Saho couldn't close her eyes. She fixated sickly on what was happening. This would be something that would never leave her.

Dad,—no, the demon—chainsaw roaring and circulating through it, was still snarling and alive, as far as that went. Saho saw a handle that looked like a joystick. She pushed it up. And so followed the blade, slicing through its face vertically, from chin to scalp. Its body fell to the wayside in two pieces, on either side of the harvester.

Saho hit reverse and backed the tractor up. Put it into drive. Towards the wall she heard the thump from earlier.

Trying not to notice that one of Dad's eyes, attached to half a face, was still blinking in the dark.

Ashiya finally opened her eyes just as the bear emerged from the husk of Alexei. It grew in height. Its rancid flesh washed off its body, as if it were snow lying in the afternoon sun. Only the skeleton remained.

The skull, devoid of eyes, drew near Ashiya as she lay suspended in the air, untouched by physical hands yet held in place against her will. Her skin split, a searing pain crackled throughout her nervous system. Her whole body became one nerve; exposed to a hard and jagged world upon which it would soon crash and be broken.

A whirring sound started up from somewhere nearby. Followed by the screams of a man. These were illusions to Ashiya. Immaterial. As transient as the shifting lights above. Fragile as her life, soon to be snuffed out. Her body, soon to be an offering to this foul god before her. Soon to be its next host.

The whirring sound got closer. Followed by a crash. She could see on the edge of her vision, just behind the bear, a huge tractor bursting forth from the wall, ripping it to shreds. The bear turned to face the threat. Whatever force held Ashiya in the air let go of her and she fell to the ground, landing on her feet, feeling the shock of the landing in her spine, feeling the further tearing of the wounds in her arms, the near amputation of her foot, collapsing to a fetal position.

The bear was too late in facing the tractor. Its long metal arm crashed into its chest like a pike and knocked it over. The tractor tried to reverse, but its rollers skidded and slipped on the snow, causing the machine to veer to side and crash into a section of the wall it had just torn out. Ashiya pulled herself to her knees. She saw Saho behind the dirty windshield, panic and terror seizing her face. She fumbled with the controls but couldn't free the tractor from the wreckage it was stuck in.

Kesagake rose to its hind legs. It lowered its bony head and charged the tractor. Saho screamed. The bear lifted the tractor off its front rollers. Ashiya willed herself to stand on her feet. Her leg bled profusely. The pain was beyond anything she could have imagined. But it also ignited a rage unknown to her. Fire burned from somewhere deep in her. The names of the dead echoed in her mind like the beat of a drum. She limped towards the tractor. Saho curled up into a ball as the bear rocked the machine, trying to shake her out of it.

Ashiya thought of Alexei's teeth pouring out over her face. Now, instead of fear and giving into the desire to turn away, she held onto that image. It fueled the anger. She kept hobbling on one foot even as she felt the bones crack in her leg. Even as she grew lightheaded because of blood loss, she walked through the pain.

The bear shook the tractor, almost knocking it over on its side. The only thing keeping it upright was the length of the arm acting as a counterbalance; otherwise, it would have been upturned already. Ashiya's foot struck something in the snow. Her bow. She bent down and picked it up. Her eyes locked onto the arrow still lodged between Kesagake's ribs. The first missed shot. Saho's cries of terror pushed her past what pain she ever would have thought a human could endure.

She jumped onto the side of the bear. Grabbed a hold of its ribs and spine. Pulled herself up its thrashing body. The bear didn't even notice her; it was fixated on Saho. Ashiya reached out and grabbed the arrow. Pulled it out of where it had gotten stuck in the bone. She squeezed her legs around the spine for balance, almost like riding a horse. The windshield of the tractor shattered, sending the shards showering over Saho. The bear tipped the tractor up to where it was about to fall to its side.

The bear's right eye was not a still target. She only caught fleeting glimpses of it.

Alexei. Taro. Ogoto. Hikari. Help me.

Squeezing her legs around the spine for support, she closed her eyes, nocked the arrow, and fired it. And then fell backwards off the bear.

Kesagake released the tractor—its front rollers bounced on the snow and Saho nearly flew through the broken window — and howled in pain, the arrow sticking out of its right eye.

"Do it! Start the chainsaw!" Ashiya cried out, lying helplessly in the snow, her body beyond its limits.

Saho woke from her terror and made eye contact with Ashiya and nodded. She reached down into the cockpit. All the while the bear shook its head and clawed at the arrow to take it out.

The chainsaw roared to life. The arm lifted up and came down over the bear, the creature too focused on its pain to notice. The teeth landed on the skull. And went to work.

Sparks flew as the metal teeth bit into the bone. The bear roared and tried to stand on its hind legs, but the metal arm held it down in place. Smoke billowed from the chainsaw. More sparks. A fire broke out on the arm. Ashiya could see Saho's face. No more tears. Her eyes were flint and her face was stone. She gritted her teeth as she pushed the throttle forward.

The chainsaw crushed the skull into pieces. Kesagake threw out its clawed paw to swipe at the arm and missed. The chainsaw ran down to its chest, cutting directly into from the center, and ground its way down to the waist, where the cutting chain flew off the guide bar. Smoke poured out to where Ashiya couldn't see what was happening. Something popped near the blade and a spurt of fire shot out. The chainsaw stopped whirring.

Saho opened the door to the cockpit and jumped out. Ran over to Ashiya and threw her arms around her neck, sobbing.

The bear's remains were stuck in the burning harvester arm. It didn't move. Ashiya feared it would come back as it had before. Could it? It had said that the bear's body was at its end, and that was before a twelve-year-old girl cut in half down the middle.

"Are we safe?" Saho asked.

Ashiya wanted to say yes. But something pulled at her insides. Something cold, like the current of the deep sea. Ashiya struggled to her side, barely able to hold on to consciousness, and turned around, facing the tree line.

And there they stood. Hundreds of pale and withered bodies. Staring at them with their black eyes.

CHAPTER 53

The dead didn't move. They were about a basketball court's length away from them. Standing on the snow, doing nothing but stare. Much like they had when Ashiya blew the head off of the bear. Without their master, they were nothing but puppets with no strings.

But was it over?

She knew deep that down that it wasn't.

"Let's go," Saho said as she tugged at Ashiya's jacket sleeve.

Ashiya looked down at her white snow-pants—what used to be white—now they were a dark red, stained by the overflow of her wounds. Her ankle was nearly severed in two. She wasn't walking out of here. She doubted she would even stay alive for another five minutes.

"Saho," she said and smiled at the girl. "I need you to run back to town." She pointed in the direction. "You need to find a working phone and a car and get out of here."

"I can't drive! And not without you! What about all the snow?"

"Says the girl who just chain sawed a demon bear." Ashiya laughed. Blood spurted out onto her chest. "Drive as far as you can. Help will come soon. But it's not safe to stay anywhere near here. I don't think it's over."

Saho finally noticed the wounds. "Are you... dying?"

"I think so. But that bear it might not be dead. You can't stay here any longer. Go!"

Ashiya tried to shove her but didn't have the strength to even push Saho's hands away. Instead, she undid her jacket and gave it to the girl.

Saho tried to protest.

"No, you must go now. Those things might wake up soon. And you need this to stay warm. Or you will die too. And then what was the point of me being here?"

Ashiya tried to smile to show her sarcasm, but it came out as a grimace. She was sure her teeth were red, anyway. She undid her boots. One came off easily. The one attached to the tenuously attached foot did not. Saho took them and put them on. They were several sizes too large for her.

"Please, please go," Ashiya said and lightly held onto Saho's hand.

Saho nodded her head, shut her eyes as the tears squeezed out of them. Let go of her hand. And started running across the clearing.

Ashiya watched her reach the hill. She turned back and lifted her hand. Ashiya did the same and smiled, no worries now of her seeing the red teeth.

Then Saho disappeared into the forest.

Please help her.

Ashiya lay back in the snow and looked up at the sky. The lights were all red. Streaking across the sky.

The sound of bones rattling.

Fuck.

Ashiya rolled over on her side and looked at the bear's body. It was shaking.

She noticed the knife she had dropped earlier, right next to her. She picked it up, knowing there was nothing left to do. If the chainsaw didn't kill it, what could?

The remains of the bear dislodged from the bladed teeth and slumped to the ground.

A black and viscous sack filled the hollowed out skeleton. It could have been black smoke. Maybe even ink in water, except it was pulsating into the air. The thick dark bled out of and consumed the bones. Two insect-like limbs shot out of the tar and came slamming down into the snow.

The sky went Thermo-nuclear. Oranges and reds and golds. It was as if the sun had gone nova. The air became heavier somehow. Had Ashiya even been able to walk, it felt like she still wouldn't have gotten very far because of the pressure building up in her head.

The limbs grew in length. Growing taller and taller out of the remains of the bear.

The dead came alive all around her. They rushed forward from their stasis and charged into the black mass. The first one to arrive was an elderly man. He ran into the tar and it shot out to meet him in a mass of tendrils, devouring him whole. Ashiya saw the tar consume and dissolve the body. Two more floppy bug limbs emerged from the mass.

More of the dead gladly ran into it. Dozens of them. On into hundreds. All racing forward, throwing their arms out as if to embrace a long-lost lover. They joyfully gave of their flesh to the thing that was emerging. Approaching. Becoming.

She even saw little Ben run by. He didn't cast her a single glance—the same as all the others—and soon become one with the darkness. None of the dead remained.

The ground shook. A heap of corrugated and rusted metal was all that remained of the now collapsed lumber mill.

Something followed the bug limbs out of the tar. A mass, both weighty in its physical presence and as ephemeral as smoke. The size of a pickup truck. And more of it was coming out. Spilling out was more like it. Being vomited out of the earth. She saw a mouth, endless in its depth, the throat of it covered in rows upon rows of teeth, spiraling down into the abyss of its stomach. Another insect limb rose from the murk and came crashing down. Ashiya used the rest of her strength to roll out of the way as the hook pierced the snow where she was just lying.

Eyes beyond count, black and glassy. A body covered in sharp edges. There was nothing for her mind to compare this thing to. She could call it spider-like, squid-like, tar-like, but that would not have done justice to the horror she was witnessing emerge from the corpse.

The mass rose higher than the mill had once stood. It stood on dozens of hooked legs. The red glow of the sky bathed the mass, yet the mass did not reflect it back. It was a living black hole. A mobile factory of death. It was an Eater of the Gods. Multiple cavernous mouths opened, and just as looked like they would suck in the world, they resealed into a dark nothingness.

It was just for a moment, but Ashiya saw it there at the center of the undulating mass. The ruined skeleton of the bear. Despite this transformation, something still bound the demon to its vessel.

It needs more death. More death and it will be free. That's why the dead sacrificed themselves to it.

Those words were both her own, and they weren't. It was her voice, as far as voice goes in the mind. It was also Taro's voice. She saw him in her mind's eye, sitting across the campfire from her, in what felt like a lifetime ago.

It needs more death and it will be free. But it is not free yet. It is bound to the bear. Bound to the bear's despair and pain and hatred. They are fuel for the demon. Take away its fuel, Anastasia.

"How?" she cried out into the flaming sky, but received no answer. None that she wanted, anyway.

The God-Eater grew further. Limbs extended into the sky as if they were tendrils or feelers going out into the world in search of... life. Life so that it may cause death. Black tar fell off the limbs and sizzled the snow beneath it. Some fell onto the metal siding of the tree harvester and ate it away.

Amid all hell literally breaking loose, she found herself back with Taro sitting by the campfire. She had asked him about Iomante. She had thought it barbaric then. But Taro didn't see it that way.

We gave the bears an honorable death, an honorable sacrifice and that let them move on and become gods once more.

Demons are nothing more than those that died without honor or love.

Iomante.

Sacrifice.

She remembered her grandmother's tales of the abaasy.

Appeasement.

Blood sacrifice.

She knew what must be done. No gun. No tool of man could do it. Only this.

She rolled to one side and tried to push herself up to her knees. The pain was a red cloud in her brain. The muscles in her arms had long torn open but had not grown numb. Fleshy strips hung from her arms, but she refused to look. The fire in her ankle swallowed her whole. She got to her knees. Knife in hand. The ground shook once more, but she held her balance. More tar fell from the creature, melting the snow into clouds of steam. Some of it scalded her face, but she did not cry out or look away.

"Hey!" she yelled towards the dark cloud of oblivion hovering over her. Rumbling like thunder echoed throughout its massive body.

It might have been laughter.

A tendril snaked its way out of one of its mouths and slithered towards her.

"I'm not speaking to you! I'm speaking to one whose flesh you stole! I am speaking to you, bear! To what you were before this darkness took you!"

The tendril stopped moving and shook.

It could have been faltering.

"I am sorry you died alone and in pain. I am sorry that we did this to you." The tendril came back to life and rushed towards her. "But I know apologies are not enough. You need atonement. You need sacrifice."

She lifted the knife and stared right into the blade. In its reflection, she saw the red sky change to a living black. She saw the tendril at her feet, just about to wrap itself around her.

She put the knife to her throat. Closed her eyes. Smiled.

"Alexei."

She slit her own throat.

The tendril smacked into her and sent her body flying. She landed some twenty feet away in the snow. It rose again to consume her, a vacuous mouth opening up in it like a worm of death. It froze.

In Ashiya's last moments, she witnessed the mass collapse in a deluge of ash and tar. The tendrils withered away. The legs snapped and the bulk of its body fell. Before it even hit the snow, it melted into a smoking heap of ash. The last thing to fall was the corpse of the bear. But it didn't look ragged and destroyed. In just a moment, she saw it alive, covered in fur, strong, beautiful. Behind it, the golden shores of a beach. Next to waves as clear as glass, she saw a man with a crooked smile who had her mother's eyes. He waved at her.

Then she saw nothing.

Not with those eyes.

Never again.

CHAPTER 54

Saho looked out over the valley from where she hid behind a wide oak tree. She never had intentions of running back to town. She wanted to see if there was anything she could do to help.

Of course there wasn't. She watched in abject horror as the monster rose into the too-bright sky. She thought it might actually grow more and blot out the lights themselves. Saho couldn't see what had caused it to fall apart. But she saw Ashiya get hit by it and her body get thrown through the air.

Then, like a bad dream, the thing melted away until nothing remained. The lights in the sky died down. Calmed to a still black, like the untroubled waters of a deep lake.

Saho ran back down the hill, across the clearing, and up to where Ashiya was lying on her back.

She didn't have to go any closer to understand. Ashiya was dead. The wounds on Ashiya's body she didn't want to see were too deep. Especially the one on her neck. Just to be sure, Saho slowly walked up to her and took her icy hand. Felt her wrist just like Dad taught her to. No pulse.

"I'm sorry."

There were no tears. Not yet, at least. Only a bottomless well dug into her heart existed.

The dead people were gone.

The monster was gone.

Dad...Mom...Taro...Ashiya.

The bear's skeleton was lying in the snow over by the mill. Not moving.

No lights in the sky save for the stars and the quarter moon.

No feeling but the cold.

Saho wrapped her arms around herself and walked away.

It must have been an hour that she hiked through the forest. More than enough time to have reached town by now. This meant she was lost. And freezing. Probably not too far away from frostbite.

The fire that was consuming the forest was nowhere near her. She didn't know if that meant it had died or just that it was moving in the opposite direction.

She sat down by the trunk of a tree that still had a blanket of moss wrapped around it.

I'm not going to make it, am I?

For once, she didn't feel like crying or feeling scared. She was too old for that by now. Amazing how one can age within forty-eight hours. She sat there with a sort of cool detachment. Otherwise, she'd go mad at the thought of her approaching death.

Just let it be. Maybe it won't hurt.

There was no one left in town, anyway. Even if there were, she'd never make it back in time. Not before her fingers turned black. Even if she made it to a car, what was she supposed to do? She got lucky with knowing how the harvester worked. The same rules did not apply to driving a car on an icy mountain road for the first time. Assuming someone had cleared the roads. Sitting there, the snow froze her butt. The ice numbed her thighs and even reached up to her stomach. The forest was silent now. No whispers or the scraping of bare feet in pursuit. No shining black eyes in the dark. No toothy smiles. No roars or growls of the bear.

It was all silence. As the cold wrapped its arms around her in a detached embrace, she almost accepted it all. The silence. The end of all things. Her body rerouted all its heat and energy to keep her alive, muddling her thoughts. She blinked eyelids that felt heavy. Each time she tried to open them again was a struggle. A kind of warmth filled her body with each shutting of her eyes. She knew deep down that it wasn't actually warmth. It was her body shutting down. Sparing her the worst of the experience of death.

A sudden burst of the desire to live sprang out of her. She forced her eyes open. But there was no fight left to stand up. Her eyes, though, she could at least keep them open. Maybe that could be enough to live until sunrise, when she might find her way back to town.

Yes! Back to town. Get warm in somebody's home. Find some food. Keep calling until the phones work or somebody comes and finds her. What did Ryoji mutter to himself while keeping her hostage? That his wife would come back today. His home was probably nothing but ashes now, but she could go there, get warmed up in a different house nearby, and wait for the wife to show up. Assuming all the dead were gone, that was. That none lingered behind instead of joining the tarry mess that the bear had become.

Live! Stay awake!

As quickly as this urge to survive rose in her chest, it deflated. She had to blink. And with each new blink, it got harder and harder to keep those eyes open.

No more feeling in her limbs. Her face felt like it was somebody else's. Like her body didn't belong to her anymore. She tried to stand one last time. Couldn't even bend her knees to try a squat.

One more blink.

The eyelids were the heaviest thing in the world now. Heavier than her grief. Heavier than her fear. Heavier than her will to live.

She felt herself drifting off to sleep.

Saho's eyes shot open. She had to shut them again because of the glare of light that stung them. A rush of warmth filled her, starting from the toes up to her legs. This wasn't the numbness that ate away at her. This was actual warmth. It soaked up into her body from her legs. It felt like she was standing in the sun. She tried to move her legs but could only manage with great effort. She opened her eyes again, wincing at the light, and waited until they adjusted.

Once the world came into focus, she expected to see the sun rising over the forest. But darkness still ruled the skies. And there was no light. She could swear she saw it as she opened her eyes the first time, but now it was gone. If it had ever been there before.

The warmth was there, though. A fire kindled in her bones. Her thoughts came back into focus. She could feel her fingers after a moment of electric tingling. She tried to stand again. Pressed her back against the tree and pushed. Her legs shook with weakness. Her stomach twisted inside her with hunger. But she could stand.

The blood rushed to her head, and she almost fainted. Put her hand on the tree and bent over, allowing herself time to feel normal again.

After a moment, she was sure she was fine. Better than fine. A surge of energy bristled inside her. The warmth filled her and did not abate.

A flicker of blue light off to her right. Saho turned her head, and for the briefest moment, thought she saw a person there. But when she set her eyes in that direction, there was no one. But she saw the tracks in the snow. They looked like a person's boots. She didn't know how she knew this, but she did. She could also tell that the steps were walking away from her. But there were no footprints before these. None to show where this person had come from, only where they were going.

She liked that thought. No worries about what was behind. Keep your eyes forward.

Saho followed the tracks.

She didn't know how much time had passed, but by the time she exited the forest, the sun had washed the town in its golden waves. She left the tree line and came onto a paved road. The snow had buried it under about a meter, but the depression it made in the terrain told her it was a road.

Knowing these things. Knowing how to track the direction of the footprints even after they had disappeared, knowing how to find her way back by tracking the North Star—she had no idea what that even was yesterday—no longer surprised her. Nor did the warmth that followed her.

These were the thoughts of someone else blanketing her own, guiding her.

As soon as Saho stepped on the road, though, the warmth left and the cold returned, but she was no longer freezing to death. The knowledge of how to move through the woods left her as well.

Fear came to her. What was she going to do now?

Until she turned and looked back at the forest.

Between the trees, she saw a woman with long black hair. Tattoos of wolves and skulls on her bare arms. Something that Saho would obsessively draw for years to come. A smile that dazzled in the sunrise. Faint blue fire pulsed around the woman. A man stood next to her with a crooked smile.

And then they were gone.

"Excuse me," came a woman's voice.

Saho nearly screamed as she felt the hand on her shoulders. She turned around and saw a middle-aged woman dressed in hot pink ski gear, complete with fluorescent orange sunglasses. She had seen this woman before. A photo of her in Ryoji's office.

"Are you okay, honey? Do you know where everybody is?"

Before she answered, she knew she was okay. She was okay now and would be okay later. Despite the cold that shook her bones again. She knew everything was going to be alright.

Because even though she couldn't see her anymore. She still felt a slight warmth off to her side. A faint flicker of blue light. She was sure it was going nowhere.

Afterword

Thank you for picking up this book and reading it!

I based the God-Eater demon off of both Ainu legends and actual history, though the entity itself is my creation.

The prologue to this book, largely, actually happened. As crazy as that may seem. Of course I embellished it and added a flare for the supernatural, but the bear attacks of 1915 are fact, not myth. Seven people were killed in Sankebetsu that winter by a rampaging male brown bear. The opening scene with Yayo is also fact. The bear indeed broke into the house where the women and children were hiding, while the soldiers were in the woods.

After local hunters couldn't find and kill the bear, the Japanese military was eventually called in to do it, dispatching fifty soldiers for the job. They also failed. The bear consistently stayed out of their line of sight and even killed more villagers (mainly women and children) while the soldiers chased after it in the wrong direction.

The bear was eventually put down by Yamamoto Heikichi, who had to shoot it once in the heart and then once in the head to kill it. Yamamoto was a rugged man who walked around in straw shoes, even in winter, and refused to be paid for killing the bear. I based the character of Taro off of him.

Another character I based on an actual person is Ryoji. Okawa Haruyoshi was a child during the bear attack and his home was used as a safe house for the people, his father being the mayor of the area. He grew up to be a bear hunter, vowing to kill 10 bears for each of the 7 victims, making 70 bears in total. He surpassed this by killing 100.

After hunters killed the original killer bear in 1915, a typhoon struck that part of Hokkaido. This led many to believe that it was—as many in the village had said before—not a bear, but a demon. Today, many think that the bear had woken out of hibernation and was driven mad by starvation and hormone imbalance. It also never attacked people until first being shot at by a hunter. Thus, starting the cycle of death.

If you visit the town of Rokusen-sawa today, you can visit a statue of the bear (actual size) next to a mock house, attacking and breaking into it. Bear statues and cartoon signs dot the town. Kamuy-Kotan is loosely based on this actual town.

To the Ainu, bears were kamuy, a representation of the mountain god Chira-Mante-Kamuy. They were ultimately benevolent and gifted the people with their meat and fur. The sacrifice of Iomante that Taro talks to Ashiya about was an actual ceremony, just as he described it, a way to send bears back to the land of the gods. I got the idea for the Kamuy-raur (literally: God-Eater in the Ainu language) from the Ainu belief that demons are born from disrespecting the dead and improper burials. Just as they gave the bear in the story neither a decent death nor an honorable send-off. The metal city and the land of the dead gods that the demon speaks about are also a part of Ainu cosmology.

I visited Hokkaido in the summer of 2024 to do the research for this novel. Spent a few days in Lake Akan, which is the center for Ainu culture today. I highly recommend you to visit. There are plays and traditional dances put on by the community practically every day. The local retellings of myths inspired the winter lights and the breaking down of the border between the spirit world and ours at the end of the story.

DEAR READER

Thank you so much for reading! I hope you enjoyed this horror and are looking forward to more to come. The Black Sun Series has 3 books out now, with 2 more coming in late 2025 and early 2026. The first 4 books are all standalone stories, but there are some minor connections between them since they exist in the same world. An example from this book is the talk about the Aomori tsunami, which is an event that happens at the end of Book 2. They can, however, be read in any order. Book 5 will be the only book that has to be read at the very end for it to make sense, and I will be tying all the books together with recurring characters at that time.

I have an ask: if you liked this story, please consider leaving me an honest review on Amazon. Reviews are the number one way for small indie authors like myself to build an audience. A review will support my writing, encourage me to keep going, and help me find new readers. I have a QR code at the end of this section that links to the US Amazon store.

If you would like to keep up on all my projects,upcoming projects, sign up for my newsletter at my website: shawnbrookswrites.com/about-5

There you will have early access to all my writing news (cover reveals, etc) and I even do book recommendations and original short stories found nowhere else. I also run free giveaways of my books and special editions several times a year.

Lastly, I have a BONUS CHAPTER for Iomante on my newsletter! This secret chapter will tie in several story threads between the Black Sun books, especially the endings for Book 1 and 3. But, for this bonus chapter to make sense and be satisfying, you will have to have read Books 1-3. The QR code for access to this chapter is also below.

Much obliged,

Shawn

Amazon review (US store):

Iomante bonus chapter:

Made in the USA
Middletown, DE
10 June 2025